Her
Boyfriend's
Bones

Books by Jeanne Matthews

The Dinah Pelerin Mysteries
Bones of Contention
Bet Your Bones
Bonereapers
Her Boyfriend's Bones

Her Boyfriend's Bones

A Dinah Pelerin Mystery

Jeanne Matthews

Poisoned Pen Press

Poisoned Pen Press
6962 E. First Ave., Ste. 103
Scottsdale, AZ 85251
www.poisonedpenpress.com
info@poisonedpenpress.com

Printed in the United States of America

*This book is dedicated to the **real** Dinah, my lucky charm from the start.*

And Billie, you are welcome.

Acknowledgments

The author wishes to thank the following writers and friends for their excellent editorial advice: Patricia Snider, Jeanne Kleyn, Joseph Winston, Sal Gordon, Gail Boyer Hayes, Joseph Massucco, A. L. H. Robkin, Judy Kimball, Ronda Taylor, Theresa Zimmerman, Katherine Berryman, Mary Brockway, Sylva Coppock, Carol Hurn, Susan Schmidt, and Gaylloyd Sisson.

For his great ideas and constant encouragement, I thank my husband, Sid DeLong.

A special thanks to my friend Michael Driver for opening his home on Samos to me and for sharing his wealth of stories, his abundance of wine, and his sense of "infinite amusement."

Introduction

The Greek island of Samos lies in the eastern Aegean Sea, a scant mile off the Turkish coast. It is the birthplace of Pythagoras, the mathematician; Aesop, the writer of fables; Epicurus, the philosopher of pleasure; Aristarchus, the astronomer who first held that the earth revolves around the sun; and Hera, the wife of Zeus and queen of the Olympian gods.

Over the centuries, Samos has been controlled by Ionia, Sparta, Macedonia, the Roman Empire, the Byzantine Empire, Venice, Genoa, and the Ottoman Empire. It was annexed by Greece after the Balkan Wars of 1912-1913 and occupied by the Nazis during World War II. There is a continuing dispute between Greece and Turkey over national air space and territorial waters. Samos' proximity to the Turkish mainland has turned it into the chokepoint for refugees trying to make their way into European Union countries. Smugglers can transport their human cargo across the narrow Mycale Strait from Turkey in under an hour, but the passage is treacherous. Many die in the attempt and the Samians, left to cope with the bodies washing up on their beaches and the horde of undocumented survivors who must be fed and housed while they await processing, feel increasingly alienated and resentful of their own government and the E.U. The Greek debt crisis and burgeoning unemployment have added to the island's hardships.

Famed for its lush forests and abundant vineyards, Samos has high mountains gashed by numerous ravines descending to the sea. Kanaris is a fictional village, a composite of several mountaintop villages that I visited during my stay on the island. All of the Samian people I met were warm, welcoming, honest, and hardworking. The scoundrels depicted in this book exist entirely in the author's imagination.

Day 1

Chapter One

The house looked like a block of melting strawberry ice cream against the intense blue of the Greek sky. The pink of the upper floors faded to cream near the door and scattered patches of reddish stone showed where the plaster had chipped. From the clay-tiled veranda, the vineyard sloped away to the Aegean. Dinah Pelerin gazed through binoculars at an enormous cruise ship docked in the harbor at Kusadasi, a mile across the Mycale Strait on the coast of Turkey. The ship had probably voyaged south from Istanbul, crossed the Dardanelles, and sailed past the ruins of ancient Troy, just two hundred miles from the spot where she was sitting. Inspired by her nearness to a place that had given rise to so many myths and legends, she imagined the still-smoldering ashes of the burned city wafting through space and time.

"It's hot as blazes," said her boyfriend. Thor Ramberg was a native of the Arctic and after less than twenty-four hours in residence, he seemed to be having second thoughts about spending his sabbatical on Samos, the sunniest of the Greek isles.

"Pull your chair into the shade and have another glass of iced tea." Dinah had grown up in the American Deep South. Heat was her preferred milieu.

Thor took off his dark glasses and daubed another blob of white zinc-oxide on his nose. He was dark-eyed and dark-complected and, in Dinah's opinion, overly fastidious about sun exposure. He scooted his chair closer under the mulberry tree that overarched the corner of the veranda. "Would you like to take the ferry to Kusadasi this afternoon?"

"We arrived just yesterday. I'd rather stay here in the village and relax." The village of Kanaris was idyllic. Situated on a rocky hilltop overlooking the sea to the east and a deep, wooded gorge to the west, it afforded spectacular views, fragrant mountain air, and a friendly taverna that boasted a wine list of two reds and two whites.

Thor gave her a teasing look. "I thought you were the restless one, always itchy to be on the go. What's gotten into you?"

She put down the binoculars and reached for her book of Greek myths. She couldn't say exactly what had gotten into her. Maybe it was the heady scent of wild thyme and oregano or the pleasant chirping of the parakeets in their cage beside the door. Maybe it was the power of the myths themselves. She had visited Turkey years ago on an archaeological dig in central Anatolia, but this was her first taste of the Aegean, Homer's "wine-dark sea," and she had never felt so drawn by the aura of a place. Samos was like no Greek island she'd read about or seen in picture books. Green and lush, with abundant water flowing down from the mountains, it was an agricultural paradise and the quiet serenity of Kanaris cast its own spell. She said, "You paid a fortune to lease this house for six months. It's beautiful, it's comfortable, and it came with a full-time servant. We should settle in and enjoy it."

"I'd enjoy it more if it had air conditioning. And our so-called servant reminds me of a prison warden. Those beetle eyes of hers follow our every move as if she expects us to break bad, throw the silverware into our knapsacks, and book."

Thor loved American cop shows, reruns of which he watched religiously on TV back in Norway. His forays into the lingo, delivered in his slightly singsong Norwegian accent, made her smile. She said, "I don't think Alcina watches us to keep us from ripping off the silver. She's not used to guests. That gossipy old guy at the taverna last night said she's been the caretaker here for the last twenty years and this is the first time it's been rented out. Don't you think that's strange?"

"The economy and the crisis with the euro have hit the Greeks hard. Taxes are going up. Everyone's looking for ways to make extra money."

"Yes, but to leave a lovely property like this vacant for so long makes no sense. It could have brought in bushels of tourist dollars over the years." She took in the vineyard with its neatly staked vines leafed out in brilliant spring green. A bush of orangey-pink roses punctuated the end of each row and a small bird with a cinnamon-colored back and a vivid yellow belly alighted on top of a stake and warbled its heart out. Under the fluorescent rays of the Greek sun, every leaf and petal and feather radiated its own brilliance. "When you met the landowner this morning and signed the lease, did he give you any reason for keeping the house immaculate, but unlived in?"

"The owner is a she. A widow, quite elderly and hard of hearing. Her name is Zenia Stephanadis and the house once belonged to her sister Marilita Stephan, the actress."

Dinah had seen Marilita Stephan in an old movie, *The Fatal Stone* or *The Lethal Stone*. Something deadly, as she recalled. Marilita had growled and purred and devoured the leading man with her huge, hot eyes. Her acting was operatic, almost laughably over the top. But she had conveyed a sort of tragic magnificence. "She must be in her eighties by now. Does she live with her sister?"

"She was executed by firing squad in 1973. Two days before her fortieth birthday."

"Jerusalem! What did she do?"

"She murdered her lover, his mother, and one of the colonels responsible for the Greek military coup in '67."

"I didn't think Greece had capital punishment."

"They don't now. But during the years when the military junta ruled, political dissidents and those regarded as criminals were routinely imprisoned, tortured, and executed."

Dinah pictured three blood-drenched people gasping out their dying breath on the spot where she was sitting now and shuddered. "Where did Marilita commit these murders?"

"On a beach on the other side of the island. Come on, Dinah. I wouldn't have booked us into a bloody charnel house." He got up, pushed her hair aside, and kissed her neck. "You want to enjoy the house? Let's go enjoy the upstairs."

She shoved the thought of murder to the back of her mind and smiled. He really was handsome beneath the white goop on his nose. "We enjoyed the upstairs this morning. Twice."

"We're on holiday. Who's counting?" He pulled her to her feet and kissed her.

"Telephone call for Miss Pelerin." Alcina materialized at the door like a ninja. She was a black-haired, top-heavy woman of about fifty with a stealthy tread and suspicious eyes. The gold cross that dangled from a chain around her neck appeared somewhat at odds with the blue-eye amulet she wore at her throat to ward off "the evil eye." She stepped out onto the veranda, gave Thor a reproachful look, and handed Dinah the phone. "You left it in the parlor. It made music and I answered."

"Thank you, Alcina." She looked at the caller ID and groaned. It was Neesha Dobbs, her uncle Cleon's widow in Atlanta. Since his death, Dinah had had the duty of trustee, doling out money from his bank account in Panama on an as-needed basis to his and Neesha's two obnoxious children. It was a complicated, aggravating, and thankless task, but Cleon had left her no choice. If she hadn't promised to administer his legacy, the children would have been cut off without a penny.

Alcina continued to hover.

"It's all right that you answered, Alcina. Thank you." Dinah waited. After a few seconds, the old busybody retreated, but only as far as the parakeets' cage. She murmured to the birds in Greek, took some fruit slices out of her pocket, and fed them through the wires.

Thor grinned and cupped his hands to his ears.

Dinah stifled a laugh and tried to muster a semblance of cordiality for her caller. "Hello, Neesha. What's up?"

"Katherine's been arrested for burglary."

"Katherine who?"

"My daughter, of course."

"I thought she'd changed her name to K.D."

"K.D. was a phase. She's changed her name back to Katherine and she's giving me a nervous breakdown. She's supposed to report to some juvenile hearing or other tomorrow, but I won't have it. It's bad enough she has to live with the stigma of her father's criminality which, thank God, I've managed to keep quiet. She can't go to jail. It would destroy her social standing. She'd never be able to come out with the other debs. You've got to help me."

"Help you how, Neesha? I'm in Greece."

"I'm sending her to stay with you."

"No, you're not. That is one hundred percent out of the question. Use your head. Skipping a court hearing isn't like skipping class. The judge will issue a warrant."

"Not right away. It'll take time. And Katherine likes you. She says you're *worldly wise*, not a slave to *convention*." Her voice fluted at the absurdity. She took an audible breath and resumed the smarmy tone. "You're so good with words, Dinah. So persuasive. If only you'll talk to her, she'll realize that she has to straighten up and behave herself."

"I've been invited to take part in an archaeological excavation in Turkey at the end of the summer. I can't drop everything to babysit a teenager. I will talk to her by phone, although I can't imagine that anything I say will make a difference."

"She needs more than a phone call. She needs a firm hand."

"I'm sure she does." Applied with brute force to her derrière, thought Dinah. "Maybe we can get her into one of those finishing schools in Switzerland. How are her grades?"

"They've slipped." Neesha emitted a tremulous sigh. "You *have* to take her."

"It's not going to happen, Neesha. There's nothing to do in this little village and besides, I'd be a terrible influence. I drink. I smoke. I swear. And I'm shacking up with a man who isn't my husband."

"I don't care about that. Dinah, please. I have my hands full with her twin brother. His ADD is worse than ever. His psychiatrist thinks he may have complications, personality disorder or something. I'm begging you. Katherine's sixteen. You can't let her go to jail. She'd just die. I'd die. It's too awful to think about."

"Can't you send her to your mother in Calhoun? Isn't she…?"

"Not well. Not at all able to look after a girl like Katherine."

Dinah sympathized, but not so much that she was willing to take on the burden of a juvenile delinquent who, even before her descent into crime, was an insufferable pain in the hind quarters. "I'm sorry, Neesha. I will wire money from Cleon's account so that you can hire an attorney. I will help you find a boarding school. I will do my best to reason with her. But I can't play nanny."

"I've already put her on a plane to Athens, flight 229."

"You did *what?*"

"She knows to transfer for a flight to Samos. She'll arrive sometime tomorrow." Neesha burst into tears and the phone went dead.

"Just shoot me."

Thor looked up from his *International Herald Tribune* and rolled his iced tea glass across his forehead. "Trouble?"

Alcina turned around and stared. Dinah stared her down. The woman fondled her evil eye amulet, muttered something in Greek, and oozed back into the house.

"You look as if you could use something stronger than tea," said Thor.

Dinah closed her eyes and took a deep breath. "It might not be a bad idea to do an inventory of the silverware, after all."

Chapter Two

Thor shaved off a few slices of Kasseri cheese and sliced an apple. "This isn't much of a lunch. There's nothing to eat in the house and Zenia informed me that Alcina will clean, but she won't cook. We'll have to fend for ourselves. Let's drive into Karlovassi and shop for groceries."

"You go. I'm going to hike down to the sea and drown myself." Dinah was stewing over the invasion of her romantic holiday by a snotty brat whose own mother couldn't cope with her. "She's a deceitful little schemer, I tell you. She's Machiavelli without the charm. She'll spoil everything."

"You're making it worse than it has to be. She'll stay a few days, grow homesick for her school friends, and realize that she has to return and square things."

"You're an optimist, Thor Ramberg. I swear you came out of the womb wearing rose-colored glasses."

"That's what you like about me. I see silver linings to all of the catastrophes that you imagine." He smiled and tickled her lips with a piece of apple.

She opened her mouth and crunched down on it. More than anyone she'd ever known, he had a gift for making her laugh and keeping her on an even keel. "I didn't say the kid was a catastrophe, but she's a major headache and there's no silver lining."

"Maybe there is. The Arctic is getting more tourists these days. I want to visit with some of the local police and learn how they handle crimes committed by and against visitors. While I'm doing that, you may enjoy touring around the island with K.D."

"I thought you planned to devote all of your time to making love to me."

"How much lovemaking can one mortal woman stand from the namesake of the Norse god of thunder?"

"It'll be interesting to find out, won't it?"

He grinned and kissed her on the top of the head. "Hold that thought until I get home from the supermarket."

When he had gone, she finished the apple and felt a lot better. She put on her bathing suit under her jeans and shirt, threw a towel into her backpack, and started to the sea, thinking mostly positive thoughts. Some men would be infuriated if their lover sprang a teenage buttinsky on them, but Thor was unflappable. Unflappable and incorrigible. Apparently he couldn't go a week without schmoozing with other cops. He was a police inspector on the Norwegian island of Spitsbergen, a place that had been virtually crime free until a contingent of U.S. senators dropped by last year and set off a crime wave. Dinah, who had tagged along as a consultant to one of the senators, teamed up with Thor, and together they had solved two murders. Crime had brought them together, but hashing over the local police blotter wasn't her idea of a fun vacation. She hoped he wouldn't turn their summer get-together into a busman's holiday.

A series of rocky, dirt switchbacks dropped away from the village past a haphazard orchard of olive trees interspersed with wild oleander and pomegranate and fig trees. Spears of dark green Italian cypress studded the hills and a massive rock face jutted up in the distance. Smaller outcrops like the teeth of giants thrust up through the green earth, and thousand-year-old rock walls terraced the upper slopes as far as she could see. Samos did not have a shortage of rocks.

A second vineyard had been planted down the seaward side of the mountain and far below, a sprinkling of red-tiled roofs gleamed amidst the green. In the bend of the fourth switchback sat a dilapidated stone cottage. It had no door and she stuck her head inside and looked around. A low stone wall divided the room in half. The wall had a hole in the bottom above a deep pit which had been partially covered with a thick stone slab.

"*Yia'sou.*"

She stepped back as a burly man in a white linen suit and a straw boater hiked up the trail from below. He leaned hard on a walking staff and panted from exertion.

Yia'sou was one of the handful of basic Greek words and expressions she'd memorized. It meant both hello and goodbye. She answered with a confident smile. "*Yia'sou.*"

The Greek that streamed out of his mouth next didn't sound so friendly.

Not sure if she had been reprimanded for trespassing, she proffered another phrase from her limited vocabulary. "*Me sink-horite.*" If she'd pronounced it correctly, it meant excuse me. She followed up with an extenuating spiel in English and hoped her apologetic smile would get the meaning across. "The cottage was open. I just assumed it was public. I didn't mean to intrude."

He leveled a penetrating look at her and came forward. "Who are you?"

"You speak English." She brightened. "My name is Dinah Pelerin. I'm staying in the Stephan house in Kanaris for the summer."

He sat down on a bench in front of the cottage, took off his boater and fanned his face. "The cicadas are bursting today."

"I beg your pardon?"

"It is very hot." His inquisitive eyes seemed to search for a way to categorize her. "Not many tourists come to Kanaris."

"Then I guess that makes me special."

"Zenia Stephanadis has never permitted guests in that house."

She said, "There's a first time for everything."

He regarded her thoughtfully for a few seconds and his face creased into a smile that spread from his mouth to his eyes. "You are right, Dinah Pelerin. There is always a first time. I am Mentor. I grow the sweetest grapes and make the best wine on Samos. My father was born in Kanaris and his father before him. I was born in the house I live in today. You will pass by it on your way to the sea."

"I'm happy to meet you, Mentor. Kanaris is a beautiful place."

"Where do *you* come from?"

"America. The southeastern part."

"America." He pulled a pipe out of his coat pocket and stuck it between his teeth. "The British think of Greece as an outdoor museum and look upon us Greeks as undeserving caretakers. They preserve the best of our antiquities in their museums, more arrogant even than the French. The Germans think we are wastrels and idlers who cannot be trusted to clean up after ourselves. Our pensions are too fat for their liking and they would impoverish us for our own good. And the Americans," he paused and lit his pipe. "The Americans can't believe that a tiny, unimportant country with socialist leanings can jeopardize their retirement funds. Is that what you think?"

She had read about the Greek debt crisis and the harsh terms imposed by Germany and the European Union, but she wasn't about to be drawn into a discussion with a Greek who obviously had a chip on his shoulder. "I don't have a retirement plan and I arrived in Greece just last night. This is my first day."

"Now you must excuse me. We Greeks have become paranoid these last two years. The world seems to have forgotten Greece's contributions to western civilization. We are scolded like children for our lazy habits and our careless borrowing."

"Americans have no right to criticize others for over-borrowing. I charged my airfare to Samos on my Visa card and it'll be months before I earn enough to pay off the balance."

He laughed. "If you need help or advice while you're on the island, ask for Mentor. Everyone knows me."

"Thank you, Mentor. That's a perfect name for an advisor."

"In Greek, it means spirit." He gestured through the door behind him. "You are a welcome guest at my *kalivi* anytime. I keep a jug of white wine in a cooler inside."

"That's very kind of you."

"It is my pleasure. In ancient Greek, the word for stranger and the word for guest was the same. Except for the hordes from Africa and the Middle East, it is true today."

That "except for" distinction implied a degree of racism. Or maybe it was just plain old xenophobia, a Greek word understood wherever the natives felt threatened by foreigners. She didn't want to wade into that discussion, either. "Is this cottage where you make your wine?"

"No. This is an old *kalivi*, used only for harvest parties and celebrations." He got up and showed her the huge stone grill and roasting spit adjacent to the cottage and then pointed inside. "On the other side of that low wall, the pickers used to crush the grapes with their feet. The juice was forced through that hole at the bottom of the wall into the well, which is lined with cement."

"It looks deep."

"Two meters, the height of a tall man. For safety, I had it covered but for a few centimeters. Wide enough to spit at the devil." He chuckled.

"Did the juice ferment inside the well?"

"No. It was siphoned into goatskin pouches and carried down the mountain by donkeys to tavernas where it was transferred into barrels to ferment. Today, everything has changed but the grapes."

"Have you always been a wine maker?"

"Only four seasons. I am still learning and experimenting. I was a professor of classical studies in Athens for twenty years. When my wife died, we came home to Kanaris. She is buried in the village cemetery. On Sunday it will be five years to the day since her funeral. You are welcome to come to the *mnimosyno* and reburial service."

Dinah's ears pricked up. Her degree was in cultural anthropology and rituals that carried over from the past fascinated her. "There's a second burial?"

"At the time of burial, the grave is filled with lime. After five years, the bones are exhumed, bathed in wine, and reburied with the blessings of the priest."

She said, "I've read about ceremonies like this. In ancient times, seeing the bones reassured the living that the soul of the dead had departed and wouldn't return as a ghost."

"We no longer bury the household furnishings with the dead or kill their horses to accompany them to the underworld and for the most part, educated Greeks no longer believe in ghosts. But I am a follower of the old ways and Kanaris has no stomach for another ghost."

She couldn't tell if he was spoofing her or being serious. "There's a village ghost?"

"It depends who you ask." He lowered himself back onto the bench. "Have you heard the story of Marilita Stephan?"

"Yes. My friend told me she was executed for a triple murder."

"There are those who still maintain her innocence. She had many friends here and is buried in the village cemetery. Her sister Zenia forbade a *mnimosyno*, but Marilita's friends went ahead with it. My mother was there. She said that when they unearthed the body, the flesh was blackened and putrid. The priest turned sick. Zenia sent him away before prayers could be said and told the mourners they had their proof. Marilita is burning in hell."

Dinah felt a vicarious revulsion. The sight of a half-rotted corpse would haunt anyone's dreams. A mischievous wind snatched at her hair and coated her shoes with dust. She shivered.

Mentor leveraged himself to his feet with the aid of his walking staff and clamped his boater low and tight over his head. "It's the *meltemi*. It blows noon to sunset, May to September. A blessing on a hot day, unless you're sailing into the wind."

Chapter Three

Dinah knew more about Greece before the birth of Christ than she knew about Greece after the Second World War. Thor, on the other hand, seemed well versed in the history of his European neighbor. Sitting under a hundred-year-old grape arbor in the courtyard of the Marc Antony Taverna, he supplied her with a junta-in-the-nutshell explanation.

"The right-wing Greek generals who instigated the coup called it a revolution, an emergency action to save the nation from communism. The Americans were all for it, of course. Anything to foil the Red Menace. The Rolling Stones, Hollywood movies, leftist academics, journalists, even Mark Twain—all of them were declared to be enemies of the Greek State."

"Was Marilita Stephan considered an enemy of the state?"

"I don't know. I've never seen any of her films, but I don't think they were banned. The military rulers probably turned a blind eye to any improprieties committed by their home-grown celebrity. In any case, she seems to have had a special relationship with the power elite."

"Why do you say that?"

"Colonels don't picnic with just anybody. Marilita was rich and famous, but she must have been special or dangerous in some other way. The junta wouldn't want to execute a popular actress, even if she went crazy and capped a colonel. They would have thrown her in prison until the public forgot about her. Instead, a military court tried her in secret and executed her in public. Somebody higher up the chain of command was covering his ass big time."

Dinah wished he wouldn't speak so irreverently. She couldn't erase from her mind the image of the casket opening to reveal Marilita's blackened body. She said, "It's a very cold case, Thor. You'll never be able to solve a homicide that happened before you were born."

"Maybe not, but I don't think anyone's made much of an effort before." He speared a piece of lamb on the end of his fork and scrutinized it as if it held some vital clue. "Zenia, the sister, has framed copies of newspaper reports of the murders hanging in the entryway of her home. They're old and yellowed and crumbling at the edges. Most are in Greek, but there was one article in a British tabloid with a photograph of Marilita and her three victims posing on the beach on the day of the murder."

Dinah dug into her *païdakia*, grilled lamb chops in English, and sipped a dry red Greek wine from a stubby, stemless glass. Thor was obviously hooked by the case and it was no use trying to distract him. Murder wasn't the most cheerful dinnertime topic, but at least she wouldn't be agitating over the impending arrival of Katherine, alias K.D. Dobbs. She said, "It's odd that Zenia would want to be reminded on a daily basis of such a horrible event."

"Wait until you meet her. I've seen more lifelike figures in a wax museum. Can you believe she uses an ear trumpet?"

"Maybe we've fallen into a time warp. On my walk this afternoon, I met a man who invited me to his dead wife's exhumation. Memorial exhumations are apparently a local custom. There was a *mnimosyno* for Marilita. His mother was there and she told him that Zenia acted like a real witch. He used to be a university professor, and yet I think he seriously believes that Marilita's ghost haunts the village. I should be taking notes for an anthropology paper."

"Maybe you should. Who was the American writer who said the past isn't dead, it isn't even past?"

"William Faulkner."

"He's the one. He could have been writing about Kanaris."

A woman two tables away set a plate of meat on the ground and a pair of scrawny cats made a beeline across Dinah's feet to get to it. The courtyard had begun to fill up, mostly couples, but there were a few lone diners. The tourists were easy to spot. They arrived before sundown carrying cameras and daypacks. If last night was any indication, the locals wouldn't start to arrive until much later, although there were a few exceptions. Two men who looked as if they'd been around since Zeus was in diapers shared a bottle of retsina and mused over a game of backgammon. A large, garrulous woman and her ouzo-sipping husband bickered companionably. Periodically, she wagged her finger and topped up his glass with water. One leather-skinned codger in a Greek fisherman's cap seemed to be taking an indecent interest in Dinah. She couldn't tell if his furtive stare signified lust or curiosity. She gave him a testy look and turned back to Thor. "Are there no young people in the village?"

"I expect most of them go to the cities to find work, although jobs are scarce everywhere these days. The E.U. austerity measures and unemployment have triggered riots in Athens." He poured himself a second glass of wine. "I can't stop thinking about that photo on the day of the murders, everyone laughing, having a good time. What changed? What sent Marilita into a rage? How did she get hold of that colonel's gun, if it was his gun? And why did she kill everyone in sight?"

"Maybe she was aiming for her lover and his mother and the colonel got caught by a couple of stray bullets." Once, in a moment of extreme provocation, Dinah had been tempted to shoot a lover. Lucky for all concerned there hadn't been a gun nearby, but she could understand how some kinds of indignities might drive a woman over the edge. Infidelity, for example. Even so, jealous rages were more apt to take place in the bedroom than on the beach and anyway, what reason would Marilita have had to kill her fiancé's mother and a military high-muck-a-muck? "The man I met today, Mentor, says that Marilita's friends believe she was innocent."

"I don't know, but I've a hunch there's a lot more to the story than the military establishment made known."

Dinah wondered if Marilita's personal life was as torrid and over-the-top as her movies. "She was probably acting out a scene, borrowed the colonel's gun, and forgot that it wasn't a prop. Judging from the one movie I saw, she emoted to excess. In fact, she chewed the scenery. Why don't we rent a few DVDs of her films and see if we can figure out what made her tick?"

"Good idea, *kjære*. There's a video rental store in Karlovassi."

Kjære. The Norwegian endearment made her feel all fizzy inside. Until yesterday, she and Thor hadn't seen each other for five months, although they'd kept in touch. When she e-mailed him that she'd received an offer to join a Turkish archaeological team near the Bay of Troy, he decided to take a sabbatical and suggested that she spend a few weeks soaking up the sun with him on Samos before the dig got underway. The timing was perfect and their romance, begun during the bitterly cold polar night in Norway, deserved a turn in the sunshine. Her innate pessimism wouldn't allow her to think beyond Samos, but this attachment felt different somehow. Easier. Less edgy. She'd rarely felt such a sense of contentment. That is, until Neesha's phone call. She glanced at her watch. In the morning, she'd have to call and find out the schedule of flights arriving at Samos International Airport.

"Hello again, my young friends." Savas Brakus, the owner of the taverna, stopped by their table smiling broadly. He was a stout, bug-eyed man with an eager manner and an unabashed nosiness. He was more direct than Alcina. He came right out and asked what he wanted to know, seemingly oblivious to the presumption. Last night he had pumped them for as much information as he could get without going through their wallets or peeking at their passports. "The wine is good, yes?"

"Very nice," said Thor.

"Lovers always want to linger over their wine and lose themselves in each other's eyes. I will bring you another carafe." He surveyed Dinah's plate with his large, lugubrious eyes, as if any uneaten morsel would reflect poorly on his kitchen. "Your lamb was good, yes?"

"Very good," she said.

"That recipe has been passed down through my family for centuries. Antony ordered his cooks to prepare *païdakia* for the feast to celebrate Cleopatra's birthday. Antony and Cleopatra were here on Samos, you know. Music, dancing, feasting, revelries of every kind. What a party *that* must have been." He took a gander around the courtyard at the other tables and inclined his face close to Thor's. "I heard that you met with your landlady this morning. Did you find her in good health?"

"As far as I could tell. Has she been ill?"

"Some people say she suffers from the *kako mati*."

"What's that?" asked Dinah.

"The evil eye. The *baskania*." He flicked a lighter and lit the little votive candle on their table. "Zenia Stephanadis is not well liked. Some say an enemy has cast the evil eye upon her. Others say she has cast the evil eye upon her neighbors. Idle minds, eh? The devil's workshop. But as the priest says, demons have no more power than we give them."

Dinah opened her mouth to inquire further about this superstition, but her thoughts were blasted out of her head by the scream of a jet so close overhead that its belly must surely have grazed the roof. The table trembled. She jumped up and knocked over her wine. "Are we under attack?"

Brakus' face flushed and he shook his fist at the sky. "*Tourkos.*"

Several customers who'd been eating inside in the dining room rushed outside, adding their angry shouts to the din. "*Sto diaolo!* Damn you and your whore mothers!"

"*Trelos diabolos!*"

Brakus returned his attention to Dinah and Thor, mopping up the spilled wine with their white cloth napkins. "I am sorry. Did it spill on your clothes?"

"No. No damage except to my eardrums."

"The Turks are a bane. I will bring you more napkins and more wine. On the house, as you Americans say." He held the saturated napkins out in front of him as if they were dripping blood and stomped off into the kitchen.

Dinah blew out a breath of relief and sat down again. The sound of the jet still roared in her ears. "That pilot cut his distance awfully close. If he crashed, the entire village would go up in a ball of fire. I can understand everyone's fury."

Thor said, "From what I understand, flyovers of Turkish F-16s occur fairly often. The Greeks buzz the Turkish coast in retaliation. Once in a while, there's a mock aerial dogfight. The dispute over who owns the Aegean and the air space above it keeps things lively."

Brakus dashed back and presented them with fresh napkins and a fresh carafe. He babbled another apology and bustled off to the next table.

A stooped figure plodded toward the taverna headed in the direction of Marilita's house. He wore a broad-brimmed straw hat, a sweat-stained work shirt over baggy jeans, and carried a magnum-sized wine bottle in each hand. Dinah watched his slow progress. Twenty yards away, the old man paused and lifted his head. He pushed the brim of the hat up with his forearm, wiped the sweat out of his eyes with his sleeve, and squinted toward the taverna as if it were a mirage he couldn't possibly reach. She said, "I've seen that man working in the vineyard."

"He's the groundskeeper, Alcina's husband. Zenia employs them both. They live in that old farmhouse where the coast road turns uphill to the village."

"He looks as old as dirt. Do you think we should go and give him a hand?"

"I don't think he speaks English. I said hello to him last evening when I went out for a run and he gave me a blank stare."

"Yannis!" A swarthy man wearing aviator glasses who'd been drinking alone at a table at the far end of the courtyard shouted. "Yannis Thoma!" He left his drink and ran down the middle of the street where he confronted the old man angrily in Greek.

Thor tensed. "Is he threatening him?"

Dinah wasn't sure. Yannis didn't act cowed. He tilted his head back and eyed the younger man with blatant contempt. The two argued for a minute, their voices loud and accusing. Yannis said something incomprehensible and spat in the street. The man in the aviators threw his arms over his head, as if in frustration, and backed away. Yannis glared at him for a moment and plodded on toward the taverna. The other man followed, gesticulating and calling out what sounded like insults. Yannis ignored him. The two walked past the taverna, Yannis in front, stooped and silent, the younger man still arguing but keeping his distance. The sun glinted off his mirrored lenses.

Thor's eyebrows spiked up. "It's going to take this Norseman some time to get used to life among the Greeks. It seems they all chew the scenery."

"Don't be silly. Greece is the birthplace of Socrates and logical thinking, although I do admit that Samos seems to foster a climate of high drama." She thought about the Norwegian propensity to coolness and restraint. Thor was probably in the throes of culture shock. She said, "You're not used to the more demonstrative nature of Southerners."

He smiled. "You mean hot-blooded Southerners like you?"

"Not me. I've had too many scenery chewers and hotheads in my life. I'm entering my Calm and Reflective Period."

The jet made another screaming pass across the roof and streaked across the Aegean.

"Not *too* calm," said Thor, rubbing his ears. He angled his chair to the west and rested an arm on her shoulder. "But that's an amazing sunset to reflect on."

They drank another glass of wine and the tensions of the day slowly dissipated. The codger who'd stared at her so intently paid his tab, adjusted the visor on his fisherman's cap low over his face, and cleared out. Dinah watched Apollo drive his fiery chariot into the Aegean and her thoughts drifted back through the centuries. What a weird and wonderful array of gods the Greeks had invented for themselves. The most wonderful of them all was Phoebus Apollo—god of light, god of healing, god of truth. He'd given Cassandra of Troy the gift of prophecy and when she rejected his love, he rigged it so that no one would believe anything she said. It struck Dinah as mean spirited and petty for a god of such sterling qualities, but the Greeks had an ironic attitude toward their deities. They invested them with the same moral weaknesses and emotional flaws as human beings. Even the god of light had a dark side.

Thor touched her hand. "Would you like more wine or would you rather walk?"

"Walk."

"Me, too." He laid a few bills on the table and they ducked out without Brakus noticing.

The way back to Marilita's house wound past whitewashed stone houses, the weathered wood of their windows and doors painted in shades of blue and aqua, still visible in the soft twilight. The air was laden with the scents of honeysuckle and pine, birds sang, and purple bougainvillea rambled over the walls in profusion. From the eaves of a low, tiled roof, a ginger cat with big yellow eyes watched them stroll past from its perch atop a rock wall. They held hands and Dinah leaned her head on Thor's shoulder. No cars were permitted in the narrow alleys of the village and they ambled down the middle of the lane.

Thor pulled her close and kissed her hair. "Happy?"

"Mmm." She was, but there was no sense tempting the gods by saying so out loud. Affairs of the heart were fraught with perils enough, and to date, her affairs had come with a higher-than-normal incidence of peril. It wouldn't do to let herself get too carried away this early in the game. She and Thor had talked on the phone and e-mailed almost daily since their fling in Norway, but all told, they had spent a grand total of three weeks and three days in actual physical proximity. How their personalities would mesh in close quarters over the course of the next three months remained to be seen.

He said, "Even after your dig starts, Samos is close enough that you could come back on week-ends."

"I suppose."

"You suppose? Why so noncommittal?"

"I don't know. Just cautious, I guess."

He laughed. "You're the least cautious person I've ever met, man or woman."

"That's not true. Sometimes my reflexes get ahead of my reasoning, but I'm working on…" She stopped cold. "What's that?"

But it was all too obvious what it was—the man who'd argued with Yannis lay sprawled face-up in the lane with a bloody, gaping hole in his chest.

Chapter Four

Dinah froze. "Is he dead?"

Thor felt for a pulse. "Yes, but his skin is warm. Whoever shot him must have done it when the jet flew over the second time."

"What do you mean whoever? It must have been that Yannis guy. Call the police."

"Do you know the emergency police number?"

"No. Don't you?"

"Go back to the taverna and ask Brakus to call. I'll stay with him."

Dinah stood rooted, paralyzed by fear. "It's too dangerous. Yannis could be hiding behind a tree. He might shoot you."

"We can't be sure he was the shooter and if he was, he has no reason to shoot me. Go. Hurry."

"Whoever it was, he might shoot me."

Thor hiked an eyebrow. "We can't leave the body to the vultures and wild jackals."

"There are jackals?"

"Some."

"Right." She took a last look at the hole in the dead man's chest and started back to the taverna in a trot. The thick fringe of trees on either side of the lane felt sinister and the stench of death fouled the air. The pleasant ambience of the island had been shattered by a gunshot she hadn't heard. Unlike Thor, she had no doubt who had fired it. She remembered the look of cold contempt in Yannis' eyes, as if the man standing in front of him were subhuman. It was creepy enough that the house she'd been sleeping in had once belonged to a murderess. Now the groundskeeper had done murder. The place positively reeked of blood. Even if Yannis was captured and taken away to a prison on the opposite end of the island, she didn't think she could go to sleep with Alcina slinking about the house and fondling her evil eye fetish.

A twig snapped in the woods somewhere to her right. She broke into a sprint and didn't stop until she tore into the taverna, frightened and winded.

Brakus' English seemed to have deserted him. It took a maddeningly long time for him to comprehend that a man had been murdered less than a mile from his terrace. It took an even longer time for him to explain the situation in Greek to the police in Samos Town. And when she asked him for a clean tablecloth to cover the dead man until the police arrived, his eyes bulged in perplexity, as if she'd asked him to hand over all the cash in the till. At long last, he produced a cloth and a couple of flashlights, instructed a waiter to direct the police to the scene of the crime, and trailed her out the door.

Dusk had begun to settle over the lane, leaching the blues from the doors and the purple from the bougainvillea. A fitful breeze rustled in the branches of the pines. Dinah walked fast. She hadn't liked leaving Thor alone and the more she thought about it, the more anxious she became. Of course, Yannis had no reason to harm him, but by definition, murderers were not reasonable people. He could have returned, found Thor standing over the body of his victim, and loosed off another lethal round. There was no jet to cover the noise this time, but he could have a silencer. Thor had only assumed that the gunshot coincided with the jet thundering overhead.

She looked back every few seconds. Brakus stumped along behind as if his legs were made out of wood. He was a ball of fire when it came to waiting tables, but out here he hobbled along like a balky mule. Past her limit of patience, she began to jog.

And then run. And then race. Her thoughts raced ahead of her feet. Kanaris was tiny and most tourists returned to their hotels in the larger towns at the end of the day. Was the dead man a resident? Maybe he was a neighbor or a relative of Yannis. Or of Brakus. Good grief. Was that why he seemed so shocked and bumbling?

Yannis had been toting a heavy wine bottle in each hand and it didn't seem likely that he would have been carrying a gun in the belt of his jeans. It probably belonged to the younger man. He'd been angry, clearly frustrated. She pictured him whipping out his weapon and pointing it at Yannis. Yannis could have lashed out at him with one of the bottles, knocked the gun out of his hand, grabbed it before his assailant could recover, and shot him in self-defense. Perhaps he had gone home to tell Alcina and call the police himself. She wondered how long it would be before the police could get here from Samos Town. She was trying to decide if the dead man bore any familial resemblance to either Yannis or Brakus when she spotted Thor. He stood with his back to her and held his phone to his ear.

"You're okay!"

He spun around and stuffed the phone in his pocket.

She bent over, hands on her knees, breathing hard. "Did you call Alcina and warn her?"

"She didn't answer. Did Brakus telephone the police?"

"Yes. He's poking along behind me."

"It's getting dark. I hope he brought a torch."

"He has two." She looked behind her. "If he ever gets here."

A circle of light bobbed along the lane and Brakus shuffled along behind it as if he were wearing bedroom slippers. Thor went to meet him and took the other flashlight. In a minute, Thor's cone of light landed on the dead man's face and Brakus uttered an exclamation.

"Do you know him?" Thor asked.

Brakus crossed himself. "It's the Iraqi."

"Does he live on the island?" asked Thor.

"I don't know. I don't know anything about him."

"How do you know he's an Iraqi?" Thor's tone was skeptical.

"It's what I've heard. Here. Cover him up." He tossed the red-checked tablecloth to Thor and looked away.

Dinah had the impression that it was fear rather than squeamishness that made him so nervous.

Thor unfurled the cloth and draped it over the body. It covered the face and torso, but not the legs.

"Had he eaten in your place before this evening?" Thor seemed to have no concept of what it meant to be on sabbatical. He was back in policeman mode full-throttle.

"He came in a few times. He never ate. He drank ouzo and occupied a table for four. Tonight, he didn't pay." Brakus sounded indignant. He looked back at the corpse as if deliberating whether it would be appropriate to remove the wallet and take what was owed him.

Thor offered him no encouragement. "Do you know his name?"

"Fathi."

"He called the older man Yannis Thoma. Is Thoma his last name?"

"Yes. Yannis Thoma has lived in Kanaris all his life."

"Tell me about him. Does he have a criminal record?"

"Criminal…?" Brakus seemed flustered by the question. "With communists, you can never be sure."

"Any history of mental illness?"

"When the wolf gets old, he becomes the clown of dogs."

Dinah had heard the expression "It's Greek to me" all her life, but it irked her to be baffled by a Greek speaking English. Was Brakus likening Yannis to a wolf and, if so, what did he mean by it? Maybe he was implying that the Iraqi had ridiculed Yannis and that's why Yannis shot him. She asked for a clarification. "What were Yannis and the Iraqi quarreling about, Mr. Brakus?"

"I have a business to run. I cannot pay attention to quarrels in the street." He tapped his watch. "Stay here if you wish, although I do not think it's required. I must go back to the taverna to work." He glanced at the Iraqi once more and made a hasty sign of the cross. "I will tell the police where you are staying in case you decide to go home."

Dinah watched as he stumped back toward the taverna. "If you ask me, that man's reaction is peculiar in the extreme."

"Murder isn't an everyday occurrence in a small village."

"It sure makes an unholy mess of the one day when it does happen." She walked a little way away from the dead man and plunked herself down on a fallen log. This was not the romantic Greek interlude she'd bargained on. She would have been more than willing to leave Thor to wait for the police, but she couldn't go back to the house until she knew that Yannis had been apprehended. Even then, she didn't think she'd feel safe. When she collected K.D. at the airport tomorrow, she would take her to a hotel in the nearby village of Pythagório to rest overnight and after she put her on a plane back to Athens the next morning, she would hop aboard the next flight to Istanbul or Antalya. If Thor wanted to romance her, he could rent a house on the Turkish Riviera. It would be just as beautiful and probably a lot cheaper.

Night had come on and her thin blouse gave no protection from the chill. She hugged herself and shivered. "The police aren't exactly Johnny-on-the-spot."

"It's a twenty-five kilometer drive."

"Fifteen miles isn't far. You'd think a report of murder would cause them to switch on their sirens and step on the gas."

He sat down on the log next to her. "I'm sorry things have taken such an ugly turn."

"It's not your fault. Maybe Alcina has cursed us with the *kako mati*. Or maybe I'm the jinx. Wherever I go, I seem to bring bad juju. Tomorrow after I've sweet-talked K.D. into going back to Atlanta, I think I'll pack up and haul my rotten luck to Istanbul."

"You're too tough-minded to be thrown by something like this, *kjære*."

She mulled the ambiguous implications of that remark. Even coming from a Viking, "Tough-minded" was a strange compliment. Maybe she was and maybe she wasn't. But she would have appreciated a little more coddling in the circumstances. "You overestimate the thickness of my hide."

"That's not what I meant." He pulled her close and wrapped his arms around her. "I know how upsetting this is, but bad things can happen anywhere. I've been looking forward to our time together. You hated the cold and I went to a lot of trouble to find a place with all the things you like—sunshine, great hiking, ancient ruins. You haven't seen the Temple of Hera yet. I shouldn't have spooked you with all that talk about Marilita. Try to put these sad things out of your mind and let's concentrate on exploring the island. And exploring one another." He kissed her in a particularly persuasive way. "Will you stay?"

Put like that, she could hardly say no, although she didn't see how sunshine and hiking could restore the feeling of romance after this horror. At the moment, all she could concentrate on was keeping the lamb chops down. Against her will, it seemed, her eyes gravitated back to the body. "He survived the carnage of Iraq to die on Samos. It seems unfair."

"That depends what kind of business he was into."

"What do you mean?"

"He could have been engaged in criminal activity."

"Why do you say that? Did you understand what he and Yannis were talking about?"

"No. But my gut tells me there's something sketchy about Mr. Fathi. I hope the police will treat his murder with respect and investigate thoroughly."

"Why wouldn't they?"

"There have been reports that some police are in sympathy with the ultra-nationalistic Golden Dawn party. They don't like refugees or foreigners in general. Whether Fathi was bent or not, I'd like to make sure his murder gets the attention it deserves."

Thor was a descendant of Scandinavia's aboriginal reindeer herders, the Sami people. Like Dinah's Seminole ancestors, the Sami had experienced years of oppression and discrimination. Thor's fellow feeling for the underdog was one of his most admirable qualities. She snuggled closer. "Are there still wolves in Greece?"

"Maybe a remnant pack or two somewhere. They were once widespread across Europe. Wolves don't adapt well to human encroachment, although they've never disappeared entirely."

She huddled under his arm and brooded until she saw the approaching headlights of a car with a flashing blue light like a gumball machine on its roof. The car stopped and Thor strode to the driver's side and stuck his head in the window. He opened his wallet and showed his ID to the driver. "I'm a policeman in Norway, here on holiday with my girlfriend. I witnessed the lead-up to the shooting and can help fill you in on the details."

Chapter Five

Dinah lay awake staring into the darkness and listening to a chorus of tree frogs outside the bedroom window. Your intuition is out of whack, she told herself. You're a worrywart who conjures up bugaboos where there are none.

She rolled onto her side and studied Thor's back. She coughed. The mattress jiggled. He didn't move. She sighed and turned onto her back again.

Maybe he was just embarrassed that he couldn't stop acting like a cop and he was afraid she wouldn't stick around and play second fiddle during his busman's holiday. He had introduced himself to the Greek officers as a tourist, but he'd made it sound like he was practically an eyewitness. He convinced them to drop her off at the taverna and take him along with them to identify Yannis. She'd sat in the taverna cooling her heels for two hours and when he finally showed up, he'd been about as talkative as a fence post. She'd peppered him with questions, but all he said was that the police found Yannis eating his dinner at the farmhouse. He had offered no resistance and the police had taken him into Samos Town where the public prosecutor would interview him in the morning. When she asked if they'd found the murder weapon, Thor just shook his head. And when she asked if he'd learned anything about the dead man or what the argument was about, his eyes wandered off into the treetops as if he were squirrel hunting.

If the local police didn't like foreigners, they might be shutting him out of their speculations and discussions. Maybe he felt snubbed and that's why he was so vague and closemouthed. Whatever the reason, his silence was keeping her awake.

A familiar, pungent aroma whiffed into the room. Marijuana. It seemed to be emanating from the veranda just under the window. The word may not have spread that the house had been let. Uninhabited, it was probably a hangout for kids sneaking away from their parents' homes to toke up. She didn't know whether cannabis was illegal in Greece, but she had no desire to be busted for possession if it was. It was Thor's responsibility to run them off, but where was a cop when you needed one? She got up, threw on her robe, and stalked across the room to the window for a look-see.

She couldn't see anything directly below, but above, a luminous crescent moon floated in the midnight sky. When the moon was waxing, as it was tonight, the Greeks believed that it was Artemis, goddess of the hunt, drawing her golden bow. Like Marilita, Artemis had killed her boyfriend, a great hunter named Orion. Different myths ascribed different motives for the murder. One story went that Orion had tried to rape her. Another held that she did it to prevent him from slaughtering too many of her beloved animals. The myth Dinah favored was the one in which her twin brother, Apollo, grew jealous of Orion and tricked Artemis into shooting him with one of her arrows. For all his sparkle and shine, Apollo came across as a jerk.

She thought about extorting a joint from the troublemakers down below in exchange for not tracking down their parents and tattling. But she'd learned that K.D.'s flight was scheduled to arrive midmorning and she couldn't show up stoned. Or at least, she shouldn't. She grabbed a flashlight and swept down the stairs to scare off the punks. To her dismay, the only doper in sight was Alcina. She lounged under the mulberry tree with a pipe in her mouth.

"Alcina, I didn't know you were here."

"It's my job to be here." She showed no guilt and made no attempt to hide the pipe.

The moon cast light enough to see and Dinah turned off the flashlight. She couldn't think of anything to say. *Too bad your husband was arrested for murder* would have been gratuitous and insensitive and *Please smoke your pot somewhere else* would have been rude and contentious. Maybe it was legal. Anyhow, the woman probably needed a hit of something soothing. Finally, she said, "I thought I sme…heard intruders."

"You're wrong if you think Yannis killed that man."

"I'm sure the police will do a gunshot residue test."

Alcina tugged at the cross on her breast. "Yannis is innocent." She seemed unfazed by the pot. Her words were clear and her voice emphatic. Disbelief, denial, loyalty—it was no surprise that she would defend her husband. But was her certainty based on something other than instinct? Some verifiable fact?

"Did you speak with him when he came home for dinner?"

"Tending this house is my job. I stay here. Yannis stays at the farmhouse. He cooks his own meals."

Thor had told Dinah that the combination bedroom-sitting room off the kitchen on the first floor was Alcina's private domain, but she'd thought it was just for rest breaks during the day. "Did Yannis telephone and tell you what he and the dead man argued about?"

"No phone calls."

Dinah's internal alert center lit up. Thor had phoned. He said Alcina hadn't answered. "Maybe there was a call and you didn't hear the phone ring."

"No calls."

Dinah didn't dwell on the discrepancy. "Do you…did you know this Fathi fellow?"

"Boatloads of his kind, Iraqis and Kurds and Afghans. Thieves, criminals, vipers. The Turks don't stop them. They're glad to get rid of them. Most end up in the migrant detention center in Samos Town."

"But not Fathi?"

"He talked his way out."

To do that, Dinah guessed he would have to have a job or a sponsor. "Did Fathi work for Zenia Stephanadis, too?"

Alcina flipped open a Zippo. In the flare, her face loomed out of the shadows like a Gorgon. If looks could turn a person to stone, thought Dinah, Alcina's could. She relit her pipe and the Zippo spanked shut. A plume of smoke rose over her head. A minute went by and Dinah inferred that she would not be commenting on Fathi's employment or volunteer any additional information. His death didn't seem to bother her so long as Yannis escaped punishment. Presumably, Yannis shared his wife's dislike of foreigners. What happened was probably one of those senseless, but all too common explosions of violence fueled by prejudice, alcohol, and testosterone.

There was nothing else to say and Dinah turned to go back inside.

"Your *gkomenos* has a gun."

"What?"

"Your boyfriend. He has a gun."

The remark blindsided Dinah. Why would Thor bring a gun with him to Greece? Norwegian policemen didn't carry guns when they were on duty at home unless there was a crisis. Oh, no! Had it been stolen? Was Thor's gun the one that Yannis used to shoot Fathi? Was that the reason Thor had been so distant and uncommunicative after returning from his ride with the police? If his gun had been used in the commission of a crime, he could be prosecuted by the Greek authorities. More importantly, he would never forgive himself. Panicky, she about-faced, ran down the hall, and took the stairs two at a time.

He was still sleeping. She brought herself up short. Would a man who'd lost his gun sleep that soundly? If he had a gun, it must still be here. Where had Alcina come across it? Was she hinting that someone other than Yannis had broken into the house and swiped it? I should have grilled her. I shouldn't have let her make such an insinuation without demanding to know exactly what it was that she was insinuating.

"Thor? Thor, wake up." She turned on the overhead light. "We need to talk."

He sat up and rubbed his eyes. "What's the matter?"

"Is there a gun in the house?"

He hesitated. "My service pistol."

So it was true. "Show me."

He opened his bedside table drawer, pulled out a sleek black pistol, and pointed it toward the floor. "Why so surprised? I'm a cop."

"A cop on holiday. Has the gun been fired?"

"You mean recently?"

"Of course I mean recently."

"No."

"Are you sure?"

He aimed it toward the window, examined the barrel, and removed the clip. "It's clean and fully loaded."

She sat down on the edge of the bed. "Why? Why do you have a gun in Greece?"

"For protection. Southern Europe isn't like Norway. *Norway* isn't like Norway anymore. Violent crime is on the increase and there are foreign criminal networks moving into Norwegian cities."

"But you told me yourself that Norwegian policemen don't carry guns, not loaded ones anyway. Not unless they're going to meet a polar bear. You didn't change your no-guns policy even after the massacre on Utoya two years ago."

"Yes, and plenty of us think that's a mistake. The Utoya fiasco would never have happened in the U.S. If Norwegian cops had carried guns, half of those kids would've been saved. We looked worse than *The Gang Who Couldn't Shoot Straight*. We couldn't shoot at all. We weren't even competent enough to get a damned helicopter off the ground because the regular crew was on holiday. The SWAT team had to take a boat to the island and the first boat sank under the excess weight of their equipment. All the while that monster continued to pick off children one by one." He raked a hand through his hair and curbed his anger.

"The point is, I have the gun because there's lots of crime in Greece, especially in the cities."

The shootings of sixty-nine teenagers by a right-wing, anti-immigrant zealot in 2011 had jolted Norwegians to the core and she could understand Thor's determination not to be caught defenseless in the future. But gun violence had already disrupted their holiday and the knowledge that he was packing heat other than the romantic sort, unnerved her. She said, "Kanaris isn't a city."

"I was in Athens for a week before you arrived. Athens has crime." He put the gun back in the drawer. "There's plenty of serious crime. Greece is a gateway for human trafficking into Europe. Thousands of women and young girls are forced into the sex industry here. There's narcotics, weapons, organized crime. And theft is on the rise everywhere."

"At the moment, theft is the only crime that worries me. Alcina knows about the gun. She could have told anyone where it is and let him walk out the door with it. Yannis or whoever could have used it to murder the Iraqi and put it back without you ever knowing."

"You ever consider a career in law enforcement?"

She scowled.

"It's a joke, Dinah. A quote from my favorite TV show. Crocket used to say that to Tubbs all the time."

"You're pretty glib for someone just roused from a deep sleep."

"I'm not used to waking up to the third degree. I don't know when Alcina caught sight of my gun, but nobody has touched it but me. Look, if it'll make you feel any better, I'll carry it in my coat pocket and sleep with it under my pillow."

"Oh, for crying out loud."

"I know you're upset, Dinah. Seeing a dead man would upset anyone. But I have a permit to carry and I'm a trained marksman."

She still felt uneasy. "Who did you phone when I went to fetch Brakus?"

"Alcina."

"She says she didn't receive any calls."

"Which one of us do you believe?"

"You, I guess."

"You guess?"

"You, completely and conclusively. But don't you dare put that blaster under your pillow."

His face broke into a smile. "Come back to bed. We'll talk in the morning."

She unhitched the belt of her robe and took a step, but his smile waned.

He wrinkled his nose. "I smell marijuana."

"Alcina's smoking a weed pipe on the veranda."

"And you said theft was the only crime I should worry about. I'd better go speak with her. We can't afford to draw more unfavorable attention to Zenia's house." He swung out of bed and went to get his robe out of the closet.

She couldn't suppress a frisson of desire as he walked across the room. He looked like a Greek god in the nude, an absolute Adonis. A shadow of superstitious fear crossed her mind. Adonis was another of Artemis' victims. She sent a wild boar to gore him to death.

Thor marched off downstairs and Dinah returned to the window. The moon had slipped out of sight like a guilty thing, but the sky was riddled with stars. She knew nothing about astronomy except that the names of the constellations had originated with the ancient Greeks. Orion was one of them. Even she recognized the three stars known as Orion's belt. She scanned the heavens looking for them, but evidently Orion wasn't visible at this time of year. She turned her head this way and that to see if she could make out Aries and the ram of the Golden Fleece or Aquarius and the image of the shepherd boy who carried cups of water and nectar to the gods. But the Greeks' ability to connect the dots and visualize rams and water carriers was greater than hers.

She tried to eavesdrop on the conversation between Thor and Alcina, but the tree frogs were too loud. Zenia Stephanadis' ear trumpet would have come in handy. She had an urge to meet Zenia and see for herself the woman who seemed to perturb everyone. Maybe after K.D. had been packed off to Atlanta, she would dream up an excuse to pay the old lady a visit. If she was going to remain on Samos, she might as well satisfy her curiosity about the Stephanadis sisters while one of them was still alive to tell.

Thor tromped back into the room, shucked off his robe, and fell back across the bed like a toppled statue. "This place is like your American Wild West. The hell with law and order. Everybody's an anarchist."

Dinah laughed. Why had she been so panicky? The Greek gods were messing with her head. The god Pan had stampeded her with an irrational fear and the goddess Psyche had psyched her out with ridiculous doubts. What was clear beyond a doubt, the real-life man in front of her needed comforting. She turned off the light and went back to bed.

Day 2

Chapter Six

Except for the marble floors, the interior of the Samos International Airport reminded Dinah of the Greyhound Bus Station in Needmore, Georgia. She sat in the sunny waiting area dreading the arrival of Olympic Air Flight 752 from Athens. It had been due at 10:50, but it was already a half hour late and the longer she waited, the antsier she became. Thor had dropped her off at ten to give her time to rent a car and organize her thoughts. It was now 11:30 and her thoughts remained as hectic and muddled as they'd been last night, and any minute now she'd have the added headache of a teenage desperado on the lam from a burglary rap.

Flight 752 was the logical connection with the flight arriving in Athens from Atlanta, but what if K.D. hadn't taken it? What if she'd defied her mother's instructions and hared off into the center of Athens? Dinah had seen K.D. operate. She'd inherited her mother's good looks and her father's aptitude for chicanery. Left to her own devices, she could wreak havoc.

A crowd of arrivals from another flight filed past, donning their sunglasses and yakking into their cell phones. Dinah checked her watch and fingered the phone in her pocket. At what point should she call Neesha and report the girl a no show? She kneaded her forehead. The fun was leaking out of her summer plans from a dozen different holes. She got up and paced. If the kid took a detour into Athens, I suppose I'll be obliged to chase her down and retrieve her. What a pain. It will be an even bigger pain if she shows up on Samos and refuses to leave. What then? Even if she acknowledges she did wrong and feels genuinely bad about it, what are the odds I can persuade her to go home and face the music? I wonder if I could petition the Greek authorities to round her up and ship her home? In leg irons, if necessary.

At 11:45, a voice announced the arrival of Flight 752. Dinah coached herself. Be sympathetic, but firm. Don't try to bully her or she'll park herself on Samos just to spite you. And don't, don't, *don't* let her wheedle a few extra days out of you. Was there a plausible threat or a bribe that would appeal to the girl's self-interest? Two years ago, she'd wanted to be a great writer. Maybe there was a school somewhere or a program or a mad professor in a distant land willing to tutor a fugitive wannabe author.

Dinah hadn't smoked a cigarette since last New Year's Eve, but she was beset by an almost unbearable craving. Did she have time to go to the snack shop and…?

"Aunt Dinah!" Dragging a large Louis Vuitton roller bag behind her, K.D. parted a sea of tourists and swooped toward her. She wore lime green harem pants that swished and billowed, an electric pink camp shirt, a pink visor, and red, heart-shaped sunglasses. She'd grown another few inches, to maybe five-ten or -eleven, and her long, straight hair had gone from sandy blond to auburn. The only thing that hadn't changed was her expression of smug entitlement. She enfolded Dinah in a suffocating embrace. "You are a perfect saint to give me asylum."

Dinah extricated herself and eked out a tight smile. "Hello, K.D. Or is it Katherine nowadays?"

"While I'm in Greece, I think I shall answer to Katarina." A gangling boy in a T-shirt that read "Raining Pleasure" rubbernecked as he walked past and she took off her glasses and gave him a flirty half smile. She held one arm of her glasses between her little white teeth and searched the crowd. "Where's your boyfriend?" Her drawl had thickened, along with her mascara, and if she still grieved for her father, she gave no outward sign of it.

"What makes you think I have a boyfriend?"

"Lucien told my mother you'd come to Greece to rendezvous. Is this one a policeman like the one you had when you lived in Seattle or an egghead like the last one in Hawaii?"

Dinah made a mental note to kill her blabbermouth brother. "I assume you didn't check any luggage."

"This is all I have in the whole, wide world." She essayed a rueful smile.

"It looks like a lot. I'm surprised the airline didn't make you check it."

"I slipped one of the flight attendants twenty American dollars."

"Terrific. Let's go." Dinah steamed off toward the parking lot and her canary yellow Kia Picanto rental. Princess Katarina and her Louis Vuitton trundled along in her wake. Dinah trained her eyes straight ahead, hoping that it was only the princess' bright colors that turned so many heads. For all she knew, K.D. was snatching purses as she went.

When they got to the car, Dinah popped the trunk, hoisted Louis inside, and took her place behind the wheel.

"It's simply too glorious!" K.D. stood beside the car and raised her arms heavenward. "I can't believe I'm really in Greece."

"I can't either." Dinah fastened her seat belt and rethought the wisdom of not bullying. "Get in, K.D."

"This is so exciting!" The girl gave a little squeal and folded her long legs into the Picanto.

Dinah turned the key, jerked the car into gear, and lurched out of the lot. Leaving the airport, she drove east along the coast road toward Pythagório, named for Samos' native son, Pythagoras. Geometry hadn't been one of Dinah's best subjects in school, but she'd memorized the Pythagorean theorem for the sheer deliciousness of the word "hypotenuse." She had read in her Samos guide book that Pythagoras was deemed the first communist, although his notions of equality were limited to his upper-crust friends and disciples. Nevertheless, he taught that money and property should be held for the common good.

She drove for about three miles, passing a ritzy resort hotel that looked wonderful, but well outside her budget. She should have reserved a hotel yesterday when her mind was clear and her temper was cool. Although in retrospect, neither of those conditions had actually applied.

Broken pieces of marble columns—Corinthian, Ionian, Doric—littered the sides of the road and ruined arches and agoras stood in the weedy spaces between the hotels and businesses. The modern town, and probably the airport runway, had been built on top of one of the oldest port cities in the world. It was an archaeological atrocity. Mentor's resentment of the British notwithstanding, anyone who cared about the grandeur that was Greece would be appalled by such casual destruction.

Traffic ground to a stop as they entered the main part of the village and she began to worry about finding a room. She inched along, immune to the kitschy charm of the cafes and shops, and irritated on many fronts. "Tell me about this trouble you're in, K.D. You burglarized somebody's house?"

"It's been blown all out of proportion, Aunt Dinah. It's really only a misunderstanding."

Dinah wasn't her aunt and she didn't regard this new form of address as an honor. "Help me to understand. Did you not do it? Were you falsely accused?"

"My friend Fiona and her parents go to dinner, okay? So Fiona leaves the back door unlocked for me and I sneak into her house to get the vibrator she's ordered for me off the Internet. I hang around for a few minutes to look at her new posters of Zac Efron and Kevin Zegers, and everybody comes home early and her father goes, 'Hey! She's stealing Fiona's *curling iron*.' I mean, I'm hiding it behind my back and he sees it for just a second, but *curling iron*?" She gave a derisive little hoot. "And Fiona totally freaks because she doesn't want her folks to know that it's a vibrator and think that it's hers and she just starts screaming and I run out and her parents call the police."

Dinah wasn't so much surprised by K.D.'s interest in sex toys as by the change in her vernacular. When last they'd met, K.D.

had flaunted her precociousness, sneering at clichés and salting her conversation with literary jawbreakers like verisimilitude and denouement. Having lost her own father at a young age, Dinah knew what it was like to go through a stage of rebellion and acting out. But she had a particular aversion to being lied to and the story K.D. had just told was seriously lacking in verisimilitude. "If that's all there was to it, the police would have dropped the case as soon as they talked to Fiona. Did you take something else?"

"No. I told you. Fiona has issues. Isn't *that* a darling little hotel?" She pointed to a small white building across from the marina.

Tired of fighting the traffic, Dinah turned in the palm-bordered entrance and parked under the portico at the front door. "Wait here."

She proceeded into the lobby and went straight to the reception desk. A young woman with long, dark hair and ravishing olive skin looked up from her book. "*Yiasou.*"

"*Yiasou.* I'd like a room with two..." Dinah stopped and reconsidered how much togetherness she could stand. "Two rooms for one night."

"I'm sorry. We are fully booked for the next three days. There is a large conference in town." She indicated a message board in front of the elevator doors.

Dinah read the list of today's meetings. MODELING RARE EVENTS, 9:00, Third Floor, Room C and RISK AND STOCHASTIC CONTROL, 2:00, Third Floor, Room B. "What kind of a conference is it?"

"Actuarial Science."

With murder so fresh in her mind, a conference of people who calculate life expectancy and the probability of disaster struck her as ominous. "Could you recommend another hotel nearby where there might be a vacancy?"

"I think all of the hotels are full. The Greek Council for Refugees is holding its conference in town and there are attendees from all over Europe. There are also several large wedding parties."

Dinah didn't want to spend all afternoon looking for a hotel. Maybe the best thing would be to take K.D. back to Kanaris for the night and hope that Alcina didn't offer her a joint. Reluctantly, she returned to the car. "No luck. They're full up."

K.D. had draped herself across the front fender of the Picanto as if posing for a commercial. "I'm not full up. I'm famishing, Aunt Dinah. Can we at least eat lunch here?"

"Why not?" Dinah had noticed a sign near the reception desk for a terrace café. She moved the Picanto to a parking spot at the far end of the hotel and the two of them wended their way along a flower-lined footpath that led behind the building to the terrace. They sat down at a table overlooking the marina, which was chock-a-block with tour boats and yachts, many of which bore German names. Bavaria and Windzerzaust and Wandervogel. Dinah gazed through the polarized lenses of her Wayfarers at the shimmering blue waters of the bay bounded in the distance by low, chalk-white mountains. A double-masted schooner glided across the horizon. She wished she were on it, en route to Troy.

A waiter delivered menus to the table and poured water.

K.D. fawned up at him. "I'll have a piña colada."

"No." Dinah's bark startled the man. "We'll have two glasses of tea, with ice, please."

"Yes, madam." He bowed and withdrew.

Dinah's brows drew together. "Don't test me, K.D."

"I was just kidding."

"I wasn't."

A truce ensued by tacit agreement and they perused the menu. The specialty of the house seemed to be mezés, small plates of stuffed grape leaves or fried vegetables or tomatoes and cheese. When the waiter returned with the tea, they ordered a selection to share. While they waited, Dinah watched the schooner sail out of sight.

"You have to go home tomorrow, K.D. I know you and your mother are frightened about this burglary charge, but it was a mistake to run away. You'll probably get a slap on the wrist and a year's probation. At most. If you pay restitution, a good lawyer can probably get you off scot-free and by the time you graduate from high school, the charge will have been expunged from your record and you can do the debutante thing with the rest of your set."

"I don't want to be like those boring cookie cut-outs. I want to experience *everything* and live life to the fullest like my daddy did."

Dinah forbore to observe that her daddy was a sociopath. She didn't know how much K.D. had been told about his criminal exploits, but it was clear she still idolized him. "Don't you want to be a writer anymore, K.D.? It's what your father would have wanted you to do."

"I'll write when I'm old. After I've *lived*. I don't want to waste any more time going to school or dragging around with an ankle bracelet. I thought I'd hang with you for a while and then move on to Sydney. I *adored* Sydney."

Dinah was about to resort to bullying when out of the tail of her eye, she glimpsed a familiar face. Savas Brakus promenaded along the marina carrying a large shopping bag. He was accompanied by a man with a mustache like Saddam Hussein's and the policeman who'd come to investigate the murder last night. When they reached a concrete walkway that led from the marina to the pool, Brakus said something to the policeman and handed him the bag. There were nods and smiles all around. Brakus shook hands with both men and split off toward the parking lot. The other two continued back along the line of moored yachts, their heads bent in conversation.

Chapter Seven

K.D. yawned and her eyelids drooped. She was probably jet-lagged and she would sound less harebrained after she'd had a nap. At least, Dinah hoped so. She decided to postpone the argument and take her back to Kanaris. At dinner tonight, she would be absolutely clear and implacable. No playing pattycake. No beating about the bush. Under no circumstances would she permit K.D. to "hang with her" for longer than one night. She didn't have to lecture the girl about the importance of staying in school or the rightness of owning up to her mischief. A murder had been committed a mere stone's throw from the house where Dinah lived and, according to Thor, the country was rife with crime. He could help impress upon the kid that Samos wasn't safe and she would save herself and everyone else a lot of grief by going home to Atlanta and turning herself in to the police.

Careful not to say anything that might give her the idea that she had won the battle of wills, Dinah paid the bill and drove back toward Kanaris. K.D. dozed and Dinah's thoughts digressed to Brakus. What was he doing loafing along in the company of a man who was the spitting image of the deceased dictator of Iraq, and the policeman who was investigating the murder of the Iraqi named Fathi? The trio didn't jibe. Brakus didn't even jibe with himself. In his taverna, he was obsequious and confidential. At the murder scene, he was nervous and sullen. But in Pythagório he swaggered, fairly beaming with self-assurance, as if one of those fancy yachts had his name on it. And what was in that shopping bag he gave the cop? Sandwiches and beer? Contributions to the policeman's ball? Payola? And if so, for what?

As they got closer to the turnoff to Kanaris, piles of garbage began to appear along the sides of the road, bits and pieces strewn by scavenging birds and sea breezes. She'd read about strikes by the sanitation workers in Athens where uncollected garbage piled up in the streets. It had seemed like a big-city problem, but with gas stations on the island charging over ten dollars for a gallon of unleaded, evidently a few Samians had decided that transporting their trash to a disposal facility was too costly. In another two to three centuries, after the detritus had rusted and decayed under layers of soil and rock, archaeologists would dig it up and label the bits as "artifacts," just as Dinah would soon be doing with the remains of Trojan culture. But at the present moment, the drifting plastic sacks and Styrofoam egg cartons depressed her and it was hard to take the long view.

The parking lot for the village sat at the foot of the hill with an unobstructed view across the Aegean to Turkey. She parked and opened the trunk for K.D. "From here, we walk. You can roll Louis up the lane or tote him up the stairs." She pointed to the near-vertical steps that climbed skyward toward the main street of the village.

"Can't you drive to the house and unload?" K.D. sounded dubious.

"Not allowed. It's longer by the lane, but with this much weight to lug, it'll be easier."

"How far is it?"

"A half mile, give or take."

K.D. hefted Louis out of the trunk, yanked up the leather handle and set her heart glasses on her nose. "Whatever." A note of defiance edged into her voice.

Dinah set off at a brisk clip and didn't look back. Maybe the isolation of the village and the lack of conveniences would help to discourage the girl.

K.D. didn't complain, although she was damp from sweat when they topped out near Brakus' taverna and turned onto the cobbled lane toward Marilita's house. Louis racketed and jounced and Dinah heard several labored intakes of breath behind her as K.D. in her T-strap sandals struggled to keep from tripping or stubbing a toe. Dinah stopped at the alley that led to the house. It was blocked by an antique, maroon-colored roadster that looked like a relic from the Roaring Twenties. A plaque in gold letters on the wood dash identified it as an Isotta Fraschini.

"You said cars weren't allowed," crabbed K.D.

"It belongs to the landlady." Instinctively, Dinah knew that this was Zenia's car. She walked around toward the veranda. No one was there. Zenia must be consoling Alcina in Alcina's private room. Or canning her. However many years she and Yannis had worked here, however reliable or devoted they might be, the notoriety of another murder associated with the property probably wouldn't sit well with Zenia.

"I'll show you to your room," said Dinah, not wanting to have to explain the presence of a new lodger. "You can take a shower and rest for a few hours before dinner."

"Will your boyfriend eat dinner with us?"

"I don't know. He's kind of busy." Dinah hurried her up the stairs, wincing with each thunk of the heavy suitcase on the uncarpeted marble staircase. At the end of the hall, she opened the guestroom door and ushered K.D. inside. "The bathroom's next door and there are fresh towels in the cupboard under the sink. Try to sleep for a few hours and I'll knock on your door around five." She turned to leave.

"Aunt Dinah?"

"Just call me Dinah, okay?"

K.D. flopped down on the bed and looked up at her with moist eyes. "Dinah, my daddy was a drug lord, my mother is totally self-involved, my brother is a head case, and I don't have one friend in the whole wide world."

K.D. was intentionally strumming on her heartstrings, but Dinah felt a twinge of empathy nevertheless. Her own family could be characterized in almost the same words. Her father had died running drugs when she was ten years old; her mother was a serial bride; and her beloved brother had lately taken to dabbling in art forgery. She did have a few friends, but they were scattered across the world and, generally speaking, they weren't people she could call at three o'clock in the morning for solace or advice.

"Your mother's overwhelmed just now, K.D. She's trying to pick up the pieces and start a new life now that your father's gone and you and your brother aren't making it any too easy. Give her a break, why don't you? You're smarter and stronger than she is and you know it. You're a survivor, like me. You'll come through the turbulence all right and when you look back some day, you'll have plenty of material for a bestselling novel. Novels about dysfunctional families are all the rage."

"If only you let me stay here until you leave to go on your dig, that will give mother a break and it will totally save my life. I won't be a nuisance, I swear I won't. Please, Dinah?"

"Let me think about it." Dinah couldn't believe she was letting this teenage manipulatrix get to her. "Keep out of my hair for a few hours and I'll get back to you at dinner."

"Oh, thank you, thank you, thank you! You are so good."

Dinah laced into herself on the way downstairs. What an idiot I am! I shouldn't have said anything that left open the possibility. Now I've shown weakness. If I'm not hard as nails, K.D. will twist "let me think about it" into an ironclad promise. Stupid, stupid, stupid!

"You're the Pelerin woman. Ramberg told me you'd be staying here, too."

She looked up into a wizened face riveted by eyes as round and alert as a bird's and as black as squid ink. The eyes were surmounted by high, penciled black brows and between the brows hung a topaz pendant. "Yes, ma'am. I'm Dinah. And you must be Mrs. Stephanadis."

"Of course, I am." Thor's wax-museum description wasn't far off the mark. A dusting of white powder coated her crinkled cheeks and a cupid's bow of magenta lipstick overtopped her pleated lip line. Thor had neglected to mention that she dressed like an avatar of high fashion, circa 1926. Her head was encapsulated in a tight-fitting turquoise cap from which the topaz had been suspended by a silver fob. She wore a beaded, dropped-waist black overdress tied in a sash around her hips and a gauzy turquoise skirt flagged around her ankles. The silver, funnel-shaped earhorn she clutched in one blue-veined hand bespoke an even earlier era.

She cocked her head and gave Dinah an appraising look. "You're darker than I thought you'd be. Gallic, I'd guess. Pelerin. French, isn't it?"

"Yes, ma'am. It means pilgrim. My father was a descendant of French Huguenots. My mother is Native American. Seminole."

"I didn't ask for your biography, although I suppose it accounts in part for the bone structure. You look a lot like your young man. More fine-boned. Prettier in a prosaic way. But the same eyes. I daresay Ramberg's fallen in love with his own reflection. Like Narcissus. Let's hope you don't suffer the same fate as Echo, the nymph who loved *him*."

Dinah knew the crux of the myth, but Zenia seemed keen to expound. "What happened to Echo?"

"Narcissus spurned her and she died of a broken heart."

Dinah got why Zenia was not well liked.

"Al-ci-na!" The old biddy called down the hallway in a clarion voice. "Bring a pot of tea and two cups. I'll be in the parlor with the Pelerin woman." She held out her arm to Dinah. "I'll want steadying."

Dinah took her arm and walked her into the front room. She gave off a strong odor of lilies, reminiscent of a funeral home.

"This will do." She perched ruler straight on a French provincial chair under a painting of a Spanish knight. "Sit down across from me so I can see you."

Dinah took that as a license to stare, which was fortunate because she couldn't take her eyes off the woman. "You speak excellent English. Hardly any accent at all."

"I can mimic any accent. That's what actors are taught to do."

"You were an actress, too?"

"I *am* an actress."

"I didn't mean…"

"What?" She raised her silver earhorn to her ear.

"I assumed you were retired."

"I can no longer play Antigone. But there are still a few roles suitable to my years. I attended the Stella Adler Studio in New York. And if that 'too' I heard is a reference to my late sister, I have always had the greater talent and the wider range. 'In your choices lies your talent.' That was Stella's mantra. Marilita's carnality reduced her to vulgar, third-rate choices." She spoke in a dispassionate, matter-of-fact way, as if carnality were neither good nor bad, but merely a limiting factor in the matter of acting roles.

"Have you acted in any films?" asked Dinah.

"I despise films. I'm a *stage* actress."

Alcina stole into the room on cat feet and set a tray on the table between them.

"Thank you, Alcina." Zenia lifted the teapot and poured two steaming cups. "I'm not foolish enough to believe that a hot drink is cooling. I drink hot tea because I'm old and old people are always cold even in warm weather. I'm accustomed to being indulged. I take for granted that you'll have a cup with me?"

"Of course."

"Cream and sugar?"

"No. Thank you."

She handed Dinah a brimming cup. Her hand was as steady as a sniper's and she didn't need eyeglasses to tong three tiny sugar cubes into her own cup. "What do you think of our island?"

"I haven't done much sightseeing yet, but what I've seen is lovely."

"Ramberg said you're an archaeologist."

"Cultural anthropologist, actually. I don't have a full-time position with a university or a museum, but occasionally I'm asked to assist an archaeology team. I'll be working with a team near Troy in a few weeks."

"There's an archaeological excavation underway right here on Samos at the Temple of Hera. Do you know your Greek myths?"

"I know that Hera was the wife of Zeus and queen of the Greek gods. She was famous for being jealous and vengeful to mortals who displeased her."

Zenia stirred her tea and pursed her lips. "She was temperamental, but she's ours. She was born on Samos. All Samian women have something of Hera in their blood. Some more than others, isn't that right, Alcina?"

Dinah looked behind her. She hadn't realized that Alcina was still lurking.

Alcina said something in Greek.

"What did you say?" Zenia raised her earhorn. "Speak up, child. Don't mumble."

"You shouldn't make sport of the dead."

"Make sport? You mustn't be so prickly, Alcina. Your mother's lack of self-control is a lesson to the rest of us to hold strong."

Dinah did the math and made an intuitive leap. "Marilita Stephan was your mother, Alcina?"

"And she was *not* vulgar. The *Athens News* calls her a martyr to the junta resistance movement and a Greek Joan of Arc." She gave Zenia a stormy look, caressed her glass blue-eye fetish, and scudded back into the house.

A drop of perspiration trickled from under Zenia's cap, rolled past the topaz pendant on her forehead, and followed the curve of a penciled eyebrow down her cheek. She dabbed it away with her napkin. "You must excuse my niece. A mousy creature with a head full of ghosts and old wives' tales. Of course, she's anxious about her husband's plight."

"She seemed more anxious to defend her mother," said Dinah.

"She has little enough cause for that. She was born…What is it the English say? On the wrong side of the blanket. Marilita scorned marriage the way she scorned every other proper institution. If there were such a thing as the curse of the evil eye, Marilita drew it onto herself with her outrageous behavior."

Dinah couldn't think of a response, but Zenia was already pushing herself up from her chair and smoothing her skirt. She had delivered her best lines and the performance was over. "I have to be at a rehearsal in Pythagório at four. An adaptation of a lesser comedy, but it keeps me from withering on the vine. You must come to my house for tea tomorrow afternoon. Bring Ramberg and that raffish young woman in the harem pants. She looks like a natural actress."

Dinah watched her drive away in the maroon Isotta. Zenia Stephanadis might be physically frail. She might be spiteful and eccentric and unpopular with the villagers. But she was the dead opposite of senile.

Chapter Eight

Dinah had run across the evil eye superstition in her studies of several ancient cultures. Jews, Muslims, Buddhists, and Christians—at one time or another, they all held the belief that certain individuals could bestow bad luck, sickness, or even death by focusing their malevolent gaze upon a victim. There were variations among the different cultures, but most people believed that the evil eye sprang from envy, which could be intentional or unintentional. She thought she detected a tinge of envy in Zenia, but it was envy of Marilita, not Alcina. Strange that Alcina would be so eclectic in her choice of protective icons, wearing both the evil-eye fetish and the Greek Orthodox cross. Dinah put it on her mental to-do list to read up on the Aegean variant of the curse and discover how it was that black magic and Christianity could co-exist so easily on Alcina's ample bosom.

At the moment, it was the story of Narcissus that occupied her mind. It hadn't occurred to her that she and Thor looked alike and Zenia's gibe had piqued her vanity. She lay across the bed on her stomach, propped on her elbows, thumbing through her book of myths. When she found the chapter on Narcissus, she flattened the book wide open and read.

Narcissus was the son of a river god, Cephisus, and a water nymph, Lirope. After the birth of her baby, Lirope sought out the prophet, Tiresias, and asked, "Will he live a long life?" In the typically cryptic style of prophets, Tiresias answered, "If ever he knows himself, he will die." Apparently, this warning flummoxed Lirope and she failed to get the memo to Narcissus. Meanwhile, he grew up to be the handsomest of men and the heartthrob of all the nymphs, but none of them could win his heart.

Back on Olympus, Zeus prevailed on pretty Echo to keep Hera distracted with a shaggy dog story while he sneaked off for a frolic with one of the other nymphs. Echo did as she was told, but when Hera tumbled to the trick, she punished her by taking away her ability to speak her own thoughts. She could only repeat the last few words that others had spoken, using *their* voices and *their* accents. Thus handicapped, she was at a disadvantage when she tried to win Narcissus' heart. She smothered him in kisses, but he was cold as ice. And then one day he saw his own face reflected in a forest pool and, like a Capuchin monkey, he thought it was a separate being. Incapable of self-recognition and too infatuated to tear himself away, he pined away beside the pool until he died—spurned by his own reflection.

Dinah closed the book. If that was what Tiresias meant by 'knowing himself,' the prophet had a cracked concept of self-knowledge. She got up and assessed her reflection in the dresser mirror, turning from side to side. Her jaw was square like Thor's. But his face was broader and his cheekbones more chiseled, which lent an exotic, slightly Ghengis Khan aspect. Apart from having dark eyes and dark hair, she looked nothing like him.

Where was he? What was he doing? It was three o'clock. In another couple of hours, K.D. would start clamoring to be fed and Dinah didn't want to go to the taverna without an escort. Besides, she was itching to tell him where she'd seen Brakus and with whom and to break the news that Alcina was Marilita's daughter. It dawned on her that she'd forgotten to let him know that she wasn't spending the night in Pythagório after all. She took out her phone and dialed his number.

"Hallo."

"Hi. The hotels in Pythagório were all full and I'm back in Kanaris with K.D. Where are you?"

"Near Karlovassi on the northwest coast."

"What's there?"

"Nothing much. I'm walking on a beach called Megalo Seitani."

"Can you meet us for dinner at the taverna?"

"Sure." It was a tardy "sure," as if he had to think how to rejigger other plans. "Around six?"

"See you there."

She had told him she wouldn't be around tonight and he had every right to make alternate plans, but still…

She moseyed over to his bedside table and debated with her better angel. Mousing around in your lover's personal belongings is deplorable and unbecoming in the extreme, argued the hypothetical angel. Guns are a special case, countered her tough-minded side. She opened the drawer. His service pistol was gone. He *had* said he would carry it in his coat pocket. She felt a touch of sympathy. For someone who hated the heat as much as he did, wearing a coat while walking on the beach would be torment.

There was a soft knock at the door. "Dinah, would it be all right for me to take a walk?"

K.D. asking permission? Dinah compartmentalized one set of suspicions and opened the door on another.

The princess had lost the eye make-up and changed into cropped jeans, a white tee with a modest pink overshirt, and sneakers. She smiled angelically. "It's such a nice afternoon. I won't go far."

"I'll walk with you. The village is small, but there are lots of confusing little alleyways. I wouldn't want you to get lost."

"Has your boyfriend gotten home yet?"

"No. He'll meet us at the taverna later on for dinner."

"I can't keep calling him your boyfriend. What's his name?"

"Thor. Thor Ramberg."

"Thor. That's the name of the Norse god of thunder and lightning. Chris Hemsworth played Thor in the movie. Does Thor look as fabulous as Chris?"

"I don't know what Chris looks like." Reading about Echo had given Dinah an idea. She hadn't yet explored the gorge that separated Kanaris from the next mountain over. Based on the map in her Samos guide book, the trail started at the western edge of the village. A couple of hours of exercise and fresh air would settle her nerves and maybe if she yelled "Go home" and Echo repeated it a few times, K.D. would get the message. "I know just the place for a walk."

She swapped her sandals for her walking shoes, put on her Wayfarers, and the two of them set out. The lane back toward the village was beginning to feel routine except for the spot where Fathi's body had lain. The police hadn't marked it, but a rabbit ran over Dinah's grave as they passed. She saw stains where blood had seeped between the cobbles and hoped that K.D. didn't notice. She walked fast, but when they had passed through the shadowy bower of overhanging trees, the terrain opened and she relaxed and slowed down. The same ginger cat lazed on the same sun-warmed tiles. The sun set the bougainvillea aflame, turning it into a near-psychedelic experience, and the fragrance of wild thyme spiced the air. She'd read somewhere that the ancient Egyptians used thyme as an embalming agent and the Greeks used it as a fumigant. Certainly, this part of Samos was well fumigated.

As they passed the rear of the taverna and cut through the alley to the main street, Dinah darted a look toward the terrace. There was no sign of Brakus. A few customers, mostly tourists, refreshed themselves with iced drinks and frosty mugs of beer. They all had daypacks stacked around their feet and water bottles. Water! She kicked herself. Well, it was too late now. But they wouldn't hike far and, from what she'd read, the trail was mostly shaded until they reached the gorge overlook.

From the center of the village, they walked down a steep hill in the direction from which Yannis had come yesterday evening. Was it less than twenty-four hours ago? It seemed like a lifetime. Where had he gotten those wine bottles? She didn't recall them having labels. Maybe the winery that processed the grapes grown in Zenia's vineyard was located along this road and he'd tapped a barrel for his private consumption.

K.D. barged into her thoughts. "Have you made up your mind about me staying? I didn't do anything that anybody should go to jail for. If you don't believe me, you can call Fiona and ask her if I stole anything. She'll tell you it was all a mistake."

"She needs to tell that to the police."

"What if you were to call up your ex-boyfriend, that policeman in Seattle, and ask him to talk to somebody in the Atlanta Police Department? Aren't all policemen sort of like a fraternity or a club or something? They scratch each other's backs, right?"

Dinah hadn't thought about the unspeakable Detective Nick Isparta in months and she had no desire to speak of him now. "I don't think that's the solution to your problem, K.D."

The cobbled street dead-ended in front of a low, rectangular building with three green, garage-type metal doors, all closed. A sun-bleached mural above the center door featured a black-bearded satyr tipping a horn of wine into his open mouth. An old-fashioned wine press with a wood-stave tank and a rusty iron screw for crushing the grapes rested on a square concrete platform in front of the building. Security cameras had been mounted above each door and the man with the Saddam Hussein mustache was sitting on a cinder block in front of the center door tossing two strands of worry beads with one hand. As the first strand hit the second, they made a sharp, clacking noise. From under lowering black brows, his eyes seemed to frisk them.

"What a skeeve," said K.D.

If skeeve meant scary, Dinah agreed in spades. She put her arm around K.D.'s shoulders and steered her toward a yellow sign to the right of the winery with a stick figure of a hiker. From there, the trail branched off through the forest. Dinah forged ahead. It was curious that a tiny winery in a tiny village would invest in modern security cameras and post a guard to protect its outdated equipment. And there was something diabolical about that man. He might be a Greek, or even a Turk. But in her mind she had classified him as an Iraqi and not an attractive one. Whoever he was, he knew Brakus and the policeman who investigated Fathi's murder. If he was guarding the winery when Yannis dropped by yesterday, he probably knew him, as well.

The trail hadn't been maintained and the farther they went, the denser the foliage became and the more closed-in she felt. Jackals and wolves were nocturnal, but murderers weren't. She remembered Thor's warning about human trafficking. She pictured herself and K.D. being waylaid and bundled off to a brothel in Burkina Faso or Kiribati or to some hideous laboratory where their organs would be harvested for sale. Thor had a quirky affinity for TV detectives, but he was no flake. He was practical and prudent and his decision to carry a gun began to seem more reasonable, prescient even. Maybe she shouldn't have ventured off without him. She stopped and waited for K.D.

"I have another idea, Dinah. You could withdraw a few thousand dollars from my daddy's account, I mean it *is* my inheritance, and I could go traveling on my own. I'm old enough to take care of myself and you know what a fanatic Daddy was about people pulling themselves up by their bootstraps and making their own way in the world. He'd be so *for* this plan. You wouldn't have to tell my mother that I ever arrived on Samos. She could think I'd vanished into thin air. It would be our secret, yours and mine, and I would be eternally grateful. Later on, of course, when all this burglary business has blown over, I'll call her and explain that I just had to grow and move on. She'll understand."

"Your mother would not understand, K.D., and she would not feel eternally grateful. She would have me jailed for interference with parental custody or contributing to the delinquency of a minor. Whatever the charge, I'd have lots of time to regret it. That much is sure. What's gotten into you?" Dinah almost laughed. She was echoing Thor asking *her* what had gotten into *her*. Samos seemed to infect everyone with the germ of anarchy.

The canopy overhead thinned, letting in more sunlight. Her jitters passed and she decided to keep walking, staying far enough ahead of K.D. so she wouldn't have to hear any more of her schemes, at least not until dinner. The trail forked. One branch appeared wider, well trodden, and less densely forested. Shafts of sunlight slanted through the trees picking out flecks of mica in the sandy soil and making them glitter like sequins.

"This way." She motioned to K.D. and started down the wider trail. She hadn't gone a hundred yards when she encountered a tall, wide-bodied monk in a long, dirty cassock. She gave him a perfunctory smile and attempted to sidle past. He stretched out a gigantic arm and blocked her. His countenance, while not overtly hostile, was daunting. His eyes were black as jet and a bristly black beard splayed wildly down his chest.

"Let us by, please. *Me sinkhorite.*"

He stood like a wall, arm out. Even if he didn't understand English, he understood that she wanted to go past. And if he understood that and still didn't yield the right of way, then he must be some kind of a crazo. Dinah had few rules that she lived by, but one of the top three was don't mess with crazy people. She whirled around, gripped K.D. by the elbow, and hissed, "Let's beat feet."

"Are you looking for the footpath down into the *lagkadi*? I will guide you."

"No, no." Dinah kept her feet moving forward. "That won't be necessary. We'll just retrace our steps."

"I can show you a beehive near the overlook." He scuffed along close on her heels, kicking sand into her shoes and breathing his dragon's breath of garlic and stale beer down her neck. "Nothing like Samian honey to cure the ills of the flesh and sublimate the baser hungers of the soul."

Dinah didn't want to find out what this bird's baser hungers might be. She stepped up her gait, pushing K.D. ahead of her.

"I am Brother Constantine. What are your names?"

"I'm Katarina," said K.D., swiveling her head. "And this is Dinah Pel…"

Dinah jabbed her in the ribs.

"Dinah Pelerin. Yes. I know who you are. You're staying in Marilita Stephan's house with the Norwegian policeman."

The back of Dinah's neck tingled. She felt exposed, vulnerable. How did this filthy, feral monk know where she lived or that Thor was a policeman?

"I can tell your fortunes if you like," said Constantine. "This mouth is a portal through which the goddess Hera speaks. Will you hear her?"

They reached the fork. Dinah prodded K.D. in the back. "Hurry up." She threw a glance behind her, saw Constantine stumble, and felt a heavy punch as he pitched head-first into her back.

She twisted as she went down, landed hard on her right hip, and yelped as more than two hundred pounds of malodorous monk flumped down on top of her. Grunting and flailing and pawing, Constantine seemed deliberately slow in rolling off of her.

With a cry of disgust, she wriggled out from under him and clambered to her feet, fear displaced by anger. "That better have been an accident, mister." She dusted herself off and started back to the village, looking behind her to make sure he didn't follow.

Brother Constantine sat up splay-legged and roared with laughter. "Give my regards to Inspector Ramberg, Miss Pelerin. And congratulations to Zenia. She has poked Kanaris in the eye but good this time."

Chapter Nine

Dinah put her head down and fumed off toward the village. Her thoughts were churning. What the hell was that old fraud talking about? Did Zenia's eye-poke have something to do with leasing Marilita's house to a policeman, even if the policeman was a Norwegian and on sabbatical? Why would the denizens of a bucolic Greek village that had not a single street light or stop sign care if a cop moved in?

Her mood had curdled. Behind her, K.D. was talking on her cell phone and her giggles grated on Dinah. As if murder weren't enough to think about, she had been saddled with a scheming, self-willed teenager, insulted by the landlady, and mauled by the scuzziest monk she'd ever seen. Her hipbone hurt from the fall and, from what she could see over her shoulder, the seat of her pants had an embarrassing stain.

Someone jostled her. Her heart skipped a beat as she looked up into the probing eyes of the codger who'd ogled her in the taverna.

He touched the side of his fisherman's cap with two fingers. "*Me sinkhorite.*"

"No problem." She stepped aside to let him pass.

"You are staying in Marilita Stephan's house with Inspector Ramberg," he said.

Inwardly, she cringed. It felt as if everybody in Kanaris had been peeping in her bedroom window. She said nothing.

He handed her a business card. "My name is Galen Stavros. I was a great admirer of the lady and a personal friend. I would like to call upon you some afternoon if that would be acceptable. It would be an honor to visit her home."

"You'll have to make an arrangement with Inspector Ramberg. He'll be at the Marc Antony later today."

"Thank you. I have an appointment this evening, but I will call later."

Dinah waited for K.D. to catch up. She had finished her phone call and Dinah looped an arm through hers to show solidarity as they walked past the winery. The man she thought of as Saddam was still there, tossing his worry beads and daring anyone to step foot on the property. She faced him with a skewering stare. She was fed up with the atmosphere of teasing intimidation.

From a distance, she espied Thor—an hour early—in the courtyard of the Marc Antony. He was repositioning a table umbrella to shield himself from the sun.

"Whoa!" said K.D. "That guy with the umbrella is gorgeous."

He really is, thought Dinah. And a lot more besides. He's smart and he's grounded and he never gives me grief for my kinks and shortcomings. He's an island of calm and I'm blowing in like a *meltemi*. She slowed down, brushed at the stain on her fanny, fluffed her hair, and took a deep breath. Whoa was exactly what she needed to do. She needed a time out and a large quantity of red wine. She would *not* be setting an example of abstinence tonight for K.D.'s sake.

Thor was still futzing with the umbrella when she and K.D. traipsed into the courtyard.

"*Kjære!*" His eyes flickered in a subtle, but decidedly amorous way. "I got back to the village faster than I thought. I've already ordered a bottle of wine."

She felt an instant uptick in attitude and a little shiver of sexual anticipation.

"This is Thor?" K.D. came on full gush. "OMG, he's blazing."

"Thor, this is K.D. Dobbs. She and her brother are…"

"Family," finished K.D., overdoing the drawl. "That's how we think of Dinah. She's the Rock of Gibraltar in our family."

Thor smiled and took her hand. "I'm very glad to meet you, K.D. You're the first member of Dinah's family I've met."

Dinah squeezed out a smile. The less said about her rogues' gallery of a family the better. "Let's sit down and unwind."

Thor pulled out a chair for K.D. and she wilted into it like a Slinky toy. "We have had ourselves *such* a day. We went for a walk in the woods and this gi-normous monk tried to lure us off to his beehive and Dinah was like, let's scrambola, and we did, but he followed us and knocked Dinah down in the dirt."

Thor shot Dinah a concerned look. "He knocked you down?"

"It was an accident. I think." She wasn't ready to delve into the encounter with Brother Constantine just yet.

Thor's fingers brushed her arm as he pulled out a chair for her. "It sounds as though you have adventures to tell."

"After the wine," she said.

He readjusted the umbrella and sat down. He was wearing an unstructured, tan linen jacket and slacks, more suitable for a business meeting than a walk on the beach. He said, "This morning I went into Samos Town and had a talk with the public prosecutor. He informed me that he had already released Yannis Thoma for insufficient evidence. No gun, no indictment."

"Are you a policeman?" asked K.D.

"In Norway. I am a police inspector in the Svalbard region."

Dinah hoped K.D. wouldn't start in on him to intercede with the Atlanta police on her behalf. "Why did you dodge the question when I asked you last night if the police had found the murder weapon?"

"I knew you wouldn't like the answer. They couldn't search without a warrant. When they returned with a warrant this morning, they came up empty."

She made a wry face. "Alcina probably went to the farmhouse and disposed of the gun as soon as the police drove off with Yannis."

"Maybe. I know you like Yannis for the murder, but I can't see that he has a motive."

"Did the police question anyone at the taverna to find out what Yannis and Fathi were arguing about?"

"No one claims to have understood."

"They were talking loud enough to be heard and there were other Greeks in the courtyard," said Dinah, looking around to see what was holding up the wine service. "And regardless of what you say, I think there's something fishy about Yannis."

Thor gave an exasperated shake of his head. "I think the good people of Kanaris don't rat out their fellow citizens. And I agree with you about Yannis. He's JDLR."

"What's that?" asked K.D.

"Just don't look right." He grinned. "I picked it up from an episode of *NYPD Blue*."

K.D. leaned her elbows on the table and cradled her chin in her hands. "It must be just thrilling to be a policeman."

Dinah was about to remark that policemen get a particular thrill protecting people's homes from burglars, but she bit her tongue.

Brakus bustled out of the kitchen with a tray and a bottle of wine. "Greetings, my friends." He set the wine on the table and offloaded a basket of bread, a bowl of olive oil, and two glasses. "And you have brought a guest. *Kalispéra*." He drew a corkscrew out of his apron pocket.

"Could we have another glass, please?" K.D. was irrepressible. "I can show you my ID if you like."

"No need. You are with a policeman, no less."

Dinah sliced a glance at Brakus. "Do you know a monk named Constantine?"

"There are no monasteries near Kanaris. No monks."

"There's one," said K.D. "He talks kind of nutty and smells as if he hasn't had a bath since the Middle Ages."

"A homeless beggar," said Brakus. "Since the austerity cuts, there are many homeless people sleeping rough, many unemployed." He seemed preoccupied tonight. He didn't ask K.D.

where she came from or what she was doing in Kanaris, or where and how Dinah and Thor had spent their day. He uncorked the wine and poured a taste for Thor, who pronounced it fine. He poured two glasses and turned to go. "It is permitted to serve the young lady?"

"Sure. Why not?" The way Dinah felt at the moment, she didn't care if Princess K got plastered so long as there was plenty for the grownups. She said, "We may want a second bottle in a little while, Mr. Brakus. And would you bring a large bottle of water?"

"Certainly."

He scurried off and Dinah imbibed a long, soothing drink of wine. "Your occupation has created quite a stir in Kanaris, Inspector Ramberg. It was a mistake that first night telling the chatty Mr. Brakus that you were a cop, even if you made a point of saying you were on holiday. He must have put out a bulletin. Everybody seems to know who we are and this Constantine character, who calls himself the 'mouthpiece of Hera' for crying out loud, implied that Zenia Stephanadis leased Marilita's house to a policeman in order to provoke her neighbors."

Thor shrugged. "It can't matter to anyone that a Norwegian cop with no authority comes here as a tourist. Now if somebody spread the rumor that I was a tax collector, I'd be worried."

"Well, I'm worried. I saw Brakus in Pythagório this afternoon in highly suspicious circumstances."

"Suspicious in what way?"

"In an up-to-no-good way. Do I have to put it in TV cop-speak or do you need an English phrase book?" As soon as the words flew out of her mouth, she felt like a louse.

K.D. smiled. "We'll have to be extra considerate tonight, Thor. Poor Dinah must be exhausted from our walk in the heat and the dirt bath she took after she was tackled by that monk."

Thor frowned. "I thought you said it was an accident."

"It was." *After my first glass of wine,* thought Dinah. *I will tell the twerp she has to go home after my first glass. I'll put her on a plane to Athens tomorrow morning and if she jumps* ship in Athens and wings off to Timbuktu, so be it. It won't be my fault. She gave Thor a contrite smile. "I'm sorry I was short, Thor. It just looked fishy to me that Brakus would be so chummy with your friend, the Greek cop."

"Sergeant Papas?"

"If Papas is the cop you rode off with to arrest Yannis. I saw Brakus give him a large shopping bag and I'm betting it wasn't a batch of baklava. There was another man with them. He looks like Saddam Hussein. When K.D. and I walked past the winery at the foot of the hill, he was sitting in front glaring at us like, I don't know, like a..."

"A total gargoyle," said K.D. "He gave us the side eye like whoa, I am one thug-nasty dude and you better not even think of coming any closer."

Dinah had to hand it to the kid. She had a gift for language.

Thor looked impressed, too. Dinah hoped he didn't start mixing teen slang with TV cop slang.

He said, "I've heard that Zenia employs refugees to work in the vineyard and around her house. He's probably a day laborer. But it worries me why Brakus would meet with Papas."

"Are you here to advise the Greek police?" asked K.D.

"Nothing like that." His eyes skimmed past Dinah's and veered off into the grape arbor. "I'm just an observer."

"Oh, what an adorable kitty." K.D. scooped up a white-socked black cat and cuddled her, or him. The cat meowed weakly. "Are you hungry, little sweetie? Would you like me to order you some tuna fish?"

Brakus' harried looking wife delivered the wine glass for K.D., gave her and the cat a scathing look, and whisked back toward the kitchen.

"What's *her* problem?" huffed K.D.

"Perhaps she has too many adorable kitties underfoot," said Dinah.

"That's cold. This little cutie is starving and she's probably throwing out gobs of food."

Thor poured three or four ounces of wine into K.D.'s glass. She set the cat back on the floor, broke into a triumphant smile, and raised the glass like a trophy.

Dinah picked up her own glass and put it to her lips.

"Wait!" K.D set down the glass and clapped her hands together under her chin. "Aren't y'all supposed to offer a toast? What do the Greeks say, Thor?"

"I *do* have a Greek phrase book, to compensate for my deficient English." He reached into the inside breast pocket of his jacket. As he did, Dinah caught a glimpse of his shoulder holster. He pulled out a small book, read for a minute, and said, "*Ya-mas*. To our health."

"*Ya-mas*," echoed Dinah and they all touched glasses. She deserved that little dig about his English, which was impeccable, and he deserved her trust and support and good humor or what was the point? She lifted her face to the sea breeze, inhaled a lungful of sweet air, and rebooted. "Somebody else bumped into me. An admirer of Marilita." She handed him Galen Stavros' business card. "He wants to visit the house. I told him he should speak with you to set up a time."

Thor read the card. "What did he look like?"

"Old," said K.D.,"but not crashy."

"Crashy?" It was obviously a new one on Thor.

K.D. translated. "Crazy plus trashy. He's sort of shriveled, but he has sexy eyes, like he could have been handsome when he was young."

Dinah hadn't noticed the sexy eyes. She had been too rattled by the fact that he also knew where she lived. She said, "He's been in the taverna before. He's tanned like a cowhide and wears a black fisherman's cap."

Thor grinned and put the card in his pocket. "Maybe he has a take on what drove the mysterious Marilita to murder."

Dinah said, "Her sister attributes her blowup to a carnal nature and a disdain of proper institutions."

"You've met Zenia?"

"It was more of a skirmish than a social meeting. She showed up at the house this afternoon to get a look at her new tenant's live-in girlfriend. I don't think she much cares for your taste in women. But here's an intriguing tidbit. She let it drop that Alcina is Marilita's illegitimate daughter."

"That *is* a surprise. Why would Marilita leave her home to Zenia instead of her daughter?"

"But she did leave it to her daughter," said K.D.

It was Dinah's turn to be surprised. "How do you know that?"

K.D. clicked her zebra-print fingernails on the side of her wine glass. "Alcina told me. She came to my room this afternoon to make sure I had everything I needed. I said her house was just gorgeous and she went all glum and said that it had been hers, but it wasn't anymore. She signed it over to Zenia when she was sixteen so that Zenia would give her the affidavit she needed to marry Yannis."

"A minor can't enter into a contract anyplace I've ever heard of," said Dinah. "Especially not one that cheats her out of her inheritance. Zenia and Marilita may have owned the property jointly and when Marilita died, Zenia took over the management. Alcina doesn't get along with Zenia. She might be exaggerating about Zenia stealing the house out from under her."

Nobody remarked. K.D. went back to nuzzling the cat. Thor broke off a piece of bread and analyzed it minutely. He seemed to grow more abstracted by the minute. Dinah sipped her wine and rubbed her bruised hip. She read an old poster on the wall next to the dining room advertising the 2010 Athens Classic Marathon, commemorating the 2500 year anniversary of the first marathon. A messenger named Phidippides ran from the battlefield at Marathon to the capital to announce that the Greeks had defeated the Persians. As Dinah recalled from some book or other she'd read, as soon as he delivered the happy news, he dropped dead.

Her glass had gone dry. This was her cue to speak up and disabuse K.D. of any hope she entertained of staying on in Kanaris. Somehow, the moment didn't feel right. She decided to put off her decision by one more glass of wine. She watched K.D. playing with the cat. Her tale of family woes had dredged up memories of Dinah's own teenage angst. The summer when she turned sixteen, she had appropriated her mother's car and a few hundred dollars and driven across the country from Georgia to Seattle to seek refuge with her Aunt Shelly. That escapade had whetted her desire to travel and Shelly, a teacher of ancient literature, had inspired in her a love of mythology. When she went home to go back to school in the fall, she'd outgrown her desperation. She had a fresh perspective and new interests. She thought, maybe I owe K.D. a week or two of refuge. Maybe all she needs is a little time apart from her mother to get her head on straight.

Dinah's stomach gurgled and she picked up the menu and browsed. "I see they have the spit-roasted goat tonight. And homemade pasta."

K.D. said, "I've already decided. I want the chicken in cream sauce and I'm going to share it with the kitties."

Thor didn't seem to hear. He hadn't even opened his menu.

Dinah settled on the moussaka with a side of tzaziki and closed her menu. She poured herself another glass of wine and studied his face. He seemed to be gnawing on an impossible problem. "What's got you stumped, Norseman?"

"Do you really think there was a payoff of some kind in the bag Brakus gave Papas?"

"I did think so. But it's probably because I don't like Brakus. I don't appreciate him broadcasting our names and address to every Tom, Dick, and mouthpiece of Hera who walks in this place. But whatever the meeting was about, I don't see how it could have any bearing on Fathi's murder, do you?"

A waiter arrived and Thor seemed glad for the interruption. K.D. and Dinah placed their orders. Without looking at the menu, Thor ordered the same dish he'd ordered the night before. When the waiter repaired to the kitchen, he refilled all of their glasses and seemed to push his worries onto the back burner. "K.D., did you know that most Greeks are named for a saint and on that saint's day, everyone with the same name gathers for a festival? It's the same in Norway. The Catholic church replaced the pagan celebration of birthdays with name days."

"Is there a name day for Thor?" she asked.

"Every Thursday is my name day. But what do you think, Dinah? As the Christian faith evolved, did the saints substitute in people's minds for the old gods?"

Conversation took off and the wine began to have a yeasty effect on everyone, bringing happier thoughts to the surface. Thor told a funny story about the Norse gods and K.D. regaled them with a blow-by-blow of the movie-version Thor's exile to New Mexico. By the time they finished their meal, Thor's mood had improved and so had Dinah's. Everything seemed to have an innocent explanation. On an island twenty-seven miles long and eight miles wide, everyone would be acquainted with the local police, Brakus included. They had probably known one another since kindergarten. And it was only natural that gossip would attend the first-time rental of the house that had belonged to a notorious murderess. As for Brother Constantine, he was probably just a vagrant who ferreted out the local scuttlebutt and used it to scam people by telling their fortunes.

As they walked back to Marilita's house in the twilight, Thor extolled the attractions of Norway, with emphasis on the nice, cool summers near the North Pole.

Dinah laughed. "Your internal thermostat is set too high, Norseman."

"He wouldn't last a week in the summertime in Georgia," said K.D.

Dinah got a chicken-skin feeling as they walked past the spot where Fathi had died, but Thor wrapped his arm around her waist, dispelling her fear. Honeysuckle perfumed the air and in one of the white-washed houses, someone was playing the piano—"Claire de Lune." Somewhere out beyond the trees, the moon was ascending over the Aegean. In the afterglow of the wine, even K.D. seemed simpatico. Maybe she wouldn't be such a bother, after all. Maybe she could hang around for a week or two so long as she minded her p's and q's and kept a low profile.

They turned down the alley toward Marilita's house and all that good feeling came to a screeching halt. The veranda was a shambles. Broken flowerpots and clumps of dirt and uprooted plants lay strewn across the tiles. The chairs and table had been smashed to kindling. The door had been egged and a stinking mound of garbage had been dumped under the mulberry tree.

Alcina stood in the center of the chaos holding a lantern in one hand and the empty parakeet cage in the other. She said, "You brought this on, Thor Ramberg. All of our trouble is because of you."

Chapter Ten

Dinah sat on the side of the bed in K.D.'s room, smoking one of K.D.'s Newports and explaining why it was too dangerous for her to stay in Kanaris. "Too much is going on. There's too much deviousness. Too much nastiness. Thor was right about there being a lot of crime on the island. It's not safe."

K.D. slouched against the wall and exhaled a long, white streamer. "Big dilly. It's only a little vandalism and people acting pissy. Like what goes on in high school? Like daily?"

"A man was murdered in the lane just yesterday, probably by...possibly by Alcina's husband. This house has bad karma."

"Karma is so *pagan*. You're overreacting."

Dinah narrowed her eyes. She hadn't smoked a cigarette since last New Year's Eve, one hundred and fifty-seven days ago, and here she'd let herself be corrupted by a willful adolescent with a subversive agenda. "You have a disturbing tendency to blow off crime as if it's hardly worth mentioning. Your burglary caper may have been just a misunderstanding and vandalism may be an everyday occurrence back in Atlanta, but murder can't be minimized and I don't think I'm overreacting. Friends or relatives of the murdered man have probably decided to take vengeance against Yannis and his association with this house makes it dangerous."

"Don't you trust Thor to protect us?"

"He can't watch over us every minute of the day and night." Dinah stubbed out her cigarette and got up to leave. "Don't unpack. I'll drive you back to the airport in the morning and we can phone your mother to expect you."

K.D. hurled herself onto the bed face-first and began to sob. Or pretended to sob.

So much for the doing of good deeds, thought Dinah, and stormed downstairs to see what progress Thor had made with the cleanup. She and K.D. had helped him broom up the dirt and debris and bag it, but left him alone to hose off the tiles and the door. On the first floor, she heard water splatting against the side of the house and the windows. Above the noise came the sound of gut-wrenching sobs from Alcina's room.

The loss of the parakeets seemed to have hit Alcina hard. If tears were any measure, she cared more about those flown birds than she did about the dead Iraqi. And where was Yannis? The police had released him. He ought to be on hand to comfort his wife.

An alarming possibility sprang to mind. What if it weren't the birds that Alcina was weeping for? Was Yannis here when the vandals struck? If they were friends of Fathi's, angry about Yannis' release and bent on revenge, they could have dragged Yannis off to do God only knows what to him.

She rushed down the hall and rapped on the door of Alcina's lair. "Alcina? Alcina, may I come in?"

She didn't answer.

Dinah pushed the door open a crack and peeped inside. The room was cloaked in shadow, lit only by candles and permeated with the tang of incense. Painted icons of Greek Orthodox saints stared down from the walls like an unfriendly jury. Alcina rocked back and forth on her knees, wringing her hands and howling. She didn't seem to be so much beseeching the saints as berating them for their ineptitude.

"Alcina, please tell me what it is you're crying about. Is it Yannis? Did the people who trashed the veranda hurt him?"

She began to ululate.

Jerusalem. She was Marilita's daughter, all right. Dinah felt a mixture of pity and aggravation. "Alcina, Thor's already phoned the police, but you need to tell us if there's something more than broken chairs and flower pots for them to investigate."

"Thor Ramberg. He caused all of this. The police turned Yannis loose with no protection. He'll have to leave Samos. They will kill him." She clasped her cross and her fetish and held them against her mouth.

"If Yannis has been threatened, I'm sure the police will do whatever it takes to protect him. Where is he now?"

"Hiding."

"So he's safe for now?"

"They'll find him and kill him and I'll have no one."

"Who's *they*, Alcina?"

"Iraqis."

"Was it Iraqis who tore up the place?"

The woman expelled a soul-searing shriek that set Dinah's teeth on edge. At a loss for comforting words, she patted Alcina's shoulder. "There, there." But Alcina only wailed louder and she gave up the effort. In the face of such an outpouring of grief, Mother Mary would have there-thered in vain. "Would you recognize the vandals if you saw them again?"

"Iraqis."

Dinah didn't doubt that Fathi might have had friends or countrymen out for Yannis' blood. But this was Zenia Stephanadis' house and any Iraqi refugee who busted up the property of a prominent Greek citizen would know that he faced certain deportation or prison. If on the other hand, the culprits were locals who resented the fact that Zenia had rented the place to a policeman...

"Did you actually see the vandals, Alcina?"

"Didn't have to. I know."

Dinah wasn't so sure. "Okay, Alcina. Try to calm yourself. I'll go and relay your concerns to Thor."

She marched back down the hall with a queasy feeling in the pit of her stomach. What sort of scary predicament had they blundered into? The sound of the water drubbing against the door had ceased and she smacked it open with force, causing it to swing back on its hinges.

Thor was coiling the hose. He said, "I don't think Zenia is going to return my deposit."

"Probably not."

"I phoned her and told her what happened. She'll stop by tomorrow to see for herself. The police will come by and confer with us in the morning."

"I'd like to confer with you tonight. I think we should move to a different island."

"You may be right." He hung the hose on a peg on the side of the house. "Let's go upstairs. I don't want to be overheard."

She led the way upstairs. Something in his body language intensified the queasy feeling .

Inside their bedroom, he closed the window and clicked on the radio. An explosion of static assaulted their ears before he located a station playing a bouncy folk tune. He turned the volume up, sat Dinah down on the side of the bed, and stood in front of her, his hands jammed in his pockets. "I quit my job in Norway at the beginning of this year. I'm not a Norwegian policeman."

"You're not on sabbatical?"

"No."

"Are you trying to get hired as a policeman here?"

"I'm already a policeman here. I'm working undercover for N.C.I.S."

"You're working on a TV show?"

"Not that N.C.I.S."

"How many are there? The only one I've ever heard of is a serial whodunit about the American Naval Criminal Investigative Service and a hotshot marine named Leroy Jethro Gibbs who discovers dead bodies like clockwork."

"Don't be flippant."

"*Me* flippant? Either the sun has addled you or you're mocking me."

"I'm not mocking you. I work for Norway's National Criminal Investigation Service and I'm violating any number of rules by telling you. But things have taken an unexpected turn and you deserve to know the score."

"Norway has an N.C.I.S.?"

"Yes. It liaises with Interpol and national police organizations. I'm here to investigate a ring of illegal arms traffickers. Samos is the entry point for migrants from all over Asia and Africa and the Middle East and it's the nexus of a number of smuggling routes for moving people and weapons north into Europe. As it happens, arms dealing is a local tradition in Kanaris dating back to the end of the Second World War."

"This little place?"

"Yes, this little place. Today Greece is awash in weapons, mostly cheap, Turkish-made guns smuggled across the Aegean from Turkey by Iraqis and sold on the black market. German arms manufacturers have also been flooding the Greek military with weapons, raking in big profits while running up Greek debt. But between '67 and '74, it was the United States that lavished weapons on the military junta."

"That was forty years ago."

"Recently, caches of forty-year-old, mint-new American rifles, handguns, and grenades have been turning up in conflict zones from Sudan to Mexico. Three months ago, N.C.I.S. detained two operatives of the Albanian mafia in Oslo. They were carrying a duffel bag full of M1911 automatic pistols like those the U.S. used in Vietnam. One of the Albanians claimed that contraband American weapons were being sold and distributed out of Kanaris by Iraqis."

So many countries. She felt as if she'd been fire-hosed with information, a crash course in the geopolitics of warfare. She couldn't digest it. "It's insane. A tiny Greek village becomes a hotbed of arms smuggling and peace-loving Norway enters the world of international espionage."

"From '95 to 2005, Norway had an elite intelligence gathering unit, E-Fourteen, that carried out covert missions abroad in Afghanistan and the Balkans. The unit was suspended and these last few years we've been living under the illusion that we are safe and secure, too far north and too non-controversial for the bad guys to take notice. But we have critical infrastructure and assets to protect and the government has opted to revive E-Fourteen to monitor new threats."

"Why in the world did this elite unit pick *you* for a covert operation, in Greece of all places?" She didn't mean to dis him, but he was a long way from Longyearbyen, Norway. "I mean, why send a policeman from a small town in the Arctic. You have no experience as a spy."

"As a matter of fact, most Norwegian intelligence stations are located north of the Arctic Circle." A spark of anger flashed in his eyes. "I don't know, Dinah. N.C.I.S. keeps U.S. intelligence in the loop. Maybe one of your American senators that I offended last year recommended me, hoping I'd die in the line of duty."

Her jaw dropped. He could fight dirty when he chose to. She said, "Bad joke. Knock wood and cross your fingers." She went to the window and stood with her back to him until she was sure her voice was under control. "Was Fathi one of the smugglers?"

He answered in a neutral tone. "I think so, but he would have been a small cog in the operation. There are hundreds of illegal arms sellers across Europe. E-Fourteen doesn't have the manpower or the resources to go after them all. It's the buyers we're interested in, the terrorists. If I can identify the sellers, it may be feasible to trace the weapons to the buyers. I'm not here to shut down the operation, but what I learn may provide clues to how it can be infiltrated in the future."

"How would somebody like Fathi be able to take guns across borders?"

"Just by getting into Greece, he could cross freely into other E.U. countries without showing travel documents. To get into a non-E.U. country like Norway, he needed an identity card and he had one. A German card with his name and photo. It would have gotten him through in the event he was stopped or questioned in any Schengen E.U. country."

She turned back from the window. "Who's running the operation on Samos? Germans? Greeks? Iraqis? Alcina is terrified that

Iraqis will kill Yannis. Is he part of the operation? Is that what he and Fathi were arguing about?"

"I don't think Yannis is mixed up in the smuggling, but I'd be willing to bet he knows something about the history of those American guns and how they came to be cached here in Kanaris. Most of the people in the village are old-time communists. They know how to keep their secrets."

"So do you." She couldn't absorb forty years of intrigue. It was all she could do to absorb the fact that Thor had invited her to Samos under false pretenses. "What was I supposed to be, Thor? Window dressing? A stage prop to make you appear more like a tourist?"

"No, of course not. Bringing you here was an added benefit."

"And all that rigmarole about the trouble you took searching out a place that I'd enjoy, sunshine and ancient ruins, and sharing a holiday in the sun with me, that was just a line?"

"It wasn't a line, Dinah. I thought you would love this place. Plans can have more than one purpose."

"Like a Swiss Army knife. Each item has a use."

He reached out and stroked her cheek. "We were going to be so close, me here on Samos, you just across the strait in Turkey. I thought we could have this time together to find out if..." Wherever he was going with that line, he stopped short and dropped his hand. "I thought I could keep my job separate. If I'd thought that what I was doing would put you in jeopardy, I wouldn't have asked you to come. I thought Fathi's murder was the result of infighting among the smugglers and my mission on Samos was still a secret. I can't be sure what this vandalism business means, but I think I've been betrayed."

"I *know* that I have. You lied to me from the start."

"Don't be self-righteous, Dinah. You've been known to tell a lie when it suits you."

"Not one that makes a monkey out of someone I care about." She grabbed a pillow off the bed and threw it at him. "Find yourself another bed. Tomorrow morning I'm out of here."

He took the pillow and started to leave. At the door, he turned. "You're right to go. I want you safe and out of harm's way. But we're good together, Dinah. Don't throw our chance away without giving it deeper thought."

When the door closed behind him, she shut off the music and pressed the heels of her hands against her eyes, already wishing he'd tossed that pillow aside and kissed her. She went back to the window and misted up. You should have known that he was on the job, that his obsession with Marilita wasn't idle curiosity and that song and dance about visiting with the local constabulary wasn't because he wanted tips on how to manage a passel of rowdy tourists. You should have known this romantic fantasy on Samos was too good to be true and you may as well quit crying and get over it.

Think about something else—the sack of Troy, the fall of Thebes, that chrome-white moon bellied out like Artemis' boyfriend-killing bow. What had Marilita thought about when she looked up at the moon from this same window? Love? Betrayal? Murder? The overthrow of the Greek state? Thor must have cause to believe that her crime related in some way to the theft of those American weapons. It would be rich if it turned out that a Hollywood actress had outsmarted the junta, stolen a consignment of American weapons, and passed them out to the communists of Kanaris.

Day 3

Chapter Eleven

"Son-of-a-bitch!" Dinah knelt down and looked at the Picanto's tires, all four slashed to ribbons and flat. "Damn, damn, damn, damn, damn!"

"The vandals again," said K.D.

Dinah walked through the parking lot, checking out the other cars. Hers was the only one to have received the special treatment. Thor's car was gone. He must have left before dawn and there was nobody else around to help. The nearest gas station was miles away and, even if the rental company sent a tow truck and a new set of tires right away, the last flight to Athens would have departed by the time she got the bill paid and the paperwork settled.

K.D. arched her back across the hood, covered her eyes with one hand, and struck a languishing pose. "Looks like we're going to miss the seven o'clock flight."

Dinah gave her the gimlet eye. The vandals weren't the only suspects. She had rousted K.D. out of bed at five to allow plenty of time to get to the airport for the seven o'clock flight to Athens. K.D. had been surprisingly speedy and compliant. Too compliant? To be fair, it would have taken more muscle than K.D. had to shred those tires.

Well, as K.D.'s daddy used to say in his phony redneck vernacular, crying don't feed the bulldog. It sure wouldn't fix four flat tires. Dinah looked at her watch and rearranged her timetable. The police hadn't showed up yet to investigate last night's vandalism and she didn't relish the idea of sitting on the curb all morning waiting for them. There was no guarantee they would come at all or, if they did, that they would waste time on her problem. She had no choice but to call the rental agency and it would probably be hours before they could muster up a tow truck.

K.D. sauntered around the parking lot. "You could call the Greek Triple A."

"I doubt that there is one on Samos."

"Then we should go back to the house. At least it'll be cool there. We can eat some yogurt and you can think about what we want to do next."

Dinah didn't like the togetherness implicit in that remark. "K.D., you do understand this is only a temporary delay, don't you? You're going home to Atlanta and I'm going to Istanbul as soon as I can get us to the airport."

"I'm resigned to my fate."

"Uh-huh." Dinah caught the handle of her roller bag and started trudging up the road. It seemed that Fate was forever ambushing her. The early Greeks believed that everything that happened was predetermined by a trinity of goddesses known collectively as the Moirai and, whatever they threw at you, it was futile to resist. Clotho spun the thread of life, giving life to both mortals and gods. Lachesis measured the thread from Clotho's spindle, allotting each life a finite length. And Atropos got to decide the manner of death and snip the thread with her ruthless shears. Dinah was thankful her thread was still spooling, but the slashed tires pissed her off profoundly.

She didn't know where Thor had gone or for how long and she did *not* want to be lolling on the veranda when he returned. *Don't throw our chance away.* That was why she had come to Samos in the first place. He was the one who had blown their chance, or at least relocated it to some other island at some unspecified future time. But it was her own fault if she felt hurt. She flattered herself that she was a cynic, but she was the worst kind of sap—a sap who was constantly surprised that people lied to each other. People lied all the time for a gazillion reasons they justified to themselves. If she wasn't a full-fledged cynic yet, there seemed to be a worldwide conspiracy to turn her into one. If Thor thought she was too "tough-minded" and cynical to get worked up over his little deception, she was a victim of her own smarty-pants rhetoric.

"You can be mean to me if you want to," said K.D., "but I think you're being immature about Thor."

Dinah sighed. K.D. couldn't have heard their argument above the noise of the radio, but maybe she sneaked downstairs in the night and saw Thor bunked on the sofa. She said, "When I need your input, I'll ask."

"Whatever you're mad at him for, you should lighten up and cut the guy some slack. He's obviously Level Ten about you and a woman in her mid-thirties doesn't have much time left for a truly great love. Thor could be your last chance. You know what Lucien said to my mother? He said, my sister is the architect of all her disappointments."

Dinah whipped around with a strong message for her brother on her lips, but was distracted by the appearance of a young man on a Vespa motoring into the parking lot. He dismounted and took off his helmet. He smiled up at her and she had a brainstorm. Mentor. He had said that if she needed help while she was on the island, she should ask for him and that everybody knew him. It was worth a try. He might know a tow truck driver or a tire salesman who could do the job fast.

"*Parakaló*," she called out to the young man, going deep into her Greek vocabulary. It meant something like "hello" or "please" or "I'm here and I have a question." It was a pointless word because her question was, "Do you speak English?"

"*Nè, málista.*" He dipped his head to the side.

She'd learned that *nè* meant yes, in spite of the fact that it sounded like no. An up-and-down nod and a word that sounded like "okay" meant no. She rolled her bag back down the hill and asked, "Do you know a man named Mentor?"

"He lives down there." He pointed along a grooved concrete path leading down the mountain from the parking lot. "The fourth house."

"Thank you. *Efkharistó*." She stowed her suitcase in the trunk of the Picanto. "Leave your bag here, K.D. Turn on your phone and go up to the house and wait for me. I'll call you if and when I get some new tires."

Dinah left K.D. chatting with the young man in the parking lot and hied off in search of Mentor. Tires weren't the only things rolling through her mind. She was thinking that thirty-three was hardly the *mid*-thirties. She was thinking that if Thor was Level Ten about her, he had a funny way of showing it. He should have trusted her enough to tell her the truth up front. Even so, she should have been less accusatory and more understanding of his dilemma. How mature did a person had to be to navigate the rip currents of a romantic relationship?

The concrete turned to dirt and the path steepened. The footing became increasingly treacherous and she couldn't take her eyes off the ground for fear of falling. She had to stop at every switchback to look for the house. Her knees began to feel the strain. Dear God, her joints were creaking. She could hear… no. Somebody was tuning a violin.

After a few sporadic twangs, the violin erupted in a wild gypsy melody. The beauty and the virtuosity were so improbable that she forgot her anger. She followed the music around two more switchbacks. As the fourth red-tiled roof came into view, she saw Mentor seated under a plane tree with the instrument tucked under his chin. He was wielding the bow like a man possessed. She approached almost on tiptoe, not wanting him to stop. When he did, a large black cat vaulted into his lap.

"*Yiásou*, Mentor. You play beautifully."

"*Yiásou*, Dinah Pelerin. That piece is from Russia. It is called 'Black Eyes.' But if you come to the taverna after ten tonight, I will play Greek music. My daughter will dance and her husband will play the goatskin."

"A drum?"

"Nothing so ordinary. The goatskin is a kind of Greek bag-pipe. You must hear it."

"That would be fun, but I'm afraid I can't be there."

"Then you must sit down with me and taste my Samos nectar. It is made from our famous Muscat grapes, acclaimed by Charlemagne and celebrated in a poem by Lord Byron." He set down his violin, petted the cat, and reached for a wine bottle on the table beside him. "After we taste, I will give you a private concert. Perhaps you will dance."

She laughed. "I'd love to hear you play more, but the house was vandalized last night and I discovered this morning that someone had slashed my tires. I thought you might know some-one who could help me."

"But that is barbaric." He threw up his hands. "First murder and now this. We are under siege. It must have been one of the refugees from the camp in Samos Town. What does your police-man friend think?"

Mentor, too? She said, "I haven't spoken with Thor about the situation yet. Things are in turmoil and I need to get my car fixed as soon as possible. Do you know anyone with a truck who could deliver a new set of tires this morning and mount them for me?"

"I know a man in Karlovassi. But it is too early yet. Taste my wine and after an hour, I will call him. Sit."

"I'm sure your wine is delicious. But it's a little early for me to drink wine and I was hoping to catch the last flight to Athens."

"You're leaving Samos so soon?"

"Unfortunately. My...my cousin needs me to chaperone her back to Athens."

"It is too bad that you must leave after two days and with such a bad taste of Samos in your mouth. I will pour you a small glass of wine and then I will call my friend and you can make an arrangement. In Greece, we are social before we transact busi-ness." He made refusal seem like a breach of etiquette.

"A very small glass, please." She sat down and, as he poured, she noticed that he wore a leather thong on his wrist with a small evil eye amulet. "I've noticed several people wear those charms."

"The *mati* is a Mediterranean custom. Jason's ship, the Argo, had an eye painted on each side of the prow when it sailed in quest of the Golden Fleece. Eyes were painted or carved on the bows of Greek war ships to keep away evil spirits. After all that has happened, it would seem that you need a protective talisman." He took off his bracelet. "Here. Take this one."

"I couldn't take your good-luck charm, Mentor."

"I have others."

"Thank you." She slipped it onto her wrist and tasted the wine. "This is very good. Almost like butterscotch."

"*Nè, nè.* Fermentation was slow, but it is aging well." He held his glass up to the light. "Will you come back to Samos after you see your cousin safely home?"

"I don't know." Much as she hated to admit it, K.D. was right. She had behaved badly toward Thor. She had been unreasonable and she especially regretted that crack that he might not be up to the job. "Yes, I think I'll probably return in a day or so."

Mentor shooed the black cat off his lap and tossed off his wine. "You and your young man should rent a room at the Lárisa. Living in Marilita's house can only bring nightmares. "

"Did you know Marilita?"

"Only a little. She was seven or eight years older, but she often visited my mother and brought me sweets and picture books. Mother doted on her as if she were her own daughter. She liked her friend Nasos, too, mostly because of his mother. My mother and Rena Lykos lived in Athens during the Nazi occupation in '41 and '42. Hundreds of thousands of Greeks starved. It was Rena who saved our family and others, too. She beguiled a German commandant to give her food, which she shared. She had the heart of a lion. She disseminated resistance leaflets throughout city, and even smuggled arms and explosives to the Greek resistance in the north. At the end of the war, Rena's husband was killed by the German collaborationists."

"Nasos' father?"

"Yes. Rena remarried after the war, but she did not forget the barbarity of the fascists. When the junta came to power, with their tanks on every street corner and their martial music blaring constantly from loudspeakers, she was distraught. But it was death, or worse, to speak out against the junta. Anyone with leftist views kept them a secret."

Dinah knew about the atrocities perpetrated by the Nazis during WWII, but she had no idea that Greece had continued such flagrant abuses with the active support of her own government. She said, "Why do you think Marilita would have wanted to kill Nasos and Rena?"

Mentor refilled his glass and held it up to the light. "With ambrosia, Hera cleansed all defilement from her lovely flesh. Do you know Homer's poems?"

"No. Is there a reason you're evading my question?"

"My mother and Marilita were close until Marilita's death and my mother spoke of her with great affection. She never accepted the idea that Marilita could kill another living being. She said it was her sister Zenia who had the heart of a killer."

Zenia was a disagreeable old crank, but the rap against her started to seem to Dinah like piling on. "Why would your mother think Zenia could kill?"

"She poisons the village cats."

Chapter Twelve

Mentor finally made the call to the tire man in Karlovassi and Dinah arranged to meet him in the parking lot at noon, four hours hence. She walked back toward Marilita's house with her phone in her hand, deciding. What would she say to Thor? That she'd been a blister? He would laugh and forgive her as he always did. That somebody had punctured her tires and she was afraid. Thor would tell her to go ahead and leave Samos and he would get back in touch with her when his mission was finished. But she had made up her mind. Danger or not, she wanted to be with him. She would take K.D. to Athens and as soon as she had put her on a plane back to the States, she would return to Samos.

With that decision, her anxiety abated somewhat and she concentrated on the arduous climb back to the village. These Samian hills were murder. So to speak. She stopped to catch her breath at the fountain above the parking lot. She had started up again when she heard the grumble of a car behind her. She turned to see the majestic grill of the Isotta Fraschini gobbling up the hill in breathtaking disregard the no cars rule. The jewel in the middle of Zenia's forehead scintillated in the sun like the third eye of a Hindu idol. Dinah jumped out of the way behind the fountain.

The Isotta surged past but lolloped to a jerky stop after another twenty yards. Zenia was no doubt on her way to assess the damage to the house. She motioned for Dinah to come forward.

"Running away, are you?"

"I'm walking *up* the hill, Zenia."

"Good. I'll want to speak with you when you get to the top."

"I'll get there faster if you give me a lift."

"Take your time. I need to speak with Alcina first." She gunned the engine and sped away, leaving Dinah to suck the Isotta's exhaust.

She trudged on feeling considerably less inclined to overlook Zenia's meanness because of her age and the tragedy of her sister. The charge of cat poisoning, if true, made her into an outright ogre. If she was bothered by too many cats, the woman was rich enough to have every cat on Samos spayed and neutered.

She's poked Kanaris in the eye but good. Dinah replayed what Brother Constantine had said. It was no mystery why terrorists or arms traffickers wouldn't want a cop in their midst. But why would anyone else give a rip about a cop on holiday? That first night in the taverna, Thor had let the cat out of the bag that he was a cop back in Norway and Brakus had obviously blabbed the fact far and wide. But the only people who could know that Thor was here on official business were the local police who had seen his credentials. Why hadn't N.C.I.S. provided him with a fake identity? She felt a stab of guilt. Thor may have nixed the idea rather than have to explain an alias to her.

When she turned down the alley toward the house, Zenia was sitting in the car and Alcina was standing over her, ranting in Greek. The engine was still throbbing like a diesel truck, but Zenia had no need for her earhorn. Alcina was bellowing. She looked up and saw Dinah and pointed an accusing finger.

Zenia cut her off. "Stop your childishness. I will send a man with new chairs this afternoon. And another cactus to protect you from the *baskania*, though the last one didn't work and you should see the foolishness. If your birds aren't back by the end of the day, you can be sure they have been eaten by a cat." She raised an imperious hand to Dinah. "I want you to come with me to my house."

"Sorry, but I'm waiting on a mechanic to repair my car. It was also vandalized during the night. As soon as it's drivable, I'll be off to the airport and Athens."

"What time is this mechanic coming?"

"Noon."

"Then you have time. I'll drive you back. This is important."

K.D. drifted outside, her eyes glued to her phone.

Dinah was curious about Zenia's imperative invitation. There were several questions she wanted to ask her about Brother Constantine, but she didn't like to leave K.D. in a house that had been the target of vandals, alone with the volatile wife of a possible murderer. "Can we squeeze K.D. into the front seat?"

"What?" Zenia put the earhorn to her ear.

"I don't want to leave K.D.," shouted Dinah. "What if the vandals come back?"

"Why would they? They've made their point. The young lady will wait here with Alcina until you return. Alcina, give the girl a breakfast. Whatever she wants."

Alcina twiddled with her cross and sulked.

"All right, then," said Zenia. "You, Dinah, get in."

Dinah couldn't resist. She slipped into the passenger seat and ordered K.D. to stay put. "Don't go anywhere until I get back unless trouble comes calling. Then run to the tavarna and stick close to whoever's there." She skewed her eyes from K.D. to Alcina and back to K.D. "And don't smoke. Anything at all."

"The wireless signal is lame," said K.D., holding up her phone. "Are there, like dead zones in the house?"

"What is it you want? Speak up."

"The Wi-Fi signal is weak." K.D. walked around to the side of the car and cupped her hands close to Zenia's ear. "Wi-Fi!"

"Alcina knows where the games are kept. There used to be a *tavli* board and maybe a checkerboard. Alcina will play with you." Zenia depressed the clutch, shifted into reverse, punched the gas pedal, and the Isotta surged backward with startling power.

Automatically, Dinah reached for the seat belt, but there wasn't one. "Some car you've got here. What year is it?"

"Nineteen thirty. It belonged to Marilita, a gift from some Italian film star."

They thudded down the rocky lane to the parking lot at a modest speed, but when they reached the curvy, asphalt road leading down the mountain, the Isotta romped forward as if it had a mind of its own. At the bottom of the hill, Zenia fumbled her foot onto the brake and they careened onto the coast road a scant foot ahead of a speeding truck.

Dinah tucked her flyaway hair behind her ears with one hand and hung onto the seat for dear life with the other. She couldn't imagine how Zenia had gotten a driver's license. "What was the point?" she shouted.

"What?"

"The vandals. What point did they make?"

"The ignorant fools think I cast the evil eye. That is how they get back at me."

Dinah covered the *mati* on her wrist and wondered if some of the rumors about Zenia enlarged on the facts. "Alcina blames Thor for having Yannis arrested for Fathi's murder and she thinks his Iraqi friends are trying to get back at Yannis."

"Alcina didn't want the house to be let. She resents Ramberg and she would defend that drunken husband of hers if he shot the Pope. Lucky for him, the man he killed was unimportant."

Then again, cat killing couldn't be ruled out. With Zenia, there was no point mouthing platitudes about the value of human life. "You seem pretty sure that Yannis was the murderer."

"Isn't Ramberg?"

Dinah didn't know if she'd been set up for the question, but she ignored it. "Yesterday I met a man who calls himself Brother Constantine. He hinted that something you'd done didn't go down well with the villagers. Was it the fact that you'd leased Marilita's house to a policeman?"

"The villagers are wary. They do clandestine business."

"Constantine looks as if he lives in a cave. How would he have heard about your tenant's profession?"

"He probably paid someone for the information."

"He has money?"

"I should think so. His monastery traded a worthless lake for a tract of expensive government-owned land. They sold it and netted millions of euros, which the financial authorities haven't been able to find. Constantine is in hiding until the next government comes into power and his crimes are forgotten. He has given the villagers a new hobby, searching for his buried treasure."

"If everyone knows he's here, how is he able to hide?"

She looked at Dinah as if she were thick. "He passes out little envelopes."

"Envelopes with cash inside? You mean he bribes the villagers not to tell the police where he is?"

"The police wouldn't arrest him. He gives them money, too."

She made bribery sound as natural and blameless as breathing. Dinah could just imagine what a straight arrow like Thor would make of the local mores.

Abruptly, she swerved onto a wooded side road, nearly losing control and slamming Dinah's sore hip against the door.

"Slow down, Zenia."

"What?"

"I said…" Dinah flinched as the Isotta's tires skidded on a patch of loose gravel. Zenia grappled with the steering wheel. Dinah reached for the wheel, but missed and the fishtailing motion of the car threw her into the door again. She pitched back across the seat and grabbed the wheel, torquing it hard to the left to keep the car from plummeting into a ditch. "Slow down!"

"I've driven this road thousands of times." Her tone was truculent, but she lightened her foot on the accelerator and the Isotta wallowed into the middle of the road.

They continued climbing up the twisty mountain road, a corniche scarcely wide enough for one car. As they gained elevation, the cliff walls appeared craggier and more perpendicular on this side of the gorge. Dinah looked across to the overlook that she and K.D. had tried and failed to reach. From wall to wall, the canyon floor couldn't be much more than a mile. A pair of hawks patrolled the airspace in between.

At the culmination of the Isotta's elongated bonnet, a winged hood ornament soared into the blue yonder. Nike, the goddess of speed and victory, Dinah supposed. The Greek gods seemed to have a plan for her life today and there wasn't much she could do about it. She anchored her posterior to the slippery seat as firmly as she could and wondered how much a taxi back to the village would cost.

"Where is your house? How far?"

"Near the summit. Kanaris is three kilometers as the crow flies, fifteen by road. The gorge is more useful than a moat. My husband did not care for the society of the villagers."

No kidding. If Zenia's toxic personality didn't deter visitors from dropping in for tea, nine miles over this hair-raiser of a road would do the trick.

"Do you live alone?"

"Not much choice since my sister killed my husband."

"The colonel Marilita shot was your husband?"

"That's right." She exhibited no emotion. She rolled on like an armored tank. "I have a house guest at present, someone I want you to meet. He's a film director. He and I are going to make a film together about 'The Regime of the Colonels.'"

Dinah was still coming to grips with the revelation about her husband. "Is that what the military junta was called?"

"I call it the last legitimate government of Greece." She sniffed. "Your boyfriend was asking questions about the junta last night. Foolish. The house splattered with filth and him asking about the junta."

"What did he want to know?"

"Whether there were armories on Samos."

"Were there?"

"I wouldn't know. My husband never discussed military matters with me."

Chapter Thirteen

Given Zenia's penchant for costumery and theatrics, Dinah had prepared herself for an architectural wallop. But it was the setting rather than the architecture that imparted the drama. The house had been built atop a massive, smooth-shouldered boulder. She had to look closely to see where nature stopped and the stone façade of the house began. Two sets of narrow, curving steps had been hewn out of the boulder on either shoulder and converged at a weathered, unpainted pine door. The house blended into the surrounding environment without calling attention to itself.

Zenia turned into a drive that circled around behind the house. She took a remote control from a side pocket, opened an inconspicuous garage door into what appeared to be a dimly lit cave, and drove the Isotta inside. "There's an underground passage into the house," she said. "Follow me."

Dinah followed her through an arched stone doorway through a tunnel that seemed to have been bored through the boulder upon which the house rested. Niches had been cut into the walls to display a collection of urns and sculptures. The only figure Dinah recognized was Asclepius with his distinctive rod entwined with serpents.

Zenia noticed her interest. "You know Asclepius?"

"He was the Greek god of medicine. His rod has become the symbol of medicine."

"He was the son of Apollo." She walked back and glowered at the statue as if it had made an obscene gesture. Her eyes fairly glittered with fury. "His mother was burned alive for adultery."

Why, Dinah wondered, would she own a statue she so obviously detested?

Zenia turned on her heels and steamed on. At the end of the tunnel, a short stairway led to a large, cheerful room with sun streaming in from two skylights. The first thing Dinah looked for was the front door by which Thor must have entered, and the photographs that had so puzzled him.

"Dearest Zenia, you are back." A slight, haughty looking man with a high forehead and slicked-back gray hair roved into the room carrying a teacup. He wore a buttoned-up brown hunting jacket, too heavy for the season, over a buff colored T-shirt from which his long neck protruded like a wrinkled parsnip.

"Egan. This is the Pelerin woman I told you about, the inamorata of the man who leased Marilita's house. Dinah Pelerin, this is Egan Vercuni, the film director."

He accorded her a supercilious smile. "Enchanté."

Zenia said, "Egan and I hadn't seen each other in forty years until I invited him to Samos three months ago to consult with me about making a motion picture together. He is staying here as my house guest while we collaborate on the enterprise."

"I am but a humble servant. Zenia is the boss."

Zenia's penciled brows crawled toward the edge of her cap. "That is because I'm paying for it. Will you take tea, Dinah?"

"Yes, thank you."

"Tell her about our project, Egan. I'll go and freshen the pot."

"Delighted." He bade Dinah to sit.

She chose a straight-backed chair across from the sofa. He set his teacup on the low table, arranged the cushions just so, and ensconced himself like a pasha. "Do you have any background in the performing arts, Miss Pelerin?"

"I'm afraid not." She tried not to let her eyes stray to the framed photographs.

"None at all? Perhaps a school play?"

"I was Madame Arcati in *Blithe Spirit* in my high school senior play."

"Only the Coward?"

"Yes."

"Pity."

In less than a minute, she had developed a major antipathy to the man. "Zenia says that you're calling your movie 'The Regime of the Colonels.' Is it based on her husband's life?"

"The Regime of the Colonels was the name for the junta of the late sixties. Zenia's husband, Phaedon, was a distinguished military officer. He helped to implement the Prometheus Plan."

"What was that?"

"A very efficient method of rounding up the anarchists and leftists."

Dinah couldn't tell if he was being ironic or politically provocative or just plain affected. Either way, he was a pill. "Were there very many anarchists?"

"Quite a large number, theoretically. NATO devised the Prometheus Plan in the event of a communist uprising and our military leaders were quick to see that, indeed, communists had infiltrated the universities, the bureaucracy, the government, even the military. The situation required drastic action."

Dinah concluded that he was being ironic in a way that he wouldn't be if Zenia were still in the room. Whatever this Prometheus Plan had meant back in the sixties, the Prometheus of Greek mythology was, as best she could recall, a Titan who stole fire from Zeus and gave it to mankind. For his generosity, Zeus had him chained to a rock where a giant eagle ripped out his liver. His fury unsated, Zeus caused a new liver to grow back every day and sent the eagle back to rip it out again every night. She was loath to ask if Colonel Phaedon's method of dealing with the communists entailed anything that grisly. "What was Phaedon's last name?"

"Hero."

"That was his real name?"

"And a most fitting one. After the coup, he was one of the brave officers who occupied the parliament and the government ministries."

"I assume Zenia chose to keep her name for professional reasons."

"Yes, and she didn't shorten it to please the philistines, as Marilita did."

"Marilita was herself a philistine," said Zenia as she pushed a teacart into the room. "She was indifferent to the refinements of good breeding and she was attracted to the same ilk." She parked the cart in front of the sofa, poured two cups of tea, handed one to Dinah, and sank onto the sofa beside Egan. "What do you think of my find, Egan? Will she do?"

Dinah was instantly on guard. "Do what?"

Egan made a moue of acquiescent distaste. "Zenia wants you to participate in our film."

"Me?" Dinah set her cup and saucer on a glass shelf beside the chair.

"That's right. What did you call it, Egan?"

"A docudrama."

Zenia sniffed. "I envision a powerful statement, one that the intelligentsia will call an epic. Governor Rigas is an old friend of mine. He has granted us permission to film whenever and wherever on the island. No restrictions. Egan is bringing in a crew from Athens. You will play the young Marilita. You have a boldness about you that puts me in mind of her."

"After the disparaging things you've said about your sister, not to mention the fact that she murdered your husband, you can hardly expect me to thank you for the comparison."

Zenia's mouth squinched into a smeary magenta smile. "There were facets of Marilita's character that were laudable. One of them was her refusal to be slighted. As you have just demonstrated, you won't be slighted either." She took a sip of tea, leaving a lipstick smudge on the cup. "My sister and I were poles apart philosophically and politically. Our father was a royalist and a distinguished member of the Greek government-in-exile during the Second World War. He died in the Civil War that followed, fighting the communists alongside your American CIA Captain Giorgos Stephanadis. There he is now. You've put your tea on his ashes."

Dinah recoiled. The glass shelf was supported by three slim, cylindrical brass tubes. "Are those cannon shells?"

Egan nodded. "Howitzer, 105 millimeter. Zenia, didn't you say that Giorgos recovered the casings after they had been fired into a nest of communists?"

"That's right. It was one of his most successful sorties. My father's ashes are in the first casing, Phaedon's are in the second. When I die, my remains will be placed in the third and entombed in the family mausoleum at Kanaris."

Apparently, Marilita had been banned from the sanctity of the mausoleum and consigned to a grave in the village cemetery. Zenia's outburst at her memorial exhumation was more understandable now. To have a loved one murdered would be anguishing enough. But to know that the loved one was murdered by your own sister—a person who shared your upbringing and your DNA, a person connected to you in such a primal way—that would embitter anyone.

Zenia cinched her lips and seemed to contemplate. "Marilita never took pride in her father's sacrifice. She had no sense of class or order."

"Now, Zenia, you must admit that she was gifted in her own way and very alluring. Nasos Lykos was something of a rake, but a marvelous fellow, clever as they come and rich as Croesus. And she did change after she fell in love with him."

"For the worse. Everyone knows that he and his mother were leftist sympathizers."

Egan tugged his jacket closer around him. "When I saw Marilita in Rome with him the year before the tragedy, she seemed disinterested in politics and her work on the set was more disciplined. In spite of his amours, Nasos had rather a mellowing effect on her and he gave no indication that he was a leftie."

"He would have been imprisoned if he did. His family's money insulated him. I daresay he and his mother donated thousands to the anarcho-communists. They drew Marilita into their cabal. Phaedon found out about them and Marilita killed him."

Dinah couldn't see the logic. "If Nasos and his mother were her coconspirators, why would she kill them?"

Zenia gave this incongruity the back of her hand. "Nasos was a womanizer. If Marilita hadn't killed him, another woman would have done it." She focused her compelling, squid-ink eyes on Dinah. "I've asked Egan to make this film about my family while I'm still alive and able to help craft it. I'll be the producer and director and I will have final approval of the script. We haven't got a big budget and the rights to use clips from Marilita's studio films would cost too much. I will speak some of the... what did you call them, Egan?"

"Voice overs."

"Louder."

"Voice overs."

"Yes, yes." She poured herself another cup of tea and cocked her head at Dinah. "You won't have to speak. All you have to do is vamp and strike an attitude. None of the women in the Samian theater company can capture Marilita's recklessness or impetuous nature. You've got the right coloring and her same rebellious eyes. You're the best we can do."

Being compared to Marilita because of her coloring was one thing. Being compared because of a perceived similarity of character was downright chilling. Still, Dinah couldn't help being fascinated. "I thought you didn't like film."

"I don't. This is an exception. All this drivel about Marilita being a martyr to the cause of democracy, I won't have it. She was depraved. I have given Phaedon's journals and papers to Egan to sort through. He has been a family friend for half a century. I trust him to tell the truth and preserve Phaedon's reputation."

And destroy any vestige of Marilita's, Dinah guessed. Egan was probably stringing Zenia along in order to bilk her out of a ton of money and the film would never be completed. But on the off chance that it was, Dinah predicted that the intelligentsia would label it fascist propaganda, whether or not of the epic sort. "I wish I could help you, Zenia, but I plan to leave Samos today."

"A day in Athens, but you'll be back. You won't be needed right away."

"Reckless, impetuous, depraved. I don't think I'd do justice to the part."

"I'm eighty-five-years old. Surely you can spare an old woman a few weeks. Of course, you will be paid handsomely for your time."

"I wish you luck finding a suitable Marilita, Zenia, but I'm not the one." Dinah stood up. "Thank you for the tea, but I have to be getting back to Kanaris to meet that mechanic. I'm sure Mr. Vercuni will save you the trouble and drive me back down the mountain."

Egan rose from the sofa, tugging his jacket around him. "Yes, of course. And don't worry, Zenia. We'll find another Marilita. I'll call one of my contacts in Athens to set up some auditions. There's always a cluster of young starlets looking for a start."

"None so damnably like my sister as this one," said Zenia and swept out of the room with surprising energy for an octogenarian.

Egan smirked. "She's not used to hearing 'no' for an answer. It's rather bracing to see. Wait here, Miss…Pelerin, is it? I'll change and drive you to town."

He left the room and Dinah nipped across to look at the framed photographs and articles beside the front door. There was a ratty newspaper clipping dated June 1973 with a picture of a hawk-nosed, thin-lipped, square-jawed man in a much decorated military uniform. Colonel Phaedon Hero, she surmised. The Greek script was unreadable. It was the kind of photo that might have accompanied a notice of promotion, or an obituary. There were several black-and-white photographs that looked as if they should have stayed in the family album. The sun pouring through the skylights had faded them badly. There was one of the Colonel, recognizable by his beaky nose, standing with his arm around an arrogant, dark-eyed young woman in a rakish feather hat—Zenia? Another photo showed a different military man standing with one hand on the shoulder of a seated woman in a high-necked dress. His heavy black brows and austere visage suggested an authoritarian mentality. No doubt he was the intrepid father whose ashes reposed in the first howitzer shell and the seated woman must be his wife. She had a vacant stare, like a marionette. It was hard to imagine such a drab looking woman giving birth to the likes of Zenia and Marilita.

Hurriedly, Dinah ran her eyes around the rest of the gallery until she found the newspaper photo that had aroused Thor's curiosity—the one taken on the day of the murders. Marilita, her hair tousled and her head thrown back in voluptuous abandon, was laughing into the camera. She wore a bikini with a man's shirt hanging open over the top. Phaedon Hero, in uniform but clearly in a jovial mood, stood between Marilita and a seemingly bemused older woman in street clothes—Nasos' mother. Phaedon lifted one of her hands high over her head as if he were about to lead her into a Greek dance. A well-muscled hunk in bathing trunks stood apart from the rest holding a picnic hamper. So that was Nasos Lykos. He certainly didn't look like a mellowing influence. He must have been at least ten years younger than Marilita and, even in the deteriorated newspaper photo, his eyes transmitted a bad-boy bent.

"Let's be off then," said Egan, breezing through the room in a short-sleeved green shirt and mustard colored tie. He opened the door with a flourish. "My car is parked in front."

Dinah put on her sunglasses and preceded him down the curved stone steps to his car, her thoughts revolving around that tableau forty years ago. If Zenia's explanation of the murders could be believed and the Colonel had found out that his sister-in-law and the others were traitors, why didn't he have them arrested? Why go to a beach and let himself be photographed smiling in their company? And who had taken the picture?

Chapter Fourteen

Egan's car was a dusty green Hyundai pocked with dents, but you wouldn't know it from his superior air. He looked as if he were holding back a nosebleed as he pulled on a pair of leather driving gloves.

Dinah couldn't wait to tell Thor that Phaedon Hero was Zenia's husband. She wondered why Mentor hadn't mentioned the fact, but maybe he thought she knew already. "How long had Zenia and Phaedon been married before his death?"

"Twenty years, I should say. Yes, twenty, at least. Perhaps longer."

Dinah did the math. According to Thor, Marilita was forty when she was executed in 1973. That would make her eighty today, five years younger than Zenia. "Did Zenia and Phaedon have any children?"

"No. They pretended briefly that Marilita's misbegotten child was theirs, but gave up the charade when the scandal broke."

"There was a scandal that Marilita had a child out of wedlock?"

"It wouldn't make the back page of the tabloids today, but at the time it made headlines in the dailies all across Europe. Marilita never denied that the girl was illegitimate. It devastated her career, but she had made most of her big films and big money in her early twenties. She had a few supporting roles in her thirties, but her star power was gone."

"Was Nasos Alcina's father?"

"Zot, no. Alcina must have been ten or twelve when Marilita met Nasos. They had known each other only a couple of years when they played their climactic scene. Marilita's execution was an anticlimax. She went to her grave without naming the child's father."

"Do you think the junta executed her because of her politics?"

"They had absolute power. They could execute anyone for any reason, but murdering a member of the junta was certainly high treason. The newspapers reported only what they were ordered to report, of course, but they embellished their stories with a rather gleeful flair. I read one or two while filming on location in Albania. *Military Court Awards Disgraced Actress, Murderess, And Convicted Insurrectionist Her Date With Nemesis, The Inescapable Messenger of Justice.* Marilita received a bit more ballyhoo than the average prisoner. The government demonized her. By the time they stood her up in front of the firing squad, she was probably longing to die. The junta's manicures were not designed to pamper."

"You mean they pulled out...?"

"Among other forms of torture, or so I've heard."

Dinah shuddered. "You said that Marilita changed when she fell in love with Nasos. How?"

"She was less outspoken. Not demure by any means, but muted. Before Nasos, her political comments would have caused repercussions were it not for Phaedon. He protected her."

"She opposed the junta?"

"She opposed conformity. I think she did a lot of things just to antagonize her sister. She was always bringing around some disreputable artist or actor to queer Zenia's parties. Phaedon rather enjoyed her slumming and laughed it off, but it goaded Zenia."

"But Zenia is an actress. Aren't most theater people nonconformists?"

"Only when it's advantageous. Zenia was ambitious for her husband. She was more interested in advancing Phaedon's military career than her own and then, well. Sadly, Nemesis is a democrat. The goddess doesn't like any one person to have too much good." He finally got the gloves fitted to his satisfaction, started the car, and eased out into the road like an aristocrat out for a Sunday jaunt.

"Aren't you headed the wrong way?"

"There's more room to turn around at the gorge lookout."

There was plenty of room here for anyone who knew how to drive, but Dinah didn't object. His dawdling would be a relief after that ride with Zenia. He obviously had no compunction about backbiting and she egged him on. "Zenia doesn't like the villagers and vice versa. Do you know why?"

"Kanaris has always been a haven for leftists and Zenia and Phaedon represented the anticommunist junta. There were demonstrations for Marilita after her arrest and some of the villagers hung banners proclaiming their gratitude that she had struck a blow against tyranny. Over the years, whenever the opportunity presents, Zenia takes pains to remind them." He chortled. "What is the line? The sins of the fathers shall be visited upon the sons."

Dinah was awed by the sheer duration of the feud. If the sons of the sinners were still alive, they'd be grandfathers by now.

Egan turned into the small, unpaved area marked with a crooked wooden sign in Greek and a badly carved horse with wings.

"What does the sign say?"

"Pegasus Point." He completed his U-turn and started to leave.

"Wait. I'd like to take a look if you don't mind."

He stopped the car and pulled up the hand brake. "You can see all that's worth seeing from the car."

"How deep is it?"

"Two hundred and forty meters."

Dinah multiplied by three and peered down. "Is there a stream or river at the bottom?"

"There used to be a small stream. Zenia's father owned all of this land, but when I was a lad, the villagers regarded the gorge and the forest as their hunting ground. After Phaedon's death,

Zenia posted trespassing signs. There's an easement for the hiking trail along the perimeter, but going into the gorge is prohibited. Of course, no one pays any heed to the postings. They do what they can to repay Zenia for her malice."

Dinah was about to question him about the *mnimosyno*, but a plume of dark, oily smoke caught her eye. It rose out of the wooded depths below like a snake swaying to a charmer's flute. Was someone burning his garbage way down there? The smell that assailed her nostrils wasn't animal or vegetable. It was noxious, burning rubber and plastic.

She jumped out of the car and leaned over the railing. The source of the smoke was an overturned car. She could see one blue door twisted askew like a broken wing. Thor's car was that exact same blue.

A sick feeling washed over her. "Do you have a cell phone, Egan?"

"Of course." He got out of the car and walked over to the railing. "What's the problem?"

"Call for help. Call an ambulance. I'm going down."

She ran along the railing, looking for a gap or a trail. Where the railing ended, she saw a chute of broken trees and scree where the car had plunged over the side. She sideslipped down a short way, climbed over a log, and sideslipped another few yards. She strained her eyes. Was it Thor's car or another blue car? Except for size, most modern cars looked alike to her and this one had landed upside down. Maybe she was catastrophizing and Thor was merrily going about his business in town this morning. What would he be doing on this side of the gorge anyway? If he'd come to talk with Zenia, either she or Egan would have mentioned that he'd been there. She felt a spasm of relief, followed immediately by a spasm of guilt. What happened here spelled catastrophe for somebody.

Above, she heard Egan talking in a high, excited voice. He alternated between Greek and English. She wished she could hear and understand the other end of the call. Did Samos have a helicopter to airlift an injured person out of this gorge? Did they have a Jaws of Life to pry apart the wreckage if someone was trapped?

Her feet slipped out from under her and she went down hard on her backside and the palms of her hands. When she got up, her hands were skinned and bleeding and embedded with grit. She wiped them on the knees of her pants and scouted around for an easier descent. A wheel had come off the car on its downward plunge and rolled at least a hundred yards diagonally through the scrub until it collided with a tree and fell over on its side. The path it took appeared less steep than the one she was on and she cut across the slope in that direction. If she were going to stay upright, she would have to zigzag down the mountain like a skier.

Belatedly, she remembered water. Why did she never have the stuff when she needed it? Not only was she getting hotter and thirstier by the minute, but water might have been the only help she could have offered the crash victim. She reached for her phone to call Egan, but she'd left it in her purse in the car. She remembered how Thor had agonized over the Utoya massacre in Norway. If the cops had carried guns, kids could have been saved. The same sense of incompetence afflicted her now. If she carried water or a phone or knew anything at all about how to control bleeding or prevent shock, she might be able to save… whoever was in that car.

Her shoes had collected a painful lot of sand and pebbles and she could feel the beginnings of a blister on her left heel, but she had too much downward momentum to stop now. Her hands felt sticky from blood and pine resin where she had been grabbing onto trees to keep from falling and her face stung from heat and sweat. She dashed a drop of sweat out of her eyes and realized that she'd lost her Wayfarers.

The heat and stink of burning plastic and rubber grew stronger and she advanced cautiously. The roof and front seat compartment had crumpled nearly flat and the rear end was charred. The gas tank must have exploded. She scrambled over a downed tree and crept around to look at the front grill. It was a Peugeot. Thor's Peugeot.

She slumped onto the ground. Nobody could have walked away from that one. He was dead. A few hours ago she'd cursed her fate over a lousy set of slashed tires. Now the Fates had shown her what they could do when they got serious. Breathing hurt, as if she were inhaling shards of glass. She wanted to cry, but she couldn't. There'd be plenty of time to cry, plenty of time to reflect on the fact that her last words to him had been mean and petulant. Time to think about all the ways she'd let him down. She forced herself to stand up, tried to steel herself against the sight of his dead body, but prayed anyway. Don't let him be dead. Please, please, please don't let him be dead.

She walked around to the driver's window. The glass had disintegrated into a mass of green rubble and there was only a small gap between the squashed roof and the chassis. Careless of the glass, she lay down on her belly. The airbag had deployed and the mass of deflated nylon curtained the interior. Was the airbag what caused that gunshot smell? She pushed the fabric aside and saw detached hunks of the dashboard. The steering wheel had mangled like a coat hanger. The seat was empty.

Had he been thrown from the car or jumped free before impact? Was he lying down here somewhere injured and unable to climb out?

"Thor?" She yelled his name over and over again, but there was no answer. It was as if he'd gone up in the plume of smoke still snaking up from the rear of the Peugeot.

Chapter Fifteen

Dinah sat on the unbroken section of the railing over the gorge and tried not to moan out loud. She drank a liter of water furnished by a baby-faced emergency medical technician who looked as helpless as she felt. The other technician, an older guy with a gaunt face and a sour mouth, was reading Egan the riot act in Greek. From what she could gather, the gist of his gripe was that they had driven their big white ambulance up this snaky mountain road to rescue a man who wasn't here. To his credit, Egan seemed to be giving as good as he got. What he lacked in stature, he made up for in hauteur.

She poured a little of the cool water on her stinging hands and scoured the slopes of the gorge for the hundredth time. This was the steeper, more sparsely wooded side. Looking across the gorge floor, she could see sections of a less precipitous trail winding up through the pines. She had climbed halfway to the top calling his name, but there was no sign that he'd walked out that way and she turned back.

Tears welled as Sergeant Papas and two other policemen drove up and got out of their car. She hopped off the railing, but her legs felt limp and she reached back and braced herself on the rail. She knew that Papas spoke English because Thor had spoken to him in English. She burst into a torrent of words. "He's not down there. His car is totaled and he's not there. I called and walked around and around. He must have been thrown free, but he's unconscious. Maybe in the trees above the floor."

Papas stepped to the railing and took in the wreckage below. "Did you see blood on or near the car?"

Her heart leapt up. "No. No, I didn't see blood. My car was vandalized this morning. Maybe somebody stole his car and pushed it over the cliff. Did he call you? Did he report his car stolen?"

"There have been no reports of a stolen car." He had a husky voice, low but oddly gentle. He had a somber face and deep-set, shrewd little eyes. He scoped out the gorge floor through binoculars. "It's possible the car landed on top of him and you were unable to see."

She couldn't let herself think along those lines or she'd lose it. "Do you have equipment to extricate him if he's trapped?"

"It's on the way."

"And if he was thrown clear, is there a search and rescue helicopter on the island? Can you radio for more searchers?"

"If we need to." Papas raised the binoculars and scanned the horizon. "Perhaps this is a strategy."

"What?"

"Perhaps the Inspector *wants* to disappear."

"Why would he want to disappear?" She rolled this two cents over in her mind. Pancake his car over the side of a cliff? It wasn't practical. It wasn't Norwegian. "He wouldn't do something like this," she said. "He absolutely wouldn't do something like this without telling me."

Papas gave her a quizzical look.

She disregarded the implied skepticism. "If you'll notice the tread marks, Sergeant, he seems to have been driving down the mountain from the other direction. Where does this road lead?"

"Nowhere. It deadends in less than a kilometer at an abandoned marble quarry. He may have gone to the end of the road to turn around."

"Does anyone besides Zenia Stephanadis have a house on this road?"

"No." He hung the binoculars around his neck, put on his dark glasses, and scribbled a number on the back of a card.

"Here is my phone number. If the Inspector is in the *lagkadi*, we will find him."

She drew in a ragged breath and watched him trek off into the abyss with the other two men.

The sour-mouthed EMT thumbed his nose at Egan and shouted after Papas. There was a curt exchange, after which the EMT climbed behind the wheel of the ambulance.

"What did they say?" Dinah asked Egan.

"The ambulance driver says he can't wait. They must be on call for other emergencies."

"But it'll take time to get another ambulance back up here. Thor may need help right away."

"Samos has limited resources," said Egan.

The nice EMT threw Dinah an apologetic look and swung up into the passenger seat. After a number of short forward and backward lunges, the ambulance took off back down the mountain.

Dinah tried to pull herself together. Zenia had said that Thor asked her about the junta last night. She turned to Egan. "Was Thor at Zenia's house last night?"

"No. I believe she did have one phone call."

"What about this morning? Did he come by before I got there?"

"If he drove past, he didn't stop in."

"And you didn't hear screeching brakes or the sound of the impact?"

"No, nothing. Of course, Zenia wouldn't hear Götterdämmerung."

Dinah had the sense that Zenia cultivated the myth of deafness as part of her dramatic persona. She heard more than she let on. "Is there a Norwegian Embassy in Greece?"

"Yes, but aren't you being premature?"

"In what way?"

"I should give more thought to the Sergeant's hypothesis if I were you. Policemen engage in all manner of covert operations. This is probably a ruse of some sort. Your inspector is probably lying doggo with a telephoto lens, spying on the gang that he's investigating."

She gave Egan a leery look. "What makes you think he's investigating a gang? How do you know he's investigating anyone?"

"Isn't he? Zenia led me to believe that the policeman who'd let Marilita's house was here to make inquiries and everyone had better be on guard."

"On guard against what?"

"Discovery, I should say. The people of Kanaris have always had a predilection to illicit pursuits and the poor economy has worsened everyone's finances. I thought he was probably investigating illegal drugs or money laundering or some such." He ran a finger around the inside of his collar and flexed his wrinkly neck. "I've already phoned Zenia with the news about Ramberg, by the way. Poor old puss. She sounded quite distressed." He went back to the cliff edge to watch the police searching down below.

Dinah grabbed her purse out of his car, pulled out her phone, and dialed Thor's number. He had his phone with him all the time. If he was anywhere near the Peugeot, the searchers would hear it ring and move in the direction of the sound. Or if he had it turned off, they could use GPS tracking to locate him. But the phone didn't ring. She didn't even get his voice mail.

She called K.D., who picked up on the first ring. "Has Thor called? Has he been there?"

"No, but I'm super glad you called. I've been thinking about our problem and the answer is so totally simple. I should have remembered. An attorney that Daddy used to work with lives in Athens, Alex Drake. He has a daughter my age and I'm sure he'd love to have me stay…"

"Shut up, will you?"

"Well, snap. You sound kind of lathery."

She told K.D. about Thor's car at the bottom of the gorge.

"Oh. My. God."

"He wasn't inside," said Dinah.

"You think he may still be alive then?"

"I don't know. I hope."

"I'll wait here, Dinah. If I hear anything or if anyone calls, I'll let you know right away."

Dinah joined Egan at the railing. She tried to think logically. Either Thor had somehow been able to scrabble out of the wreckage and was lying hurt somewhere, or Papas and Egan were right and he had faked the crash. She would like to believe that Thor had disappeared for some cloak-and-dagger reason, but her intuition...no, her common sense told her that he hadn't. If he wanted to disappear, it would be supremely stupid to cause a flaming crash guaranteed to draw police and spectators for miles around.

If somebody wanted to kill him and make it look like an accident, they'd leave his body in the car. But if they just wanted him temporarily out of the way so he didn't interfere with their plans, he might have been dragged off and locked up in somebody's wine cellar. Killing an international cop would cause more trouble than it was worth. Whatever the situation, the people he was working for needed to know that he'd gone missing.

She Googled the National Criminal Investigative Service of Norway. N.C.I.S. Incredibly, a telephone number popped up. She moved out of range of Egan's ears and dialed it. Not knowing which person or office to communicate her concerns to, she left an urgent message with the receptionist that one of their agents was missing on the island of Samos in suspicious circumstances and she requested that someone in authority return her call ASAP. She repeated her cell phone number twice, very clearly, and hung up. It crossed her mind that this phone call could end Thor's career if N.C.I.S. was finicky about their agents confiding in their girlfriends, but she couldn't think about that now.

She scrolled through the list of embassies in Athens, but stopped. Interpol. Thor had said that N.C.I.S. coordinated with Interpol. They probably had dozens of agents operating in Greece. She Googled Interpol for a contact number and found this: *When to contact Interpol. Never. Interpol does not provide investigative services directly to individuals. However, it never*

*hurts to ask local law enforcement of member countries if they are
coordinating with Interpol.*

Egan turned back from the railing. "The search could go on
for hours. I need to be getting on. Where shall I drop you?"

"I'm not leaving until they find him."

"As you wish. But if I were you, I would take care to have
independent transportation available in the event you decide to
remain on the island. Zenia and I have work to do on the film.
We can't be counted on to provide you taxi service."

Egan snailed along as if he were leading a funeral procession.
Dinah fidgeted and pressed her feet against the floorboard as
if she could impel the Hyundai forward. She felt stymied and
feverish. The air conditioning gave her goose bumps. Thor would
have loved it.

Where was he? If he had faked the crash, for whatever
reason, he would have left her a letter. Even if he believed she
was breaking off the affair, he would have left her a letter. She
hadn't looked inside the Picanto. He could have taken her keys
before she woke up this morning, placed a letter in the car where
it wouldn't be seen by Alcina, and returned the key. Maybe he
was delivering a letter when the tire slashers showed up. They
might have stabbed him, stuffed him in the trunk of his own
car, driven it up here, and sent it hurtling off into the gorge. She
shivered. The trunk had been mashed flat.

A sheep pounced out of the trees into the middle of the road.
Egan braked hard and they watched as one by one, a whole rau-
cous, baa-ing flock bowled down a steep dirt path and bunched
in front of the car like a rockslide.

Dinah ducked her head and looked up through the dust
cloud to her left. "Where are they coming from?"

"From overgrazed pastures to new." Egan pulled up the emergency brake. "Rather quaint. One forgets how pastoral parts of
the island still are."

A young man with long, curly hair bopped out of the woods,
rotating his shoulders and wagging his head to whatever music

his iPod was channeling into his ears. When he saw the car, his face broke into an ebullient smile and he plucked the buds out of his ears. "*Kaliméra!*"

Dinah rolled down her window, stuck her head out, and returned his good day. "*Kaliméra.* Can you herd them to the side of the road, *parakaló*? We're in a dreadful hurry."

He frowned and shook his head.

"Tell him in Greek, Egan."

"I don't see why you're in such a hurry. There's nothing you can do."

"Just tell him."

Egan harrumphed and spouted a stream of Greek at the boy.

"*Nè, málista.*" The boy smiled and prodded the nearest sheep in the rear with his staff. A few more deft prods and he had maneuvered the flock onto the verge where they trotted along like a line of obedient, but noisy school children. The boy refitted the ear buds in his ears and resumed his head-wagging dance-walk.

Egan released the brake and rolled on. "Not my nostalgic image of the humble shepherd, but with fifty percent unemployment among Greek youth, it's good to see that at least one has a paying job."

Dinah leaned out the window and called out behind her. "*Efkharistó.*"

The boy waved and smiled.

She fished Papas' number out of her pocket and punched the numbers into her phone.

"*Yia'sas.*"

"It's Dinah Pelerin. Have you found anything?"

"A pair of dark glasses, non-prescription."

"They're probably mine. Anything else?"

"We pried open the trunk."

"He wasn't…?"

"No. We found a man's shoe a few meters distant from the car. It was of Norwegian make."

"So he must have been thrown from the car. He must be down there somewhere."

"It seems so, yes, but..." He faltered.

"But?"

"There is blood on the shoe."

She swallowed. "A lot?"

"Yes. We don't know if it is Inspector Ramberg's blood or if there was someone else in the car. We don't know if the scene is real or if it has been," he hesitated again, "staged. We will keep searching. You may rest assured."

Dinah didn't think that she could rest at all, much less assured. She couldn't understand why Papas was so doubtful. Why would he think that Thor had staged the scene? The shoe proved that he had been in the car at some point and that he'd been hurt.

"Did they find him?" asked Egan.

"Not yet."

"Were you and the Inspector engaged to be married?"

She shook her head. The lump in her throat ached so she couldn't speak. She didn't have much faith in the institution of marriage, but she hadn't ruled it out. Having the option taken away by death filled her with misery. Anger, too. She may have been the architect of some of her disappointments, but this one came courtesy of outside forces. She said, "You speak as if you know Samos well, Mr. Vercuni. Are the police trustworthy? Are they honest?"

"Honest in what way?"

"Zenia seems to think they can be bribed."

"In the Balkans, the trading of favors is looked upon as a show of good will. *Rousfeti* is how things get done. It has nothing to do with honesty."

Dinah didn't think of Greece as part of the Balkans, but of course it was the southern end of the Balkan Peninsula. She had been on a dig in the Balkans in 2000 when the ethnic tinderbox that made up the former Yugoslavia had erupted. The Albanians attacked the Serbs, the Macedonians attacked the Albanians, her Bulgarian archaeology professor was caught smuggling weapons to the Kosovo Liberation Army, and everybody assumed that everybody else was lying and taking bribes, which justified their doing the same. She was picking up a similar vibe here. "Do you know Savas Brakus?"

"I knew his father Aries well. We grew up together, served in the army together."

"Along with Phaedon Hero?"

"Under Phaedon's command. After Aries left the army, he opened the Marc Antony. Savas took it over when his father began to sugar the lamb and salt the pudding." Egan chortled. "Poor old Aries. Eventually went stark mad. That must have been twenty years ago. Savas aspired to be a great runner and represent Greece at the Olympics, but his mother couldn't run the taverna by herself. An eight-hundred-meter man, I think Zenia said he was. Of course, Zenia never cared for Aries or Savas. *Agroikos*, she called them. What you would call yokels. I haven't thought about Aries in years. Marilita was his Aphrodite. He worshipped her. Pity he was married and Catholic to the marrow. I think he would have killed for Marilita if she had said the word."

"Was there ever any suspicion that she had?"

"Asked Aries to kill Nasos, you mean? That's rather farfetched."

Dinah kept coming back to Kanaris' allergy to the police. "Have you ever heard of anyone on Samos whose illicit pursuits included arms dealing?"

"Gangsters on Samos? There's one for the books." His laughed a dry, hacking laugh that made his Adam's apple bob up and down. "Not likely. Of course, I've been away for decades. There's more economic hardship and less respect for law and order. And of course a lot of foreigners have moved in."

"Samos is a stepping stone from Turkey and the Middle East into Europe. With so many foreigners passing through, the island would be a perfect transit point for smugglers, don't you think?"

"Samos has its share of minor villains, but no arms smugglers."

His neck squirmed inside his starched collar and she could see that the subject bothered him. "Did you know the Iraqi who was murdered?"

"No. Why would I?"

"I thought you might have seen him at Zenia's house. She hires refugees as day laborers, doesn't she?"

"I'm not the gardener. You'll have to ask her who she hires to prune the shrubbery."

"I intend to. What happened to Thor was no accident and I mean to find out who was behind it."

His forehead puckered and his Adam's apple bobbed, as if he'd just thought of something galvanizing. She could almost hear the cogwheels whirring.

"What are you thinking, Egan? Do you know something about arms trafficking on Samos? Do you have an idea who it was that ran Thor off the road?"

He made a series of dry, raspy sounds that she construed as a laugh. "Zot, no. I was thinking what a coincidence this would be if your Inspector Ramberg is never found."

She clenched her fists. "What do you mean?"

"You and Marilita would have more than your rebellious eyes in common. They couldn't find Nasos' body either. He fell into the sea after she shot him. The police speculated that the currents carried his body into Turkish waters."

Chapter Sixteen

Dinah sat on a bench in the Kanaris parking lot staring out at the Aegean and waiting for the mechanic with the new tires. A tide of morbid thoughts swamped her. She thought about Marilita's boyfriend, perhaps not yet dead of his wounds, swept under the waves and drowned. Egan was a jerk to suggest that Thor wouldn't be found. It was worse than tactless. It was cruel. But it had deflected her questions about arms traffickers, which may have been what he had in mind.

So many coincidences. Zenia waited for decades to lease Marilita's house and then leased it to a policeman. Thor had been engrossed by Marilita's crime. His car crashed on the road where Zenia and only Zenia lived. And he had called her last night to ask about armories on the island. Dinah believed in coincidences, but they didn't come in swarms. Those American weapons that Thor was investigating were tied in some way to Marilita or the coterie of people who surrounded her.

A service truck rumbled up the mountain and nosed into the parking space next to the Picanto. The mechanic didn't speak English, but he had brought the right sized tires, thanks to Mentor's earlier explanation, and he set about his job without any social preliminaries. While he jacked up the Picanto, she paced around the parking lot, lobbing an occasional look across the Aegean. The *meltemi* had come up and the water was rough and choppy. Bad news for anyone sailing against the wind, or swimming against the current.

Heat radiated off the pavement and, with the incessant wind, she began to feel as if she were being baked in a convection oven. Thor would be miserable in this heat. Beyond rational thought, at some elemental level of cognition, she knew that he was alive. If he had been in the car when it crashed, he had obviously escaped the brunt of the impact. He was hurt, but he was strong and resourceful. He could have climbed out of the gorge, been picked up by a passing motorist, and taken to a hospital. Maybe the hospital had called the land line at Marilita's house and the message hadn't gotten through. Maybe Alcina wasn't around to translate for K.D. But if Thor wasn't in the car when it crashed, where was he and how did his bloody shoe wind up in the gorge?

The mechanic blotted the sweat off his face with a greasy towel, slung the fourth tire out of the truck, and started to mount it. Dinah took out her phone and called K.D. Suddenly, she wasn't so gung-ho to hustle her off to Atlanta. In Thor's absence, she had become by default the closest thing Dinah had to a friend on the island.

"Dinah!" She sounded breathless.

"Are you all right?"

"Yes, but Yannis is here. He knows about Thor's accident. I heard him say it served him right for mixing in."

"I didn't think Yannis spoke English."

"Well, he does. He's speaking Greek right now with Alcina, but they shift in and out of English."

Dinah's chest tightened. How could Yannis know that something had happened to Thor? Had Papas or one of the other policemen phoned to give him a heads-up or had he been there when the car went over the cliff?

"I think he's getting ready to leave again," said K.D., "but if you want me to, I'll stall him."

"No." Dinah was still assimilating the fact that he knew what had happened. Had he run Thor off the road to get back at him for having him arrested? She couldn't think what to do. Did she dare question him face to face? Would he pretend he didn't understand? Would he turn violent?

"He's walking down the hall right now. Should I…?"

"Stay out of his way, K.D. I'll be there as soon as I can."

The mechanic was tightening the lugs on the last tire. Dinah counted out a wad of euros, roughly the amount Mentor had said it would cost.

"*Efkharistó*," she said, thrusting the money into his hand. "Thanks very much."

She gave a second's thought to calling Papas, decided he couldn't help, and hopped in the Picanto. Stoked on adrenalin and suspicion, she barreled up the road without regard to the town ordinance or the safety of its inhabitants. She took the corner past the taverna too fast, hit a pothole and bonked her head against the roof. The pain slowed her down and reminded her that she hadn't the foggiest idea what she would say to Yannis. She bumped down the lane to Marilita's house, rubbing her head and racking her brain.

She parked beside the veranda. Before she cut the engine, K.D. flew out the door.

"I told him you wanted to talk to him and he'd better not run or you'd have him arrested again."

Well, that should set the tone for a productive dialogue, thought Dinah. She got out of the car and tried to rally her courage. This was the man who, regardless of a lack of evidence, may have gunned a man down in cold blood. He could be armed to the teeth right now.

He shambled out the door wearing the same ratty straw hat he'd worn when Fathi confronted him.

She squared her shoulders and stepped up to meet him with a bravado she didn't feel. Up close, she saw that his eyes were a disconcerting Celtic blue, not unlike Alcina's glass *mati*. They regarded Dinah with undisguised animosity.

"How did you hear about what happened to Mr. Ramberg's car, Yannis?"

"*Dhen katalamváno.*"

"In English, please. I know you understand."

He snorted. "I understand you have no power. You have no right."

"I do have power. I know American senators, important people who can pull all kinds of strings with the Greek officials. They'll make sure you tell the truth or send you to prison until you do."

A piercing yip made Dinah jump. She looked up and saw Alcina hovering in the doorway.

Yannis muttered something in Greek to her and turned back to Dinah. "He missed the curve. It has happened on that road before."

"Did you see it? Were you there?"

"No."

She didn't believe him. "This is the second violent incident connected to you. If you're innocent, you need to cooperate. If you weren't at Pegasus Point, who told you about the car?"

"The monk."

"Brother Constantine? How did he know it was Inspector Ramberg's car?"

"The police. They are everywhere in the *lagkadi*."

Dinah supposed that Yannis had called or visited Constantine to inquire about his little envelope and the brother had filled him in. She probed deeper. "What did you and Fathi argue about?"

"Yannis didn't kill him," cried Alcina.

He raised a hand to shush her. "He tried to sell me stolen *komboloi*. Worry beads. Coral and silver. I told him to go to hell."

"If you didn't shoot him, who did?"

"I wasn't there. I didn't take the gun."

Her phone rang and her stomach knotted. She glanced at K.D., walked to the edge of the veranda, and answered.

Sergeant Papas said, "He's not in the *lagkadi*."

"You're sure?"

"Very sure. We have combed the area."

"What does that mean?"

"Either he was not in the car when it crashed or if he escaped, he was able to leave the scene."

She said, "He's been kidnapped."

"It is possible." Papas put a good deal of reluctance into the admission.

"It's got to be what happened." Thinking that one's lover has been kidnapped shouldn't boost one's spirits, but considering the alternative, it boosted hers. People who are kidnapped have value. They aren't killed until and unless the kidnappers' demands aren't met. "Can you trace him through his cell phone?"

"If it is turned on."

"He keeps it on all the time. Maybe the kidnappers don't know about cell phones."

"It is possible." His voice carried an unmistakable note of *what planet do you live on?*

She had to acknowledge that he was probably right on that point. "Will you contact the Norwegian Embassy and notify them that one of their citizens has been kidnapped?"

"I will ask my superior to make the call and report the Inspector missing."

She turned around. Yannis had vanished, but Alcina was still loitering and listening. She lowered her voice. "Did you find beads on Fathi's body, Sergeant? Coral and silver *Kombolói*?"

"Only his wallet with two hundred euros."

"Could you tell if anything had been taken?"

"There was no appearance of robbery."

She said, "He wasn't a refugee. He had an identity card that permitted him to travel anywhere in Europe."

Papas had nothing to add. He cut her off with a crisp, "I will keep you informed."

"Thank you." She ended the call, feeling marginalized, alone, and alien. She didn't know if or when Norway would send in the cavalry. She didn't trust Papas or the local police who took bribes. She didn't trust Egan or Yannis or Brakus or the villagers who also took bribes. Mentor seemed honest enough, but what could he do? What could she do?

What was it Yannis had said? *I didn't take the gun.* Was that what Fathi was trying to sell? An American gun?

"Now you know how it feels," said Alcina. "This is what happens. You have someone and then the *astrapi*. In a flash of lightning, everything changes and you are alone."

Dinah didn't need any truisms about lightning strikes. She experienced her first when she was ten and the knowledge that life was uncertain had been etched indelibly on her consciousness. But Thor was missing, not dead, and what she needed was a Greek she could trust, someone who could help her set the wheels in motion for an intensive, organized, island-wide search for him. She knew only one person who fit the bill. Zenia was too old to be involved in gunrunning, she had friends in high places, and she wanted something, however crazy, that Dinah was uniquely constituted to give her.

"What are you going to do?" asked K.D., sounding worried.

"Take a shower," said Dinah, dabbing at her skinned palms and scraping the dirt from under her broken nails. "After that, I'll do what everybody in the Balkans does. Trade favors."

Chapter Seventeen

Dinah spent a long time in the shower. The steaming spray pelted against her face and washed away the tears. This was her catharsis. Catharsis was the word coined by Aristotle to refer to the purging of pent-up emotions, of which she had a superfluity. They ranged from stubborn hope to forlorn despair and back again like a mad pendulum. She had to make up her mind—hope and action or despair and tears. If she were going to be of any use to Thor, she would have to foreclose the possibility that he was dead and emerge from this room dry eyed and determined and cynical. In a place with so many secrets, cynicism would be an asset.

"…in there?"

She shut off the water. Before she did anything, she should send K.D. home. It was the height of irresponsibility to let her stay on in the circumstances.

"Dinah, are you in there?"

"Yes."

"That man who bumped into you is downstairs."

"Brother Constantine?"

"No, the one in the fisherman's cap. Stavros. He says he'd like to speak with you. He came to offer his condolences about Thor. He brought a bouquet of flowers."

Dinah stepped out of the shower and massaged her temples. How had *he* found out about Thor? The admonition about

Greeks bearing gifts leapt to mind. His visit was most likely prompted by morbid curiosity, but he'd acted weird at the Marc Antony. He had seemed to be staring at her, but had she misinterpreted the object of his interest? He might have been staring at Thor, stalking him and waiting for the chance to jump him.

"Hello? Dinah? What do you want me to tell him?"

She cleared her throat and blew her nose. "Put the flowers in a vase and tell him I'll be down in a few minutes."

She toweled off and opened the bathroom window to clear the fog. She had paid no attention to his business card except for his name and an Athens address. Thor had been in Athens for a week before she arrived. What if this Stavros person had followed him to Samos? What if he had come here today to issue a ransom demand?

N.C.I.S. hadn't returned her call. Maybe her message had been dropped in somebody's inbox and wouldn't be read or acted on for days. Norwegians were uncompromising about their summer holiday, the *fellesferie*. They deserted their posts in droves, regardless how essential their jobs, and practically the whole country shut down. The *fellesferie* was usually not until July, but the N.C.I.S. slackers had obviously deserted their posts and the kidnapping of their agent had been left for her to contend with.

Swabbing her nicks and cuts with iodine and wincing, she ran through her mental archive of friends and relations. Her brother Lucien had scads of money, but she didn't know where he was offhand and there was nobody else she could rely on for a large sum on short notice. In a crunch, she could raid Uncle Cleon's bank account in Panama and figure out how to recoup K.D.'s inheritance later. The key was to keep the kidnapper happy until a rescue could be mounted. She ran a comb through her wet hair, dressed, and jogged downstairs barefoot. She felt each step pounding her sore hip to a pulp.

Galen Stavros stood up when she entered the room. His leathery skin bespoke long years in the sun, but his eyes retained a youthful alertness. A thick red scar trenched across his scalp and parted his white hair from just below the crown to his left ear.

"I was wounded in a student protest."

Dinah felt her cheeks grow hot.

"Don't be embarrassed. Everyone stares. It's why I wear a cap." His face was intensely earnest. He held out his hand to her. It was soft and smooth, not calloused or rough as a fisherman's or a laborer's would be. "I came to offer my help."

"How did you hear about Inspector Ramberg's misfortune?"

"One of the policemen who conducted the search ate lunch in the taverna today. He described the scene."

"Sergeant Papas?"

"I didn't hear the name."

K.D. swanned into the room carrying a vase filled with peonies and purple asphodel. "Thank you for the flowers, Mr. Stavros. They smell divine."

The crying must have plugged Dinah's sinuses. She couldn't smell anything but the pail of bleach Alcina had left beside the front door and a whiff of falsity emanating from the gentleman with the smooth hands. She said, "Please sit down, Mr. Stavros."

"Thank you." He settled in the corner of the sofa with his hat on his lap and swung one leg across the other.

K.D. set the flowers on the table under the painting of the Spanish knight and planted herself on the sofa next to him. "Mr. Stavros was telling me that peonies get their name from the Greek god of healing. How did you pronounce him, Mr. Stavros?"

"Paieon. He was a student of Asclepius. Homer called Paieon a deliverer from evil and calamity."

"The perfect flower to bring to a calamity," said Dinah. "K.D., I'd like to speak with the gentleman alone if you don't mind."

"Why, that wouldn't be polite, now would it, Mr. Stavros?"

Stavros had the grace not to respond.

Dinah skimmed K.D. a black look and sat down across the room. She didn't have the energy to strangle her and she had no inclination to be polite to Stavros. If he had something to say to her about Thor, it was on him to say it.

He said, "Marilita was a dear friend. I came often to this house."

Dinah couldn't put her finger on what it was about him that kindled her suspicion. He seemed almost too sincere. "You must have been staggered when she committed the murders."

"She was a kind woman."

"I take it you're one of the people who doesn't believe she did it."

"That's right."

"If Marilita didn't shoot those people, she must have told the police who did."

"I'm sure she did."

His hand stole to his scar. Dinah didn't know if the gesture implied that Marilita had been tortured or that he had. The peonies aside, he was remarkably uncommunicative for a man who'd come to offer his help. She said, "Did you see Inspector Ramberg last night or this morning?"

"No." His eyes roamed about the room as if analyzing and recording every chink in the wall. Either he was remembering the times he spent in the house with Marilita or casing the place. His eyes came back to Dinah. "Did the inspector indicate that he knew who was behind the vandalism?"

"No. Alcina thinks it was friends of the murdered Iraqi. Did you know him?"

K.D. interrupted. "Do you think the police will find new evidence that clears Marilita some day, Mr. Stavros?"

"It is possible. An investigative reporter in Athens is trying to rehabilitate her reputation." The corners of his mouth lifted ever so slightly, like the archaic smile on a Greek statue. "The mills of the gods are late to grind, but they grind small."

Dinah eyed him askance. Had he really known Marilita or was *he* the reporter foraging for grist for his newspaper?

"The mills of the gods," chimed K.D. "That's so poetic."

"A quote from the Greek philosopher, Sextus Empiricus." His eyelids twitched. In a younger face, the effect would have seemed flirtatious. "You have an ear for poetry, Katarina."

"I'm considering becoming a writer."

"Alcina wrote poetry when she was your age. It was of the fantastical sort. Her mother's execution traumatized her. I think she sought to lose herself in the supernatural."

That wasn't something a stranger would know. It would be an easy detail to make up except for the fact that it sounded so true. He could be both an old acquaintance *and* a reporter.

His eyes came to rest on the wall above Dinah's head. "I was with Marilita the day she bought that painting. It was shamelessly overpriced, but she had to have it. She said the knight reminded her of someone she couldn't be with. I thought she must have meant Alcina's father."

Dinah turned and looked. It was a face made melancholy by unusually prominent eyes that sagged into soft cheeks. There was an undeniable likeness to Alcina. A high-bridged, patrician nose and somewhat martial set of the jaw redeemed the knight from blandness, but he was no dreamboat. "Have you kept up a friendship with Alcina through the years?"

"Not as I should have. Even before her mother's death, she was shy and insecure. Afterward, she turned more inward. If it hadn't been for Yannis, she would have had no one to cling to. They married when she was very young."

"Have you spoken with her recently?"

"No. I've spoken only with Yannis."

"If you're serious about wanting to help, please explain to her that she and Yannis have no reason to blame Inspector Ramberg for their problems. If they know where he is or what's happened to him, they should tell me at once. And if Yannis had anything to do with his disappearance…"

"He has given me his word that he knows nothing about the Inspector. Yannis is a good man, salt of the earth."

"There is strong circumstantial evidence that he murdered a man."

"As you say, the evidence was circumstantial."

A fresh apprehension percolated into Dinah's thoughts. Stavros had been at the taverna on the evening of the murder and witnessed the altercation between Yannis and Fathi. He left shortly after Fathi passed by. "You were there that day. What did Yannis and the Iraqi argue about?"

"The Iraqi was selling. Yannis did not wish to buy."

"Worry beads?"

"Yes."

"Did Yannis steal them? Because the police didn't find them on Fathi's body."

Stavros' voice became impatient, as if she had shunted him into a conversation he'd rather not have. "Yannis would do nothing to bring more attention from the police. His pension has been reduced and, like many Greeks, the things he does to get by may not be strictly legal. People can hardly be blamed for improvising."

"Or for taking bribes?"

"I have known Yannis for many years. He is a man of principle. He opposed the junta and its repressive policies when he was young. He is a Christian and a liberal."

"If he shares Alcina's opinion of foreigners, he's no liberal now."

He spread his hands. "With the influx of foreigners and the economic war being waged against us by the Germans and the E.U., many Greeks feel they are losing more than their jobs and their pensions. They are losing their cultural identity. They are afraid for their future as they were when the junta came to power in the sixties. Then, it seemed that our civilization was being degraded by the American culture of *anything goes.*"

Dinah bristled. "And so to avoid the degradation of rock and roll, the Greek people resorted to a military dictatorship."

"My brother is into scum punk," said K.D. without looking up. She was hunched over her cell phone, her thumbs moving busily. "Anything would be better."

"No," said Stavros, acknowledging Dinah's sarcasm with a wintry smile. "The junta was brutal, but your President Nixon supported it and, for a while, it made Greece stable and prosperous. The danger today is that we will remember the prosperity and forget the brutality."

"Did you protest the junta?" asked Dinah.

"Yes. Yannis protested, too. I don't believe that he has forsaken his ideals. The Greek people invented democracy. We have no desire to relinquish our fate to a new mob of fascists, or to the German bankers, for that matter. But that is a separate crisis."

It struck Dinah as a kind of irony that the Greeks had also invented the word crisis, varieties of which abounded in this complicated country. She tried to bring the focus back to her own crisis. Thor didn't believe that Yannis was mixed up in the gun smuggling operation, but he suspected he knew something about the American guns. She said, "Yannis lied about what Fathi tried to sell him. It wasn't worry beads. It was an old gun. I think you know that."

Abruptly, he uncrossed his leg and leaned forward. "Is that what the Inspector told you?"

She self-censored. "I can draw my own inferences."

"What did he tell you about Fathi?"

"Nothing."

"What time did Inspector Ramberg leave the house this morning?"

"I don't know."

His eyebrows pinched together over his nose and his voice was freighted with gravity. "Have you spoken with anyone else besides Yannis and Alcina?"

"No."

"No one at all?"

"No."

"You may have said something about the Inspector or his plans without knowing that the person to whom you spoke would feel threatened by him."

She couldn't believe it. The guy was interrogating her. "No."

"She didn't have to talk to anyone," said K.D., looking up from her texting. "Everybody knows about all of us without our saying anything. Brother Constantine, Mr. Brakus, and you also spoke with a man whose dead wife was about to be exhumed, didn't you, Dinah?"

Stavros leaned forward. "Mentor Rodino?"

Dinah stood up. "I appreciate your concern, Mr. Stavros, but I have to be on my way. If Alcina has any additional information, please let me know and if you have any clout with the police or government officials, that would be helpful. The regional governor is a friend of Marilita's sister. I'm going to ask her to call in a favor and request that he send additional search teams and investigators from other places to expand the search."

Stavros' mouth hardened. "So Zenia still brags about friends in positions of power."

"Is she lying?"

"She has towering flaws, but she doesn't lie, except to herself." He stood and fitted his cap over the scar. "Zenia Stephanadis is not someone you should trust. If your friend has fallen into the wrong hands, I may be able to help."

The skin on the back of her neck prickled. *Wrong hands*? Did he know the kidnappers? Was there a ransom demand implicit in that if-maybe overture? "What sort of help?"

"Where the wolf has been there will be tracks."

Dinah scowled. Enigma was another word derived from the Greek language and the Greeks seemed determined to confound her with riddles.

He said, "I have connections. I can put out antennae."

Can, not will. Her throat felt dry. Was this the time to ask the price? It required no effort to sound dumb. "Are your connections in the police force or government administration?"

"Suffice it to say that they are well-placed." He shook her hand and then K.D.'s. "Will you be staying on here in the house?"

"Oh, yes," said K.D. "We'll be right here until Thor's found, won't we, Dinah?"

Stavros smiled. "Then I will be in touch. I'm staying at the Sunrise Hotel in Iréon and this is my cell phone number if you need to contact me for any reason." He handed her a card. "What is your number?"

K.D. reeled it off and he wrote it down.

"Thank you. You should not discuss the matter with anyone else until you have heard from me."

Dinah balked. If he was a kidnapper, he should cut the tease and lay out his terms, and if he was a Good Samaritan he had no business dictating terms of any kind. She said, "Unless I have a clear reason, I will discuss the matter with anyone I choose."

His lip kinked. "If you think Zenia will condescend to help you, by all means ask her."

She followed him to the door. "Why don't you like her? What has she done to you?"

His forehead crimped and he seemed to cast about for words. When he spoke, his voice was cold and his eyes bitterly sincere. "She has a stone tablet of shalls and shall nots where a heart should be."

Chapter Eighteen

Nobody had a good word to say about Zenia. Egan had praised Marilita's allure and Nasos' charm and Phaedon's heroism, but said nothing complimentary about Zenia even when she was sitting in the same room with him. Behind her back, he called her malicious. Brakus spread the rumor that she cast the evil eye and Mentor claimed that she poisoned cats, but Stavros' put-downs were the most poetic and the most damning. Toweringly flawed, a braggart, a snob who wouldn't condescend to lend a helping hand, a prig with a stone where a heart should be. His criticisms were tempered only by a backhanded retort that she didn't lie. In Dinah's book, not lying was a rare virtue. And if "thou shalt not kidnap" and "thou shalt not murder" were also graven on her stone heart, so much the better.

It wasn't yet five o'clock in the afternoon on what was turning out to be the longest, most grueling day of her life, but she had to keep moving or go mad. She grubbed through her purse with mounting agitation. Where had she put her car keys?

"Aren't you hungry?" K.D. waltzed into her bedroom without knocking. "I'm starving. Do you think the taverna has opened yet?"

Dinah swore under her breath. K.D. was an albatross. It was too dangerous to leave her behind in the house and too trying to take her along. If only she could be stashed in an airport locker like a piece of baggage and reclaimed when it was convenient.

"There's cheese and bread and fruit and yogurt here."

"Alcina and I ate most of the cheese and bread for lunch. We have to eat something. We don't want to show up on Zenia's doorstep and faint from hunger."

"Don't worry about it. You won't be going with me."

"But Alcina went to the farmhouse to spend the night with Yannis. You're not going to leave me here by myself, are you?"

Dinah pondered her options. She could drop her off at the taverna for the duration of the evening, ask Mentor if he would babysit, or duct tape her mouth closed and take her along. She said, "Let's see if we can scrounge up something here."

Downstairs, she opened the refrigerator and shifted various cartons around. She hadn't eaten all day, but she didn't think she could choke down a bite. Her throat felt tight and the ticking of the clock weighed on her. It would be dark in another three hours and the thought of Thor in the *wrong hands* roiled her stomach.

She could scramble some eggs and somewhere in the cupboard was a package of Greek doughnut holes drizzled with honey, which Thor had bought to satisfy her sweet tooth. Absent-mindedly, she buttered a sauté pan and started cracking eggs in a bowl.

K.D. found a chunk of cheese and grated it into the eggs, and sat down at the table with a bowl of grapes. "It's strange the house doesn't have a real dining room. Do you think Marilita cooked in here?"

Dinah looked up from her egg-beating. "Yes, I do. It's a lovely room and she had a lot of friends."

The kitchen was large and airy. The heavy oak dining table had an aged patina and the floor-to-ceiling windows looked out on the vineyard. She pictured Marilita sitting across from Nasos, flirting and laughing in that abandoned way of hers. Phaedon and Zenia would probably have been frequent guests along with Galen Stavros and Egan Vercuni and a succession of disreputable artists or actors Marilita invited to annoy Zenia. Aries Brakus may have come to cook his specialties for her, a culinary expression of his Platonic love and, at some point in time, the man whose face she saw in the painting of the Spanish knight must have dined here.

Dinah scrambled and plated the eggs and went hunting in the cupboard for the doughnut holes. She reached for the package and her hand froze. Propped in front was an envelope with her name on it. Her insides did a somersault. Thor had left her a message after all.

"What's wrong?" asked K.D.

"Nothing." She stuck the note inside her shirt and put the doughnut holes on the table. "Go ahead and eat. I'll be back in a few minutes." She started back to her room, but her knees buckled midway up the stairs. She sat down and tore open the envelope.

> *Dinah,*
>
> *I was wrong to mislead you. It was selfish to think I could have my pleasure and also do my duty. But my country has sent me to thwart a possible terrorist attack and that must come first. I'm sorry for what I said last night about your senators wanting me to die. It was a stupid thing to say. I don't know why I was chosen for this job except that I love my country and, if I lack craft and experience, perhaps my strength is that I know how to hang on one minute longer. For now, I must be like Rick in the movie Casablanca, walking away from love to do the right thing. If I disappoint you, forgive me and don't worry. I have an ally on Samos.*

She choked up. How like him to see the world in terms of a movie—"Casablanca," for crying out loud. She hated that movie. It made no sense to her that Rick couldn't simultaneously do the right thing and hang onto Ilsa, the woman he loved. Love and duty weren't mutually exclusive. And if Ilsa loved Rick, she shouldn't have let him hand her over to Viktor like a tarnished consolation prize. In real life, she would have made Viktor miserable, forever yearning for the love that got away.

Dinah's phone rang and she flinched. She pulled it out of her pocket and looked at the caller ID. Neesha. Of all the hairballs she couldn't handle at the moment, Neesha topped the list. She stalked back to the kitchen and tossed the phone to K.D. "It's your mother."

"Shit. Do I have to talk to her?"

"Yes."

K.D. rolled her eyes. Dinah rolled hers and wandered out to the veranda. The late afternoon sky was a fierce blue and the green leaves of the repotted plants shone like phosphorous. The colors of Greece exaggerated reality, heightened her sense of foreboding and her sense of guilt. If she'd been more understanding and willing to listen to Thor, if she'd been less self-centered and dismissive, she would know where he was going and who he planned to meet when he left the house this morning. She'd at least have an inkling of the kind of danger he was facing. She didn't know whether she loved him deeply or seriously. She might. But guilt had to be the worst possible reason to decide that she did, and deciding after he'd been snatched by kidnappers was hands down the worst possible time.

The good news was that Thor had an ally. That note was written after he knew he'd been betrayed, so there was someone on the island he could count on. If only she knew who that person was. If only she could go to him now and join forces. What would an ally be doing at this moment? Was he pursuing leads among the police or searching the gorge floor or...?

Her thoughts hit a snag. Did this ally even know that Thor had disappeared and that he may have been abducted? The air of Samos contained more gossip than nitrogen or oxygen. Surely he knew. But what if the bad guys had attacked him, too? What if he and Thor were roped together in some horrible dungeon? What if that bloody shoe belonged not to Thor, but to his ally?

She had to get a grip. Conjuring up dire possibilities didn't accomplish anything. She had had her catharsis, vowed to be brave and determined, and here she was backsliding into despair. She needed to proceed step by step. Tonight, she would enlist Zenia's help and the help of her friend, the governor. Tomorrow, she would follow up with the Norwegian Embassy and N.C.I.S. She would pay a visit to Papas' superiors and find out who Galen Stavros was and what his talk of well-placed connections was all about.

She raised her chin and sailed back into the kitchen. K.D. stood at the end of the table holding a meat fork in the air. A large black pistol hung by the trigger guard from one tine.

"Looky what I found in the cupboard."

"Mother of God! Put it down. Gently! Gently!"

"Don't have a cow." She set it on the table with a clunk. "I used the fork so I wouldn't mess up the fingerprints."

Dinah walked around for a closer look. Had Yannis lied about not taking Fathi's gun or was this a different one? She nudged it with the meat fork. Zigana. Not an American make. Forensics would be able to ascertain whether it was the gun that fired the bullet that killed Fathi. The question was, whether to trust Sergeant Papas and the Greek police and hand it over or trust no one and hide it until Thor and his ally could take charge. Or maybe she should stick it in her purse for her own protection.

She didn't know anything about Greek law, but they probably had something on the books equivalent to what U.S. lawyers referred to as "chain of custody." If the chain of possession was broken, the gun would be useless as evidence in court. The smart thing was to hide it here in the house. As events developed, she'd know better what to do. One thing seemed both smart and necessary. She said, "Get your things together, K.D. I'm taking you to Pythagório tonight. You'll be safe in a hotel and tomorrow morning, I'll pick you up and take you to the airport."

"I can't go home."

"Yes, you can. Go pack."

"My mother left Atlanta. That's what she called to tell me. She's taken my brother to a shrink in Switzerland. He went off his meds and dumped a bag of dead rats on our neighbor's lawn. It's total pandemonium. She said she'd text me when and where she wants me to meet her."

"Did you tell her what's going on here?"

"I told her Greece was the most glorious place in the world and we were having a fabulous time."

"And she believed you?"

"She wouldn't believe me if I'd told her the bad stuff. She doesn't want to know anything about me that will add to the heartache of motherhood." K.D. flipped her long auburn hair with a practiced show of indifference. "She said to thank you for being such an angel and could you wire her eight thousand dollars for Thad's new shrink?"

Dinah didn't know who she felt sorriest for—the disaffected daughter, the deranged son, the overmatched mother, or the dead rats. She picked up the gun with the meat fork. "Where did this come from?"

K.D. pointed. Dinah went to the opposite side of the cupboard and hid the gun behind a jug of olive oil and a sack of chickpea flour. She closed the door and tried to regenerate a little of the spunk and determination she'd walked in with.

Chapter Nineteen

Dinah parked the Picanto in front of Zenia's house and mar-
shaled her thoughts. Egan's car was gone and that cheered her
up. She hoped Zenia was at home. She had her emotions sewn
up tight, but a long wait might unravel them again.

She said, "I need you to stay quiet, K.D. This is about getting
Zenia to call in a favor to help find Thor. Nothing else. Don't say
anything about Galen Stavros or Yannis or Alcina or anything
at all. Is that clear?"

"I know when to keep my mouth shut."

"If you do, you've acquired the knowledge since running off
at the mouth to Galen Stavros."

"I didn't run off at the mouth. And anyway, he's elegant and
cultured and soulful. I trust him."

"Fine. If you want me to trust you, don't talk."

K.D. rolled her eyes. "Fine."

They got out of the car and Dinah charged up the curving
steps to the front door. There was no bell and no knocker. She
hammered on the door with her fist. The house was solid as a
fortress and Zenia was partially deaf. She cantilevered herself over
the handrail and clonked her fist against the window. "Zenia!
Zenia, are you in there?"

She tried to open the door, but it was locked. There was no
point walking around to the back. From what she'd seen on
her last visit, the only entrance was from the garage through an

underground passageway. She pummeled both fists against the door and shouted.

Zenia must be in Pythagório at one of her rehearsals. She turned away in frustration, but stopped halfway down the steps. What if the same people who vandalized Marilita's house had brought their campaign of terror to the woman who had introduced an outsider with the title of "Inspector" into their insular little world? What if Zenia were cowering in a closet, afraid to come to the door, or worse, what if she'd been hurt?

She went back to the door and gave it another hard wham. "Zenia! Please! Open the door!"

And it opened.

"Easy peasy," said K.D., rubbing her hands on her jeans. "There was an orange tree right under the kitchen and an open window over the sink."

Dinah blew out her cheeks. She so hadn't planned to add breaking and entering to her list of problems. "Is Zenia at home?"

"I haven't checked every room. Come on in. We may as well look around since we're here."

Corrupted again, thought Dinah, and walked into the living room. "Let's make sure she hasn't fallen and broken a hip or something." She walked down the hall, reconnoitering the bedrooms and calling Zenia's name. Satisfied that she wasn't in the house, Dinah returned to the living room.

K.D. was browsing the book shelves. She said, "I think we should search the house."

"I think we should go back to the car and wait for her to come home."

"You trust her?"

"What do you mean?"

"You don't trust anybody else. How can you be sure that Zenia had nothing to do with Thor's accident?"

"She's eighty-five," snapped Dinah, but the idea jarred. Zenia's reasons for putting the word out about Thor being a policeman puzzled her. She said, "I suppose we could just walk around the house. Don't touch anything."

"What should we look for?"

"I don't know. See if there are any books about the military junta or the weapons they had. They called it Regime of the Colonels."

"Most of these books are in Greek."

"Then you won't find anything useful."

Dinah went back down the hallway to the bedrooms. It was easy to spot the mistress' suite. It was papered over with theater posters and enlarged photographs of actors and actresses. Zenia seemed to specialize in the classical Greek tragedies. She had played Jocasta in "Oedipus Rex" at the famous Odeon of Herodes Atticus amphitheater in Athens. She had played Antigone and Electra. And she was Clytemnestra in "The Agamemnon." The largest and most lurid poster featured a much younger Zenia as Medea. She wore an expression of ghastly righteousness and held over her head a dagger dripping with blood. Dinah had read the story of Medea and seen the play while she was in college. Medea had fallen in love with Jason and helped him in his quest for the Golden Fleece. When he threw her over for another woman, she poisoned her rival and followed that up by murdering her own children, the sons she had borne to Jason. Zenia must have been a powerful actress in her heyday to portray such a difficult character.

Dinah felt like a peeper, which of course she was. She had come to ask for Zenia's help and here she was prowling around her boudoir like a cat burglar. Zenia had said rehearsals began at four. It was six o'clock now. She probably wouldn't be home for another half hour at least, but Dinah didn't want to be caught inside the house and there was no telling when Egan might walk in the door.

"The only title I've found in English is *Timeless Tales of the Greek Gods*," called K.D.

"Look in the console behind the sofa."

Dinah was on the way out when her eyes lit on the bedside table and a book in English, a copy of Agatha Christie's *Death on the Nile*. She smiled. So Zenia's taste wasn't limited to high tragedy. Absent-mindedly, she picked up the book and riffled the pages. An envelope had been placed in the center. It was unstamped and addressed to Zenia Stephanadis. The sender was Nasos Lykos.

She caught her breath. Egan's words reverberated. *They never found Nasos' body.* She bit her lip. The envelope looked new. Nasos was probably a common name, but Nasos Lykos? It had to be Marilita's boyfriend or a namesake—a son or grandson. She could feel the edges of a letter inside the envelope. Curiosity trumped scruples. She slipped it out, unfolded it, and looked at the slanting scrawl—all in Greek. Indecipherable. She put the letter back in the envelope and, impulsively, crammed it in her pocket. Her corruption was compounding faster than the interest on her Visa bill.

"What's this?" Zenia's voice sounded high pitched as an incoming missile. "Come away from there. I will shoot you."

"No!" Dinah ran into the living room. Zenia stood in the door that led from her garage. She wore a silver-beaded skull cap and a flapper-era dress and she was aiming a shiny black pistol at K.D.'s head. "Zenia, please put down the gun. This is my fault."

"What are you doing here?"

"We knocked and when you didn't answer, we thought you might have fallen and couldn't get up."

"Liar. How did you get in?"

"I climbed up your orange tree," said K.D.

"What?"

"I climbed your orange tree and crawled in through the kitchen window. We're here to ask for your help finding Dinah's boyfriend, Thor."

"Pah!" Zenia's lips compressed to a pinkish-purple gash. "What's that in your hand?"

Dinah slued a glance at K.D. She was holding what looked to be an old scrapbook.

"I don't know," said K.D. "A book. I haven't opened it."

"Please, Zenia," pleaded Dinah. "Put down the gun." She wouldn't have bet one way or the other on the marksmanship of an octogenarian who was apparently too vain to wear eyeglasses, but she noted that the hand holding the gun was rock steady. "Aim that thing somewhere else. You know that we mean you no harm."

She transferred her aim from K.D. to Dinah. "Snooping through my personal belongings, that's harm."

"It's a misunderstanding," said K.D. "Alcina told me about the orange tree. She said you sometimes didn't hear her knock and we could come in the back way."

K.D. might be a liar, but she was a damned good one. Dinah regained a semblance of composure. "*Is* there someone you're afraid of, Zenia? Is that why you have that gun?"

"Any woman who lives alone should have a gun."

"But you're not alone," said Dinah. "You have Egan."

"The only thing Egan knows how to shoot is a movie." She lowered the pistol, nestled it into her drawstring bag, and laid the bag on the console. "Put that book back where you found it. I'm going to brew a pot of tea. Come along and tell me what it is that you want."

Dinah and K.D. followed her into the kitchen. It was a grimy little galley with the smell of many suppers embedded in the walls. The window through which K.D. had climbed opened above a sink piled high with dirty dishes. Dinah looked away from a sauté pan containing some congealed, meat-resembling substance and said, "I'd like you to telephone your friend, the regional governor, and request reinforcements to search for Thor."

Zenia filled a kettle and set it on an electric burner on the counter next to the stove. "The police have already searched the gorge, doing a great deal of damage to my trees and property in the process. Where else would you have them search?"

"I don't know." Out of the blue, she remembered that Thor had been at some beach yesterday afternoon, Megalo something. "The police should go everywhere that he's been and talk to everyone who saw him. I'm afraid he's been kidnapped."

"Pah. Who'd kidnap a policeman? Will you eat biscuits?"

"Yes ma'am, thank you." K.D. regarded Zenia with a respectful, almost reverent gaze. Having a gun pointed at her head seemed to have had a chastening effect.

Zenia opened a package of sesame-topped cookies. "*Koulourakia*," she said. "They're my favorite."

Dinah watched her empty the cookies onto a plate. What was going on in the brain behind that topaz pendant? "I need your help, Zenia. I don't trust the local police. You said yourself that they take bribes. I want outside police brought in."

Zenia spooned loose-leaf tea from a tin canister into a sterling tea ball and plopped the ball into a Victorian silver teapot. "Do you think it wise to place such confidence in your young man? You aren't married. He has no obligation. Perhaps he doesn't wish for you to find him."

Dinah saw what Galen Stavros meant about Zenia's shalls and shall nots. "I understand that you're a stickler for the proprieties, Zenia, but this is a matter of life and death. Thor and I aren't married, but we care about each other. He wouldn't disappear without telling me."

"Sentimental rubbish." The old woman's eyes showed not one mote of compassion.

Dinah trotted out the only thing she had to barter. "If you call the governor for me, I will help you make your docudrama. I will be your Marilita."

"You're too late. Egan has made another woman an offer."

Anger mingled with frustration and Dinah lashed out. "If you haven't the humanity to help save a man's life, it's your prerogative. As a matter of fact, I've had another offer. A man who also has important connections."

"I won't have another mob trespassing on my property."

Dinah was seething. "No one gives a rip about your trespassing signs. If Thor is in that gorge or anywhere else on your property, we will find him and the men who kidnapped him. Where the wolf has been, there will be tracks."

Zenia paled beneath her rouge. The kettle shrilled and the plate in her hand wobbled and tipped. Cookies hit the floor and skittered in all directions.

Dinah took the plate and lifted the kettle off the burner. "You'd better sit down and tell me what or who it is that you're afraid of, Zenia. And if you know anything about Thor's disappearance, you'd better not leave that part out."

Chapter Twenty

Zenia reclined on her sofa under a heavy quilt, her head supported by a plump bolster. Dinah had removed her beaded skull cap and poured her a double shot of twelve-year-old Metaxa, which K.D. had found concealed behind *Timeless Tales*. Zenia sipped the liquor and glowered at Dinah, who glowered back.

"I'm not afraid of anyone," said Zenia. "If anyone threatens me, I'll shoot him." She had her crust back and parried Dinah's questions in a waspish temper.

"Has someone threatened you? Is that why you keep a gun in your purse? Is that why you leased Marilita's house to a policeman and told everybody to be on guard?"

"If you're looking for a gossip, go and badger that talebearer at the taverna. He tells everyone who complains about his stomach flu or his lost goat that I've hexed them."

"I don't mean to badger you, Zenia. I came to ask for your help. I need you to telephone your friend the governor to ask for additional police, people who don't have friends or relatives in Kanaris and aren't susceptible to bribery."

"This morning you said you were leaving for Athens. Your man has been unaccounted for less than twenty-four hours. I see no reason to bother the governor."

Dinah felt her objections to waterboarding ebb. She thought about the letter written by a ghost, the rich and clever boyfriend whose bones were never found and she had an idea. "K.D., the least we can do to make amends is to wash the dishes for Zenia. Come on."

K.D. gave her an are-you-nuts look, but put down the book she was leafing through and followed. Dinah turned on the kitchen tap full-blast and took the letter out of her shirt. "I took this out of a book on Zenia's bedside table. Here's what I want you to do."

Dinah washed most of the dishes and set them on the drain board. She left K.D. to do the drying and returned to the living room.

Zenia raised her head off the bolster. Her face was gray, like crinkled wax paper. "Egan leaves things a mess."

Dinah took the glass of Metaxa off the table and handed it her. "Here. You'd better drink some more."

Zenia held the glass in both hands and regarded Dinah over the rim. "I have no need of your housekeeping services. You are free to leave."

"In a few minutes. I was thinking about Nasos Lykos. Did he have children?"

"If he did, they would be bastards."

"Egan said they never recovered his body. Is it possible he's still alive?"

"There was a double funeral for him and his mother in Athens. Dignitaries and courtesans from all over Europe came." The contempt in her pronunciation of *courtesan* was palpable. "He is quite dead."

Dinah rested one hip on the arm of the sofa and snugged the quilt around Zenia's feet. "You didn't find Nasos as charming as Egan did."

"He was a frivolous man. Spoiled by his family's money. His debauchery would have humiliated any other woman. Marilita laughed it off. She was no better than a courtesan, herself."

"Did you know Rena Lykos, his mother?"

"She had a dignified carriage and wore couture dresses. After her death, I read in the newspaper that one of her legs had been nearly torn off by a badly thrown grenade which she had purchased for the guerillas fighting the junta. Her allegiance was misplaced, but she had mettle."

K.D. walked out of the kitchen carrying a glass of iced tea. She set the glass on a napkin on the coffee table. "May I use your bathroom, Zenia?"

"Is it the custom in your country to break into a person's house, snoop through their private possessions, but ask permission to use the *loutro*?"

"Second door on the right," said Dinah. When K.D. left the room, she turned back to Zenia. "Nasos sounds like the sort of man Americans would call a wolf. Were you thinking of Nasos when I mentioned the word wolf? Is that what upset you?"

"The only thing that upset me is finding you snooping about. I felt dizzy for a moment. My high blood pressure."

So she did lie. Stavros got that wrong. She had been frightened white. Was it possible that it was Nasos' ghost, and not Marilita's, that haunted Kanaris? Dinah walked across the room and studied the photographs. Presumed dead and washed out to sea left plenty of latitude for doubt. Who other than Nasos would write Zenia a letter using his name?

Zenia said, "What are you gawking at?"

She went back to the sofa. "Do you know a man named Galen Stavros?"

"No."

"He appears somewhere in his seventies. He lives in Athens, but he gave the impression that he had lived on Samos at one time."

"Is he the man who offered to help you find Ramberg?"

"Yes."

"What did he say?"

"That he was a friend of Marilita's. He doesn't think she murdered your husband or anyone else."

"If he believed she was innocent, he should have spoken up before it was too late."

Dinah conceded the point. Why hadn't he come forward? Fear of the junta, she supposed. A wild notion swam into her head. What if Stavros *was* Nasos? He was old enough, and seemingly familiar with all of the players. He could be lying about where he got that scar on his head. It could be an ugly souvenir of that last picnic with Marilita. If he were the real murderer, that would have been a very solid reason not to come forward.

Zenia said, "This Stavros person must be one of those creatures who chases the *foreio*."

"What is that?" Dinah asked.

"The ambulance. He heard about the accident and tracked you down, hoping to see his name in the newspaper. Maybe he's a newspaper reporter."

"That's possible, but he sounds like a family insider. He speaks as if he also knows you personally."

Her black eyes gleamed with Medea-like ferocity. She threw off the quilt and sat up. "I don't know who this Stavros is, but if he claims to be Nasos Lykos, he is an imposter. Nasos is dead."

"Is that what you think, Zenia? That someone is pretending to be Nasos?"

"No." She drank more of the Metaxa, handed the glass to Dinah, and lay her head back on the bolster. "Whoever he is, he is of no interest to me."

It was plain from the fear on her face that he was of enormous interest, but Dinah didn't have the time or the patience to draw out truths she didn't want to divulge. "Let's start over, Zenia. If Thor is alive, he's in big trouble and it's important, urgent, that we find him fast. Trust me, your friend the governor will want to throw all of his resources into a case that involves arms smuggling."

"Arms smuggling?"

Dinah thought she discerned a flash of suspicion in her eyes. "That's right. Guns that the American CIA supplied to the junta are being smuggled north from Samos. Did Phaedon ever talk to you about a lost or missing shipment?"

"Phaedon would never breach his duty by revealing military secrets."

Dinah pulled out her phone. "Give me the governor's number. I'll go through the hoops with his secretary or assistants and when he comes on, you can speak with him directly."

"Governor Rigas is on Malta. I will call him when he returns."

There seemed nothing left to say or do. Defeated, Dinah picked up K.D.'s tea and took a sip. She choked and began to wheeze and cough. It was eighty proof.

The toilet flushed. She was just recovering her breath when K.D. sashayed back into the room. She saw Dinah holding her "iced tea," rolled her eyes, and crossed the room to turn on a lamp.

Dark had fallen and Dinah dreaded the helpless, unavailing hours until morning. She could phone Stavros to see if any of his connections had come through with information. She could phone Papas and pester him to follow up on all the places where Thor had been the previous day. Or she could go home and ransack the house to see if Thor had left any clue to the name of his ally on Samos. She said, "We're going now, Zenia. I would appreciate anything you can do or suggest to help." She scribbled her phone number on a piece of paper and set it on the table. "And if you need help, or if you want to talk about anything at all, call me. Day or night."

The front door banged open. Everyone started, but it was only Egan.

"What an enchanting scene, Zenia, dear. I see that all is forgiven."

"I had a bout of dizziness. Dinah and her young friend have been playing nurse."

"Shall I call for the doctor? You didn't forget to take your pills, did you?" Egan adopted a custodial tone.

"No. I feel quite well." She sat up ramrod straight. Damp tendrils of hair stood out on her head like pilled wool and she primped and tried to smooth them down. "Hand me my drink."

Dinah handed her the glass and wondered if she had more than a friendly interest in Egan.

"I'm Katarina Dobbs from Atlanta, Georgia," said K.D. "Dinah's niece." She held out her hand to Egan as if she expected him to kiss it.

"I'm Egan Vercuni." He appeared vaguely taken aback and shook her hand somewhat brusquely. "What is that you're drinking, Zenia?"

"Metaxa. These girls are on their way out. You must come and have a drink with me. I've had a new idea for the film."

"Which of the muses has whispered in your ear?"

"Mnemosyne," said Zenia. "The goddess of memory. I've remembered something interesting about Marilita."

"And what is that?" he asked.

"She had an absurd love of gypsy music. Decadent, as you'd expect, but we may weave in a few tunes to the musical score."

"Brilliant." He took a sip of Metaxa from her glass, moved the quilt aside, and sat down beside her.

Dinah picked up the note with her phone number and placed it in Zenia's hand. "Take care of yourself, Zenia. Watch out for wolves in sheep's clothing."

Egan shot her a look. "Is there some innuendo in that warning?"

"Not really. The wolf seems to be a popular figure of speech in Greece." She pushed K.D. ahead of her and started for the door. Hand on the knob, she turned back. "Egan, do you know the name Galen Stavros?"

"Doesn't ring a bell. Is he in the theater or the film industry?"

"Not to my knowledge."

"Then I've probably never met the fellow."

Dinah lofted a last look over her shoulder at Zenia. For all of her meanness and perversity, she looked small and frail and defenseless.

Chapter Twenty-one

As the Picanto spiraled down the mountain toward the coast road, Dinah searched for the moon, but Artemis was a truant. A haze dimmed the stars and the lineless road was black as widow's weeds. Her eyes felt sandy and irritated from too many unprotected hours in the sun and the dark of night brought no relief. "Did you copy it down exactly?" she asked K.D.

"I think so. The handwriting would have been hard to make out even if it weren't in Greek, but I have mad skills. I copied the Desiderata in Arabic script in my calligraphy class."

"And you put the original letter back in the book?"

"Page ninety-six, just like you said."

Dinah didn't like to admit that she was finding K.D.'s mad skills useful. "You were in the bathroom an awfully long time."

"What? You think I do Robitussin or something? That sucks."

"That drink you concocted from Zenia's liquor cabinet is what sucks. It tasted a lot worse than cough syrup and your sneakiness about the alcohol doesn't inspire confidence."

"Well, you can relax about the pharma-fun in Zenia's medicine chest. All that's there is a bottle of mouthwash and a bottle of pills. Probably for her blood pressure."

"So you *did* look."

"I checked it out, okay? I checked out the bedrooms, too. But the really interesting thing I found was in the console in the living room."

"What?"

"Oh, it's probably nothing."

Dinah took her eyes off the road. K.D. was admiring her fingernails, smug as a cat.

"Don't act so pleased with yourself. What did you find?"

"I lied when I told Zenia I hadn't opened that scrapbook. I paged through it before she walked in on me with the gun."

"Did you see any other letters or anything from Nasos Lykos?"

"No. There were a few scraps of writing, but they were all in Greek."

"Did you copy down any of those?"

"I didn't have a chance."

"Were there photographs?"

"Tons. Most were glam shots of old movie stars that had been cut out of fan magazines. Well, I guess they weren't so old when the pictures were taken. There were a couple of Paul Newman and Marlon Brando when they were young and hot, and there were quite a few of Marilita. She looked bangable."

"Slutty, you mean?"

"That, but she was kind of like, I don't know. Like the pouty lips and the cleavage was an inside joke or something. Like she was looking past the camera and the droolers to somebody she really cared about. Maybe the lover who looked like the Spanish knight." K.D. might have an overly romantic sensibility, but even when she seemed not to be paying attention, she didn't miss much.

Dinah couldn't see Zenia poring over movie mags, much less scissoring out glam shots. "It seems way out of character for Zenia to have those kinds of magazines and mind-boggling that she would paste pictures of the sexpot sister she hates in a scrapbook."

"I don't think it's Zenia's scrapbook," said K.D. "It seemed more like the pictures a kid would collect. There are photos of a girl, twelve or thirteen, playing with a camera like she's some kind of paparazzi."

"Alcina?"

"For sure, but she must have been way immature for her age. The heads and arms and legs had been cut off of some pictures and their outfits glued next to pictures of Marilita and Marilyn Monroe. Like paper dolls. I saw something else that was *pret-ty* amazing." K.D. twisted the rearview mirror around, turned on the overhead light, and tweaked her eyelashes.

"Can the suspense. Just tell me."

She twisted the mirror back into place. "In one of the photos, Alcina is pointing the camera at Marilita. In another, she's zeroing in on a woman with bird eyes and penciled eyebrows, Zenia for sure, and the dude in the bathing suit whose picture is by the front door. I'm thinking she took the picture of Marilita and her boyfriend on the beach the day of the murders."

"Dear God. If Alcina was an eyewitness, no wonder she's traumatized." Dinah's first impulse was to race back to the house and question her, but asking her to relive that day in memory could unhinge a woman who teetered permanently on the brink of hysteria. "Could you tell where they were taken? Indoors or out?"

"Out. There were trees and water in the background."

They reached the coast road and Dinah turned back toward Kanaris. The Aegean was black and foreboding tonight, or maybe her mood made everything appear that way. Across the strait, the lights of Kusadasi twinkled like fragments of crystal. She wished she had a crystal ball. Did the key to finding Thor lie in the past, or was she chasing figments? "Damn it, I wish Alcina weren't so emotionally combustible and I could ask her without sending her into conniptions."

"She'll talk to me," said K.D. "The two of us sort of bonded this morning over our off-the-chain parents."

"What did she say?"

"She was like, 'my mother was executed by a firing squad,' and I'm like, 'my father blew his brains out before they could take him to trial.' And she goes, 'my mother didn't do what they said she did.' And I'm like, 'how do you know that?'"

"And?"

"She said it was bandits."

"Bandits." Dinah let it simmer for a minute. "Bandits killed the other people?"

"That's what she said. They wore black ski masks and carried rifles."

"Why didn't you tell me this earlier? Before I talked with Stavros and Zenia?"

"I don't know. I guess I didn't believe her. I mean, she had a hissy fit when she saw one of my sandals lying sole-up on the floor. She went all over the room spitting and said I should touch this bat bone she carries around for good luck. Serious ick. I was like, no way and she got all fussed. She can sound pretty batty when she gets cranked up."

Dinah was on board with that assessment, although bandits made far more sense than an actress in a bikini running amok with the Colonel's gun. But what could bandits hope to steal from a party of picnickers? Their cooler of beer? Nasos was rich, but he wouldn't have much cash on him at the beach. Ditto, the ladies. That left the Colonel. What if he had access to, or knowledge about, the junta's weapons? The bandits' object could have been to force him to reveal their location and after he did, they killed him and Mrs. Lykos and, probably, Nasos. But why didn't they kill Marilita and Alcina? And why, if they had scored a load of valuable weapons, hadn't they sold them before now?

K.D. said, "With an evil old skank like Zenia in the family tree, it's not surprising that Alcina's freaky. Those posters in Zenia's bedroom grossed me out. The dagger dripping blood wasn't too griz, but the severed head? Ugh! How can she sleep at night?"

Dinah had missed the severed head. It must have been the head of Medusa or else Pentheus, the king of Thebes. She had read the story of Pentheus just recently. Dionysus sent him to spy on a ladies-only drinking party, but the ladies spotted him ogling them from behind a tree and his own mother lopped off his head, not realizing until she sobered up that she'd killed her son. It was the same with Oedipus. He didn't realize he had killed his father and married his mother. As in so many Greek tragedies, the characters' crimes derived not from any willful disobedience to the gods, but from a simple misunderstanding of the facts. What was it that *she* misunderstood?

K.D. steepled her fingers under her chin. "How's this for a plot? Alcina doesn't want her mother to marry Nasos because he's taking up all of her time and attention. So she's playing with her camera and shooting pictures, but then she puts down the camera and asks the Colonel to let her see what it's like to look through a gun sight. Maybe he's one of those men who likes to show off his expertise. Daddy was like that, if you remember. So anyway, the Colonel gives her the gun. Alcina turns it on him and shoots everyone but her mother and when the police come, Marilita does the noble thing and says *she* did it. Alcina didn't count on her being executed and ever since, she's been racked by guilt and collecting bat bones and evil eye charms and religious stuff she thinks will keep her from going to hell."

"A child would have had trouble holding a gun steady," said Dinah, "let alone hitting anyone. Almost any adult could have knocked it out of her hands before she did any harm. And what reason would she have had to kill Nasos' mother or the Colonel?"

"You never know. Maybe her father was a born killer like mine. Maybe she's got badness in her blood."

Dinah felt a tug of sympathy. Over the years, she had come to terms with her own father's bad acts. She'd like to help K.D. do the same, but there was no way to distill twenty years of attitudinal evolution into a pithy maxim. She said, "It's all right to love someone who's done bad things, K.D. I loved my father. You loved yours. That doesn't mean we replicate their moral failings. Our conscience is our own."

"Jeez, you don't have to preach."

I'll get back to her, thought Dinah. She said, "I don't think Alcina murdered anyone, although if she was there when it happened, she knows who did."

"Maybe we could find somebody to hypnotize her," suggested K.D.

"Not practical."

"I'll bet Mr. Stavros could persuade her to talk if you trusted him."

"But I don't."

"Then who will you get to translate the letter?"

"I don't know."

"We could bring up a Greek dictionary on the Net and do it ourselves."

"There could be hidden meanings. Nuances a dictionary might not give."

"You don't even trust the dictionary?"

"You've made your point, K.D. But all of the Greeks I've met have been metaphorical to a fault. I wouldn't want to miss some esoteric idiom a dictionary wouldn't show." She considered driving into Karlovassi and showing the letter to a young person, someone who'd never heard of Nasos Lykos or the Stephanadis sisters. But she had to trust somebody sometime. Maybe it was time she rolled the dice. She decided to park K.D. at the house and spend the rest of the evening at the Marc Antony listening to gypsy music. Until the morning, she was in limbo. All she could do was hitch her hopes to Thor's self-assayed strength. *I know how to hang on one minute longer.*

Chapter Twenty-two

The courtyard tables at the taverna were filling up early tonight. The little votive candles glimmered pleasantly and a hum of conviviality belied the very idea of trouble. Dinah looked around for Mentor, but she didn't see him or recognize any of the other patrons. They seemed to recognize her. An awkward hush fell as she walked past the grape arbor. She supposed they'd heard about Thor and congregated at the local watering hole to gossip about it.

Brakus' wife hurried out the door carrying a tray loaded with mezés and Brakus filed out behind her with a carafe in each hand. He saw Dinah and his brow furrowed. He delivered the carafes to nearby tables, said something to the occupants in Greek, and stepped up to greet her. "I am sorry to learn about Inspector Ramberg. It is unbelievable."

She nodded, glancing around at the audience of attentive listeners.

He dropped his voice. "Have you come for dinner?"

"If you have a table."

"Yes, yes. Come." He led her to a table inside. She took the chair facing the courtyard and he unrolled her napkin and dropped it onto her lap. "The police say that he has disappeared. Have you heard from him?"

"No."

"It is the *kako mati*. Murder, vandalism, and my dumpster upended. That is where the *bandalos* got their ammunition. I showed the police. One bag of garbage taken away and another spilled on the ground. But the police said they threw eggs. An expensive waste." He paused, as if he sensed there might have been a gaffe in there somewhere, but he couldn't quite pin it down. He shook his head and kept going. "What did Zenia Stephanadis have to say for herself?"

Again she had the feeling that her every move was being watched and reported and the Kanaris grapevine seemed to sprout directly from Brakus' mouth. "She was extremely helpful. She telephoned her friend Governor Rigas even though he's on vacation in Malta and he promised to send additional police from other areas in the region. They should begin arriving tomorrow."

"Is that so?" His eyes widened, whether because he was titillated by the gossip or alarmed by the prospect of more policemen. "You must have wine. Tonight the wine is free for you and everything on the chalkboard is fresh. I will be back to take your order."

"Thank you. Perhaps when you aren't so busy, you could stop by the table and we could share a glass of wine and talk."

"*Nè, nè, nè.* Yes, I will do that." He skipped a look over her head and bustled off toward the terrace.

She looked at her watch. Nine-thirty. Mentor probably wouldn't arrive for another half hour. She kept a close watch on the courtyard. His daughter and goatskin-playing son-in-law could be one of the couples taking their seats at a long table under the grape arbor. She hoped to catch Mentor before he brought out his violin and the entertainment began.

The white-socked black cat scampered from the courtyard into the dining room inches ahead of a little girl, maybe three-years-old, with unruly blond curls and a tenacious countenance. Behind her came the mother, smiling indulgently. The cat slunk behind a table leg as the mother tried to outflank it and shoo it toward the girl, but it moved farther under the table. Undeterred, the girl crawled under the table after her prey. The large Greek family through whose legs she grabbed and poked at the cat, laughed indulgently. After a while, the grandfatherly gentleman at the head of the table swept up the cat in one hand and presented it to the girl, who clutched her prize to her chest and beamed. There were no thanks or apologies and clearly none were expected. Mother and child returned to the courtyard with the cat and Dinah wondered if all Greeks spoiled their children so lovingly.

Mrs. Brakus, even more harried than she'd been the last time Dinah saw her, appeared at her elbow with a notepad and a carafe of red wine.

"*Dorean,*" she said. "No charge." She had dark circles under her eyes and puppet lines around her mouth and chin. With her husband gadding from table to table swapping gossip, she probably had to do more of the work of running this place.

Dinah thanked her and ordered the homemade noodles with myzithra cheese. As Mrs. Brakus hastened back to the kitchen, her husband returned.

"It is Katogi Averoff," he said, tapping the carafe his wife had brought. "Our best bottle. I took the liberty of decanting it." He poured her a glass.

"Please pour a glass for yourself and sit down, Mr. Brakus."

"Thank you. I know this is a tender time for you. Did the Inspector tell you where he was going this morning?"

"He went looking for stolen weapons."

His eyes bugged as if they might jump out of their sockets. "On Samos?"

"You make guns on Samos sound stranger than guns on the moon. Why?"

"We are a quiet island, far from the riots and upheaval in Athens. We are like the moon. It is bizarre. First the Iraqi and now a policeman has been murdered."

The instantaneous assumption of murder stunned her. She found herself rubbing the evil eye fetish Mentor had given her. "I believe he has been kidnapped. Do you have any idea who might have wanted to get him out of the way? Someone with an illegal sideline who didn't want a foreign policeman nosing around the neighborhood?"

"Illegal sideline?"

"I've been told that the bad economy has forced some people into shady dealings."

"Not Samians. If weapons are stolen, it is al Quaida or the Taliban who steal them. They are here from Iraq and Afghanistan, Syria and Pakistan. Some come to escape their wars, but many are parasites and terrorists. They should be deported. All of them."

She tasted the Katogi and pondered. Was he flogging the case against foreigners too hard? He hadn't appeared as if he wanted to deport the Iraqi he was consorting with in Pythagório. "When you identified Fathi's body, you said it's *the* Iraqi. Are you sure you didn't know him?"

"No."

"Do you know any other Iraqis?"

"No."

She watched his face as he tried to read her mind. "Would any policeman that you know have a reason to harm the Inspector?"

"A policeman?"

"Yes. I've heard rumors that some can be bought off."

"*Nè, nè, nè.* It is Zenia Stephanadis who has given you this idea. Whenever you hear a slander, it comes from her mouth. She hates us peasants. Did you know that she poisons the village cats?"

Loud exclamations and laughter erupted from the kitchen and Mrs. Brakus emerged with a transforming smile on her face, followed by a laughing young woman in an apron and, behind her, a grinning Mentor. He was obviously privileged to enter the kitchen through the back door. Other diners shouted greetings and he waved his violin case in the air and said something to the crowd in Greek.

"*Kalispéra*, Mentor." Savas got up and shook his hand. "You bring a smile to Irene's face when no one else can, and your music brings in the customers."

"If I make you rich, Savas, you must share the gravy."

"No one gets rich in Greece, but I will put extra *saltsa* on your meat. Irene has made a pork roast tonight."

"*Exochos!*" Mentor laughed and kissed Irene Brakus on both cheeks.

Brakus demeanor stiffened noticeably. "Will you drink wine, Mentor?"

"*Nè, málista.*" He saw Dinah and waved, but his smile faded. "I will sit with Dinah Pelerin for a few minutes."

"I'll bring another glass," said Brakus. He gave Irene a sidelong glare and went into the kitchen.

Mentor set his violin case in an empty chair and sat down across from Dinah. "I am sorry about your friend. Is there any news?"

"If there were, everyone on the island would know it."

"It is hard to keep secrets of any kind in Kanaris."

"Of any kind? I was hoping I could trust you, Mentor. Don't start out by telling me a lie."

"All right. Kanaris does keep some secrets. Most of them stem from pride, people covering their embarrassment at having to skimp and barter to get by."

"Is there anyone who would kill to keep his secret?"

"I know no one so vicious as that."

Brakus returned with a glass for Mentor. "What will you eat, Mentor?"

"I must have some of Irene's roast, but later. In the kitchen, after I have finished my concert."

"Later, then."

When he was out of sight, Dinah pulled the copy of Nasos' letter out of her purse and handed it to Mentor. "Would you translate this for me?"

He knitted his brow, held the letter close to the candle, and read.

The wolf is old and his fur white, but his memory is long. I thought it purgatory enough that you should live for so many years with the stain of your sin. But you have no remorse. You have only hubris and now you have awakened the wolf. He is at the door. It is time for you to pay.

He said, "This is a threat against an old person by an old person."

"It seems so."

"Who wrote it? To whom?"

It had occurred to her that Galen Stavros might be Nasos. But now, looking at Mentor, she vacillated. He had been away from Samos for many years. Come to think of it, so had Egan. Zenia hadn't seen him in forty years. A man's face could change a lot in forty years.

"If you will not tell me who wrote this, will you tell me where you found it?"

She fixed her eyes on his. "Someone named Nasos Lykos sent it to Zenia Stephanadis."

"But Nasos Lykos died many years ago. Marilita killed him."

"Do you believe that?"

"It is the received wisdom, even though it seemed a lunatic idea at the time. Someone killed him. He has been dead for forty years."

She studied his eyes. "Why do people in Kanaris make so many allusions to the wolf?"

"The wolf is a common motif in many Greek sayings. One of the cult names of Apollo was Lukeios, from the word *lykos*. It means wolf."

The young woman who'd followed Mrs. Brakus out of the kitchen brought Dinah's noodles to the table and untied her apron. "*Mpampas*, let us begin. The food is all prepared and I want to dance."

"Dinah, allow me to introduce my daughter, Jacey."

Jacey smiled. She was a lithe, attractive woman with the same parenthetical laugh lines from mouth to eyes as her father. "I am happy to meet you."

Mentor said, "Jacey has a degree from the music conservatory, but there is no work and no students can afford to take lessons. She and her husband are looking at the possibility of emigrating to Australia, but for now she is helping Irene at the taverna. We are hoping her husband can find work on Samos. I don't know if I could live without my family."

"We will all be fine, *mpampas*. And tonight we will dance." Jacey nudged his arm affectionately. "Dance with me, Dinah. Come, I will show you how."

"Not tonight, thanks. I'd rather watch you."

Mentor opened his violin case and stood. "We must talk more, Dinah. Come to my house tomorrow morning."

Father and daughter went out to the courtyard and the music began. Dinah put the letter back in her purse and picked at her noodles. As the music built, she asked herself whether she was conflating the uncertain fate of Nasos with Thor's disappearance and whether her desire to keep Nasos among the living had more to do with the hope of finding Thor alive than it did with real possibility.

"I should tell you something," said Brakus, stopping by the table again. "I do not like to speak ill of my neighbors, but what you asked has made me think. Mentor Rodino has what you said..."

"*Opa! Opa!*" The music ended and the crowd applauded and shouted.

"He has an illegal sideline," said Brakus.

"What?"

"Stolen antiquities. He hides them in his *kalivis*."

"But I looked inside his *kalivi*. There were no antiquities, only a cooler and a jug of wine."

"No one knows how a teacher can be rich with his pension cut to the bone, but he is. He supports his daughter and her husband. All he does is make wine and play music and yet he has bought three *kalivis* in the last five years. Trust me, he would not want the police to look inside."

Chapter Twenty-three

A police car pulled up in front of the Marc Antony, lights flashing. The music stopped in mid-tune. Dinah watched as Sergeant Papas got out and walked across the courtyard. She swallowed hard. He said something to Brakus and Brakus pointed her out in the dining room. She felt as if Papas were walking in slow motion. She searched his face for portents, but his expression was deadpan. She held herself in. Even if the worst had happened, she willed herself not to cry in public.

"May I drive you to your house?"

"Have you found him?"

"No. But I have news."

She let out a breath and stood up. "What?"

"Nothing worse than what we know already."

She walked out ahead of him, nerves taut as Mentor's bow strings. If Papas didn't know anything more, why was he here? Had Brakus called and warned him that she was asking questions about the integrity of the police? He opened the front passenger door for her and she slid in. He stood outside the car for a minute outside her range of vision. Her thoughts went into overdrive. He might be Thor's betrayer, or his undercover ally, or an ordinary cop trying to deal with a missing person case that had ramifications he didn't understand. Whatever he had to tell her, the personal visit and the flashing lights added a worrisome significance.

He got in, turned off the lights, and drove down the lane to Marilita's house.

"What is this about, Sergeant?"

"I would rather speak when we get to the house."

She tried to anticipate him, but could read nothing in his stern profile. With every bump and cobble, the tension built. The car bucked into Marilita's drive and he shut off the engine and pulled up the brake. "May we go inside to talk?"

"Yes, of course. I'll make coffee."

As they crossed the veranda, the mulberry branches swayed and jittered in the wind, creating a shadow show on the side of the house. She saw that Zenia had sent new outdoor furniture and the birdcage had been rehung. She couldn't tell if it contained replacement parakeets.

K.D. met them at the door, an expectant look on her face. "Did you find him?"

"Not yet," said Dinah. "Is Alcina in her room?"

"She went down to the farmhouse with Yannis."

"Sergeant Papas wants to speak to me alone. Would you mind waiting in your room?"

"Not at all. I'll leave you grown-ups to do the heavy brain work in private." She smiled and sallied up the stairs.

The jab wasn't lost on Dinah, but she couldn't be sidetracked. She led Papas down the hall to the kitchen and flipped the light switch. "Sit down, Sergeant. I don't have anything to offer you except coffee." She took a bag of Starbucks out of the cabinet. She'd bought it in the Athens airport after seeing TV footage of protesters firebombing a Starbucks store in the heart of the city. "Are you politically averse to American coffee?"

"No, but if you like, I will make Greek coffee."

Dinah had tasted Greek coffee, which had the taste and consistency of coal tar. She said, "I don't think we have any."

"There is always Greek coffee in a Greek house." He opened a canister on the counter and sniffed. "Ah. This is Greek coffee." He looked around. "And here is the *briki*." He picked up a small metal pot with a handle, measured two cups of water into it, added two spoons of sugar and two heaping spoons of coffee.

Dinah couldn't understand what he was waiting for. "Sergeant, if you've got something to tell me, don't leave me on pins and needles."

"We have found a phone."

She sat down. "Under the car?"

"No. It was found on the road a mile below the *lagkadi* overlook, crushed by a rock or a boot heel or a passing car. It is being examined by people who can ex—I don't know the English word."

"Extract the data?"

"Yes."

Her pulse quickened. "If someone took his phone, then that proves he was kidnapped."

"We have no proof yet that it is his phone. Even if it is, he could have destroyed it himself. Policemen have backup phones, the same as drug dealers."

"I know he's alive, Sergeant. You *have* checked all the hospitals and clinics, right?"

"I came to tell you that everything is being done. The Samian police are doing everything the Athens police would do, what any European police force would do. The *astynomia* of Samos are up to the highest standard." He turned away and went back to making the coffee.

She deduced from his defensiveness that Brakus had conveyed her suspicions. She hadn't told Brakus that she'd seen him with Papas in Pythagório. Maybe if she played it cool and didn't light into him with accusations, she could extract some data about their connection. "Is there a special technique to making Greek coffee?"

"Each step is important. You must start with very cold water and it should warm up slowly."

Like a good interview, she thought. "I suppose that everyone knows everyone on Samos. You probably know all the residents' names and the names of their children and their pets."

He lit the stove, set the pot on the flame, and began to stir. "A policeman must have, how do you say in English, *gnosi?*"

"Knowledge."

"Yes, knowledge." He began to stir the coffee. "I have knowledge of all of the people who live on Samos. What happened to your Norwegian friend was not caused by any Samian."

"A stranger then. A refugee?"

"Yes. We are questioning the usual suspects."

She covered her mouth. Did Papas realize he was lifting a line from "Casablanca," or that it was intended ironically in the movie, or that it had become a standard one-liner? She tried to look simple and credulous. "What do *you* think happened at Pegasus Point, Sergeant?"

"Inspector Ramberg must have seen a boat landing, illegals crossing from Turkey. They followed him and, how do you say? They *sampotaz* his car."

"Sabotage."

"Yes. The brakes, maybe. Or the steering."

She accepted the idea that someone might have tampered with the brakes and she didn't doubt that illegal immigrants might be involved. But Thor was tracking weapons, not immigrants. Like Brakus, Papas was eager to scapegoat foreigners. "Do you think the Iraqi man who was murdered might have been engaged in weapons smuggling?"

"No. Fathi wore nice clothes, an expensive watch, Italian eyeglasses. He showed his money too proudly. His death was an attempted robbery."

"You've changed your opinion then."

"It is the best explanation. When the robber heard you and the Inspector coming, he fled into the forest without taking anything."

Dinah had the feeling that he had rehearsed the robbery scenario. "Where would an unemployed immigrant like Fathi get two hundred euros?"

"Robbing another man. Who can say?"

"How would an Iraqi arriving in Greece from Turkey get a German identity card?"

He turned back to the coffee pot and his stirring became more vigorous. "I have no knowledge where he entered into Europe or when. He may have arrived first in Germania and migrated to Greece."

She said, "An official ID must be like gold to a refugee. If he were stopped at a border for any reason, it would be like a get-out-of-jail-free card."

"Inspector Ramberg asked us to talk to Fathi's associates and search his apartment. We, the police, did what he asked. We found no guns. There was no evidence of any wrongdoing."

She tried to think of an oblique way to ask her burning question, but she'd run out of patience and subterfuge was getting her nowhere. She said, "I saw you in Pythagório yesterday."

He didn't look around. The spoon clattered against the pot like rapid gunfire.

"You were with Savas Brakas and a man with a big, black mustache."

If he had an innocent explanation, now was the time to give it, but he didn't say anything.

Her eyes dilated on the gun strapped to his hip. Tread softly, she told herself, but her tongue had a mind of its own. "Did your friend Brakus call and tell you that I was asking questions about the honesty of the police?"

Silence.

She said, "You meet secretly with Mr. Brakus, he gives you a bag of something—and Inspector Ramberg turns up missing. It doesn't feel right to me."

Still without turning, he said, "You are upset and so I understand how you can make an elephant of a fly."

"If I've misinterpreted the purpose of your meeting, please set me straight."

Finally, he turned. "Savas Brakas is my business partner. Nothing to do with Inspector Ramberg. Nothing to do with my job as a police officer. I have children to feed. It is *sympliroma*."

He managed to inject both defiance and self-righteousness into the speech.

"What," she asked, "is *sympliroma*?"

He went to the sink, filled two glasses with water, and set them on the table. "I don't know how you say it in English. To make ends meet. It is what all Greeks must do in this time. The police do not condone what is not legal, but when the law is too harsh or unnecessary…" He gave an almost imperceptible shrug and resumed his rapid-fire stirring at the stove.

"I have no interest in how you or anyone else pads his income, Sergeant. But I believe that someone disclosed Thor's undercover mission to people with reason to want him neutralized."

"The Widow Stephanadis told everyone on the island that she had let Marilita's house to an *astynomikos*."

"I'm aware of that. The question is, who would have been the most worried by that?"

"Samos has many policemen. Another would make no difference."

She had expected him to follow Brakus' lead and point the finger at Mentor. She said, "It obviously made a difference to somebody. I mean to find out who."

He didn't turn around. "It's important for the sugar to dissolve completely and after it dissolves, you boil it for a few minutes."

She didn't know about the sugar, but her courage was dissolving fast. "Why did you come here tonight, Sergeant? Are you trying to intimidate me, because if that's your intention, you won't succeed."

He turned around, the *briki* of hot coffee in one hand, the other resting nonchalantly on the butt of his gun. "I don't know who would have tried to kill or kidnap the Inspector, if that is what happened. Here is what I know. Your friend was sent here by his government. Governments have no care for the feelings of people. You are not his wife or his sister, or even the same nationality. Whatever is done, you do not have the, how do you say, status? Yes, the status to be informed."

Her certainty skated out from under her. The matter of her unofficial status hadn't occurred to her. She went to the cabinet, brought out two mugs, and returned to the table.

Papas poured the coffee and sat down. "The most important thing is the foam."

She blew a wisp of steam and took a sip. It was scalding hot and strong enough to strip enamel. She took a cooling gulp of water and tried to reconcile the Thor she thought she knew with Thor, the secret agent man. *I love my country and I have my duty...don't worry. I have an ally on Samos.* It crossed her mind that Papas may have come to pass her a message from Thor in a veiled, off-the-record way that circumvented the government ban on informing girlfriends. Was he speaking in code? She tried to elicit a more particular hint. "Did the Inspector say anything of a personal nature to you, Sergeant?"

"Personal, no. But I have brought your lost eyeglasses." He pulled her Wayfarers out of his pocket and set them on the table.

She picked them up, half-expecting a message to be taped to one arm. She looked back at him, imploringly. "Did he not give you a message? Who he trusted? Who he didn't?"

"I will tell you what your Inspector said. He didn't trust the Syrians. Two boats came ashore from Turkey the day he arrived. He said to me, 'Papas, their revolution has turned them into animals. They are greedy for weapons. I will center my investigation on them.'"

"Those were his exact words?"

"*Nè, málista.* He said, 'They have destroyed their country. They will destroy yours if you let them.' And he was right. The fools at the foreign ministry have promised hospitality to twenty thousand of them, converting the hotels of Crete and Rhodes into barracks. Samos is overrun with *prosfyges*, but the Syrians are the worst."

She sighed and crossed Papas off the list of potential allies. If Thor had confided in him at all, which she doubted, he totally misrepresented what Thor had said. The Sergeant sounded like a member of the anti-immigrant party Thor had told her about, Golden Dawn.

"You should take your young friend and go to Athens tomorrow. It is not wise for you meddle in police matters. We will continue to search for Inspector Ramberg and when he is found, you will be informed."

She thanked him for the sunglasses and the coffee and he saw himself out. She lingered at the table. Everybody on Samos seemed to be running some scam or other. Even Mentor, if what Brakus said was true. She hated to think that Greece's cultural heritage was being looted by a professor of classical studies, no less. But then, she didn't have children to feed. She didn't care what the citizenry did to make ends meet, so long as they had no part in Thor's disappearance. Papas warning not to meddle scared her, but she had a gun of her own behind the chickpea flour in the cupboard and she would not be bullied into leaving Samos.

His remark about her inferior status rankled. She might not be Thor's wife or his sister, but she had a right to know if he was alive. If she showed up at the Norwegian embassy in Athens and threatened to sic her U.S. senator friends on them, perhaps somebody would deign to tell her the truth. She polished off the last of her coffee and spat a mouthful of sludge into her napkin. She felt fluttery from the caffeine and the tension. She walked out onto the veranda for a dose of fresh air.

The cicadas and tree frogs were shrilling and the smell of thyme enveloped her.

"Isn't it just the most gorgeous night?" K.D. lay across one of the new chairs with her legs dangling over the arm. "Just look at those stars. It's better than the Fernbank Planetarium."

"I don't feel like talking right now, K.D."

"I found something that might change your mind." She swung her long legs around, bounced out of the chair and strode across the veranda. "Looky here." She handed Dinah a laminated card, about the size of a credit card, with the photo of a black-haired man next to the multi-color holograph of an eagle and lots of greenish-brown curlicues. The name on the card was

Mohammed Al Masri and the place of issue was Bundesrepublik Duetschland.

"Where did you get this?"

"Trooper Papas had a stack of fifty of these thingummies in his glove compartment. I took one out of the middle of the stack. They didn't look kosher for a Greek cop. What d'ya think?"

Dinah turned the card over. The back showed the Brandenburg Gate and gave the man's eye color, height, weight, and place of residence—Berlin. This must be the same kind of identity card that Fathi had, a card that would allow him to move about the continent at will. "Did you notice any of the other names?"

"There were a lot of Abdullahs and Mohammeds."

Day 4

Chapter Twenty-four

Dinah woke up at nine and hugged the empty pillow beside her. She breathed in the ferny scent of Fitjar soap, the Norwegian brand that Thor liked, and brooded. Love was such a hackneyed little verb with an infinite variety of meanings and applications. She loved her brother, she loved mythology and folktales and tomato sandwiches and fried okra and fountains, almost everything French, and the music of John Barry and George Gershwin. She sprinkled the word like confetti and yet she'd never told Thor that she loved him. Did she, or did the fact that he'd been spirited away in such a shocking way make her think that she did, or should, or might someday?

She had lain awake rehashing the interlocking mysteries until three. Murder, betrayal, vandals, a bloody shoe, an anonymous wolf, a missing lover, an unknown ally, and a cop with a deck of German identity cards. The potter's wheel in her head kept spinning, but no unifying theory took shape. The one thing she'd decided, and this was instinctive and absolute and contrary to all efforts to convince her otherwise: Thor had not gone missing of his own volition.

Sunshine flooded the room with a cheery warmth, as if Apollo were mocking her, and the smell of cinnamon made her mouth water. She didn't think that baking breakfast treats was in Alcina's repertoire. K.D. must be showing off an unexpected skill. If her knack for pastry was half as impressive as her knack for larceny, she'd be a shoo-in for a job in a prison kitchen somewhere.

Not that Dinah wasn't glad that she'd filched that card. It gave the potter's wheel a wicked spin. The fact that the cards had been issued by Germany argued against a Greek police sergeant having a stack of fifty in his car for any legitimate reason. Was he stealing or forging them and retailing them to illegal immigrants? That must be the business he and Brakus had going and now that she thought about it, it explained why Brakus was so nervous when he saw Fathi lying dead in the lane. He knew he'd sold him a bogus card and he was afraid it could be traced back to him. When he phoned to report the murder, he must have made damn sure that Papas would be the responding officer. Thor had looked at the card, but obviously not carefully because he thought Fathi was in Greece legally.

A devil's advocate for Papas would argue that the cards were, in fact, authentic. Stolen, perhaps, and Papas was on his way to surrender them to the proper authorities when K.D. boosted that sample. If the cards were forgeries, he might have confiscated them from the forgers or intercepted them at the post office. Dinah bridled her tendency to jump to conclusions, but fifty German ID cards with Arab names in a Greek cop's glove box did not add up to a favorable defense.

The smell of cinnamon was irresistible. She showered and dressed and followed her nose to the kitchen. Alcina sat at the end of the table unbraiding a fat, gooey bun and dropping ropes of dough into her upturned mouth.

Dinah took out a plate and helped herself to a bun from a baking tray on the stove. "Did you bake these?"

"Katarina," said Alcina, her mouth full. "They are *nostimmos*, better than baklava."

"Where is Katarina?"

"Gone for a walk."

"Did she say where?"

"To the village."

"Did she say what for?"

"For the beauty."

Dinah's nervous circuitry could handle only so much. A breaker had tripped and she had no capacity to worry about K.D.'s antics. She put on a pot of Starbucks to brew and looked out the open window. Roses bloomed and birds chirruped and the Aegean sparkled in the sunshine, but the beauty was wasted on her. All she could think about was Thor. She should have been more observant, more sensitive to those fjord-like, Norwegian depths. If he were here this morning...but he wasn't. The old adage was true. You don't know what you've got 'til it's gone.

She sat down and tried again to jimmy a little information out of Alcina. "I know I've asked you before, Alcina, but please. Try to remember the last time you saw Thor."

"Yesterday morning."

Her prompt cooperation astonished. "Did you speak with him? Did he say anything at all?"

"Not to me."

"Was someone else here?"

"Just Ramberg, talking here in the kitchen."

"You didn't hear any other voices?"

"Just his."

A phone call, thought Dinah. "Did he call anyone by name? Did you pick up any words?"

"Grouch." Her bosom heaved with indignation.

Dinah didn't think that Thor would complain about Alcina to anyone other than her. Maybe he had been talking to his ally. She took a bite of her cinnamon bun. It really was delicious. She made a mental note to ask K.D. for the recipe on the off chance that someday there would come a morning when she'd feel happy enough to bake pastries.

The coffee pot burped. She got up, poured herself a cup, and changed the subject. "Tell me about your friend Stavros."

"Tell you what?"

"He seems fond of you. Do you see him often?"

"He went away when I was young."

"Has he been back to visit you?"

"*Okhi.*"

"No? Not ever?"

"He writes letters." She took a second bun and licked the icing off the corner.

Getting information out of Alcina was like tapping a sugar maple on a cold day. The desired product didn't flow. She wished she could see one of his letters to see if the handwriting looked anything like Nasos' scrawl. She remembered that the words were large and loopy and slanted to the right. She shouldn't have bothered to have it copied. She should have snitched the original. "Do you still have Mr. Stavros' letters? Or some of them?"

"Some."

Dinah perked up. "What does he talk about in the letters?"

"He says nice things about my mother. He told me not to let anyone tell me she was a bad person."

"Do you remember her friend Nasos?"

"He gave me presents." She tilted her head back and lowered a braid of the cinnamon bun into her mouth like a rope down a well. A dollop of white icing dribbled down her chin and her eyes shone with an expression akin to ecstasy. Dinah watched, transfixed. The woman seesawed between extremes, one day bawling her eyes out and the next exulting in epicurean rapture. How much was owing to bipolar syndrome and how much to put-on was debatable. In some ways, she seemed childlike and coy, but Dinah sensed an underlying guile.

"What kind of presents did Nasos give you?"

"A Pentax ES Two. I still have it, but it's hard to buy film."

Dinah didn't want to evoke painful memories and set off the waterworks, but she felt compelled to ask her about the day of the murders. "Were you with your mother and Nasos the day of the shooting? Did you take their picture on the beach?"

"Zenia says I wasn't there. She says I dreamed it after seeing a horror film at the *sinema*."

"But *you* think you were there?"

"I was. We went on a picnic to Megalo Seitani. Nasos was teaching me how to swim. Three masked men with guns came and then Brakus took me away."

"Brakus?" She must mean Brakus Senior. "Do you mean Aries Brakus? Did he come to the beach with a gun?"

"No. One of the bandits walked me back to the road and called him to come. When he got there, the man told him to take me and leave." She licked her fingers, wiped them off on a kitchen towel, and stood up. "Yannis doesn't think it was a dream. Neither does Galen."

Dinah wasn't sure what to think, but Alcina's "dream" certainly reshuffled the possibilities. She wondered what Thor had seen at Megalo Seitani all these years later. "What do you remember about the men with guns? What did the bandits say to Colonel Hero and Nasos?"

"I don't know. But my mother didn't shoot anybody. She was a great heroine, an *iroida*. An *ieromartyras*, like the paper says. Galen says her justice will come."

"Did you talk with her after that day? Or did Galen?"

"No-oh-ayee!" Her voice piped out of control and tears started down her cheeks.

Dinah couldn't quite believe those tears. Crying on cue must be second nature to the daughter and niece of actresses. "Did Marilita speak at her trial? Did you testify?"

From her violent head-shaking, Dinah presumed not. Alcina was one of those people whose testimony would be easy to discount. Even if she were entirely credible, a story of masked men attacking a party of picnickers would have been a hard sell, although Dinah found it easier to picture masked men as the perpetrators than a bikini-clad actress. But why would they spare Brakus Senior and Alcina?

Alcina continued to bawl and Dinah could think of no words of comfort. She tried to tune her out and construct a plausible bridge between then and now. The more she dug into the past, the more certain she became that the past held the key to the present.

"What an awesomely divine morning," said K.D., pirouetting into the room with an expansive wave of her arms. She halted in mid-stride and pulled off her red, heart-shaped glasses. "Whoa! What's the matter with Alcina? Is she stoned?"

Suspicion rippled through Dinah's veins like ice water. She pushed away the last bite of her cinnamon bun and glared.

Chapter Twenty-five

Dinah eagle-eyed the cinnamon buns and found no suspicious specks of marijuana. "Lucky for you," she said to K.D. "Has Alcina shown you her stash?"

"I've seen where she keeps it, if that's what you mean. But you needn't worry. I don't smoke dope."

"I'm glad to hear there's one vice you leave alone." Dinah rationalized the hypocrisy of what she was about to say. "Alcina likes you. This afternoon, after she's had a few hits of her tranquilizer, I'd like you to wangle your way into her room, get her to show you Stavros' letters, and when she's not looking, slip one of them into your beach bag."

K.D. blew a mare's tail of cigarette smoke out the side of her mouth and regarded Dinah with a sardonic little smirk.

"What's that look about?"

"Oh, nothing. I was just remembering that sermon about how you wouldn't do anything to contribute to the delinquency of a minor."

Dinah eyed the cigarette, but fought down her craving. "Your delinquency was in full flower before you left home. Anyhow, I just want to look at the letters. As soon as I get them translated, you can return them." She rinsed the plates and cups, placed them in the dishwasher, and unplugged the coffee pot. "I wish I'd copped the original of Nasos' letter to Zenia. I'd like to compare Stavros' handwriting."

"Don't you watch crime shows on TV? Only an expert can match handwriting."

"Without looking at the writing side by side, I don't expect a match. I just want to know if they're similar."

"They won't be because nobody writes letters by hand anymore. Galen probably printed them off his computer."

"If you can get hold of one of them, we'll know, won't we?"

"Are you going to tell me what it is that you suspect or treat me like a dorkbrain?"

K.D. had many shortcomings, but dorkiness wasn't one of them. At this point, Dinah couldn't see a reason to keep her in the dark and it would be helpful to have a sounding board. "I don't believe Nasos Lykos died on that beach with his mother and the Colonel. I think he's come back to Samos, either to avenge Marilita and his mother or because he knows something about the missing weapons Thor was investigating."

"You think Nasos is Galen?"

"Conceivably. He's been away a long time, but then so has Egan. Mentor, too, although he claims to have been here since his wife died five years ago."

"You think Nasos, whichever one he is, had something to do with Thor's disappearance?"

"I don't know. That's what I'm trying to work out. If Alcina is to be believed, three masked men with guns crashed Marilita's picnic."

"Bandits, like she told me."

"I don't think they were bandits in the ordinary sense. Zenia insists that Alcina was dreaming, but I'm inclined to believe the dream was real and for some reason, Zenia doesn't want to believe it."

"Or doesn't want anybody else to believe it."

Dinah was beginning to enjoy K.D.'s astringent observations. Zenia hadn't been at the scene of the crime and yet she sat like a spider in the center of the web. What terrible sin was Nasos accusing her of and why had he waited until now to come back? She said, "It's possible that Nasos was in cahoots with the gunmen and they let him get away. But surely he wouldn't have stood by while they killed his own mother."

"Maybe his mother killed his father," said K.D. She fiddled with her cigarette, shaping the ash on the side of a seashell ashtray. "Orestes and his sister Electra murdered their mother Clytemnestra because she murdered their father."

"When did you become such an authority on Greek myths?"

"I borrowed your mythology book this morning."

"You sneaked into my room?"

"With Thor not here, I didn't think it was like, a *forbidden* zone. You were zonked and I needed something to read while the cinnamon buns were baking."

Dinah took the cigarette out of her hand, ground it out in the ashtray, and tossed the ashtray in the trash. Before she left the house, she would have to remember to count her money and make sure that her bank card was where she'd put it. "In the photograph, Nasos' mother looked like a pleasant, respectable woman. I'm sure she didn't kill Nasos' father or anyone else."

"It was just a brain wave." K.D. flopped onto the bed on her back and scrutinized her fingernails. "So what do you suppose the bandits wanted?"

"I think they were after information that only the Colonel had. They forced it out of him and then they killed him. They killed Nasos' mother and they must have thought they'd killed Nasos, too. But either he played possum or he fell or dived into the ocean and saved himself."

"But why," asked K.D., "didn't they kill Marilita? They'd already killed one woman."

"I don't know. I can understand they might have shrunk from killing a child, but why didn't they kill Aries Brakus? Was he a co-conspirator?"

"Not necessarily," said K.D. "They needed somebody to take Alcina away and they knew he couldn't identify them because they wore masks."

"But why didn't he stay and help them fight off the bandits? Egan told me that Brakus had been in the army under the

Colonel's command. He was a friend, or at least a comrade in arms at one time, and he was smitten with Marilita."

"Maybe he didn't know what they planned to do."

"That's possible. But when the shooting was over, he knew that Marilita was innocent." Dinah tried to glean some logic from the various players' actions and inactions, but if there was a link that made sense, it eluded her. She decided to relegate the mysteries of the past to her subconscious to marinate and concentrate on the present. "I'm going out for a while. I want you to stick to Alcina like a cocklebur. See if you can induce her to say anything else about her mother or Nasos or Galen Stavros."

"Steal the letters, interrogate the witness, anything else, chief?"

"It would be great if you could find an old map of Samos, the more detailed the better."

K.D. sat up cross-legged like a yogi. "Where are you going?"

"To look for Thor. How many places can there be to hold someone captive in a village the size of Kanaris?"

The walk into the village energized Dinah. She breathed in the tonic scents of thyme and honeysuckle and kept up a steady, purposeful gait. Someone was playing the piano again, "Flight of the Bumblebee." The tempo caused her to quicken her gait. Where the lane curved toward the village, she peeked through a flimsy, flowering hedge to the back entrance to the Marc Antony. The windows were shuttered and she didn't see anyone about. It was just ten thirty. They wouldn't begin serving lunch until one or two.

The village seemed strangely deserted. She met no one on her way down the hill toward the winery and, to her surprise, the winery was deserted. Either the bruiser with the black mustache hadn't arrived at his post yet or it was his day off. Of course, he could be inside. A whole battalion of bruisers could be inside. She glanced up at the security camera and kept walking.

At the sign to the trailhead, she casually strolled into the woods and continued on for about fifty yards. The woods were

thick, but there wasn't much underbrush. She darted a sur-
reptitious look behind her, filtered into the trees to her right,
and doubled back toward the winery. If she had guessed correctly, she should emerge near the rear entrance, if it had a rear
entrance. She'd brought along a couple of paper clips in the hope
that she'd encounter just a simple padlock. If there were more
sophisticated locks and security cameras mounted on the back,
she wasn't sure what she'd do. Knock on the door and ask for a
liter of wine, maybe. She would have to wing it, but one way
or another, she was determined to see what was so precious it
had to be guarded like Fort Knox.

She dodged from tree to tree, skittish at the slightest noise
or movement. When the rear of the winery came into view, she
stopped to collect herself. Windowless and barn-like, the back of
the building looked more ramshackle than the front, although
there were two roof-mounted cameras trained on the overgrown
yard below, one at either end. Weeds grew knee-high in front
of a single wooden door, as if no one had entered or exited that
way in a long time. There was no padlock, only a rusted knob
and lock plate. She edged closer. Did that mean there was no
alarm system? Were the cameras just for show?

She gauged the distance between the electronic eyes. Fifty feet,
give or take. In order to reach the side door, she would have to
cross at least ten feet of ground surveilled by the camera at the
near end of the roof, but the sun was high and almost directly
behind her back. In a backlit situation, focusing an ordinary
camera was practically impossible. How much better could a
security camera be? If it caught her, she might be obliterated
by the lens flare. In fact, the weeds were tall enough to hide her
if she crouched low and moved quickly. The movement might
look no more suspicious than a gust of wind whiffling through
the brush.

Hunching her back, she broke for the door. The weeds
thrashed against her arms and legs and she swatted them out
of her face. When she got to the building, she turned around
and leaned her back against the door. So far, so good. She took

a few deep breaths, pushed her hair behind her ears, and was turning to face the door when she saw the snake approximately two inches from her left foot.

It looked like a decorative rope, charcoal-colored diamonds against a gray, scaly background. Its head was raised inquisitively above its coils, round coppery eyes fixed on her left shin, tiny forked tongue flicking in and out to detect the nature of the disturbance. In South Georgia where she'd grown up, copperheads and cottonmouth water moccasins were common. The white lips and pointy snout of the water moccasin indicated that it was venomous. She studied the physiognomy of the customer at her feet. Did that distinctive horn on the end of its snout indicate the same?

She stood stock still. Except for its constantly moving tongue, the snake didn't budge either. It seemed unable to decide whether to attack or retreat. She counted off the seconds. A minute dragged by, then two. It was a Mexican standoff and she had no idea how long it might go on.

She was starting to sweat. Did she smell like predator or like prey? Afraid even to lift her wrist to look at her watch, she kept her eyes glued on the serpent. If a water moccasin was threatened or riled, it bared its fangs and lunged or else crawled away. She wasn't used to a snake that couldn't make up its mind, like freaking Hamlet.

The sun burned the back of her neck and she began to feel like a bug under a magnifying glass. She thought of Ladon, the never-sleeping, hundred-headed serpent that Hera installed in her orchard to protect the tree that produced her golden apples. Had the man with the mustache sown this field with snakes?

Her left foot cramped sharply and she whimpered, which didn't matter vis-à-vis the snake because snakes are deaf, but if anyone inside the building was listening...

A sound like the crack of doom exploded overhead. Her hands flew to her ears. She looked up as a pair of F-16s scorched across the sky directly overhead. The door vibrated against her back and the ground vibrated under her feet. She looked down and in one quick, sinuous movement, the snake uncoiled and slithered off into the weeds.

She sagged against the door. Seldom had a deus ex machina come with such heart-stopping sound effects. She gave silent thanks to the Turks and waited for her heart to quit thumping like a rabbit's. Wiping the sweat off her face, she stood on one foot, removed her left shoe, and massaged away the cramp. When the pain and the noise subsided, she laced up her shoe and tried the door. The knob didn't turn, but the primitive keyhole lock was ridiculously inconsistent with the security cameras.

She fished out a paper clip, untwisted it, and threaded it into the keyhole. She wiggled it around and presto, the tumbler snicked and the knob turned. Even as she congratulated herself on the simplicity of the lock, she allowed for the possibility that it was irrelevant and the real protection lay on the other side—a nest of the snake's relatives, perhaps, or the mustachioed Iraqi holding an assault rifle.

She ran her tongue around her lips, wishing it were as sensitive to danger as a snake's. Summoning all her courage, she pushed the door open and stepped inside. The gloom was Stygian. She slid her sunglasses onto her head and tried to adjust to the murkiness. Somewhere in the shadows, an air-conditioner hummed, lowering the temperature by at least thirty degrees. She took out her keyring mini-lite and tiptoed across the concrete floor, deeply alert to the threat of snakes of all species. A musty, cellar-like smell permeated the place, which felt far larger than it appeared from the outside. A bank of wooden casks had been stacked against the back wall. She eyeballed a few of them up close. They exuded the smell of fermenting wine, but short of tapping into each barrel, she couldn't be sure of the contents.

Two canvas cots occupied one corner. She lifted a blanket off one of them, held the light between her teeth and ran the blanket through her hands inch by inch looking for blood, but to the naked eye it was clean. Near the cots, a camera like the ones used in drivers' license bureaus stood mounted on a tripod and there was a large, business-sized laminating machine. It seemed that she had discovered the facility where Papas and his accomplices manufactured their German identity cards. What Papas was doing was undoubtedly criminal. Was he also into arms trafficking, or did his identity cards merely ease downtrodden refugees across borders into a better life?

In front of one of the metal doors that faced the street was a folding card table. Piled on top of the table was a clutter of newspapers and coffee cups. She rifled through the papers and found a Michelin atlas of Europe. She opened it to the map of Greece and shone her mini-lite from Samos to Athens and north to the border with Albania, Maedonia, and Bulgaria. There were no added markings or notes.

She traversed the space again, shining her light into corners, eyes peeled for any sign of weapons or any sign that Thor had been here. But there was nothing. She doused her light and returned to the back door. Her hand was reaching for the knob when the door flew open and a flash of sunlight blinded her. She caught her breath and when the world came into focus, she was staring into the disconcerting blue eyes of Yannis Thoma.

Chapter Twenty-six

Yannis looked simultaneously astounded and angry. "What are you doing?"

"Searching."

"You must go. Get away from here now."

"Are you a part of what goes on in there? The forged cards?"

His eyes moved side to side and up toward the security cameras. "You must leave. Follow me."

He turned and bushwhacked through the weeds in his big boots. Dinah followed, not without fear, but relieved to have someone else blazing a trail through snake habitat.

"Are the snakes on Samos poisonous?" she called out to his back. "I saw a large one with black diamonds on its back."

He ignored her, slogging ahead of her with his old-man stoop just as he'd slogged ahead of Fathi. She wasn't unmindful of how following Yannis had worked out for Fathi, but Stavros had raised doubts about Yannis' guilt.

"Yannis, wait." They were back on the beaten path through the woods now, almost to the trailhead sign.

He turned and faced her. "I don't know what happened to Ramberg, where he is, who to ask. I can't help you."

"Have you been pressured to keep quiet? Has someone threatened you and Alcina?"

"No. I don't know anything about your man. Do you understand me?"

"I understand that you're afraid. Why does Alcina think the Iraqis want to kill you? Is she believable?"

"Alcina is not weak-minded. She was a beautiful girl, shy and mystical. She has seen too much cruelty. She has learned to expect it."

His English became fluent once he decided to talk. "You don't believe that Alcina dreamed the masked men who murdered Zenia's husband. Why?"

He hooked his arm around the sign and rested his weight against the post. "You ask me what I believe? I will tell you. The masked men were not bandits. They were soldiers. The junta killed their own man."

"Why would they do that?"

"The junta pandered to farmers and herders, but they were hypocrites who lined their pockets the same as the thieves in power are doing today. Phaedon Hero was a fool. He did not hide his wealth or his wealthy friends. He embarrassed the hypocrites. They killed him and laid the blame on a *sinema* actress."

Galen had been right about Yannis' ideals. Only a disappointed idealist could sound so bitter. She rushed to take advantage of his unexpected outbreak of talkativeness. "Did you know Nasos or the Colonel?"

"Nasos chartered my fishing boat a few times and invited his friends. Phaedon Hero, Egan Vercuni, and Aries Brakus. Nasos was the only one who didn't serve in the army. He was born to wealth. His mother was the heiress of a shipping magnate. He became what you call a playboy, always pictured in the news with a pretty woman."

"What about Galen Stavros? Was he one of their friends?"

His eyes hooded. "They knew him."

She registered the ambiguity. "He seems to know you very well. He vouches for your good character."

No comeback. His willingness to talk was obviously winding down.

"Can you think of a reason why Aries Brakus would be singled out by the masked men and sent away unharmed with Alcina?"

"Maybe he paid them."

"Nasos and his mother could have paid, but they weren't given that option."

Again, no response.

"Where was Egan when the murders took place?"

"He had served his time in the army and gone abroad."

She said, "Egan told me that Zenia suspects that some of the villagers had a hand in her husband's murder. Do you know who or why?"

"You ask questions I can't answer."

"Can't or won't?"

"Can't."

"Did she suspect Aries Brakus?"

"If she did, it is past. Aries is dead." He unhooked his arm from the sign, rolled his shoulders, and seemed ready to go.

Dinah was still wrestling with why the junta would assassinate one of their own. The Colonel could hardly be faulted for associating with his sister-in-law and her fiancé, even if they were rich. But suppose he had embarrassed them in a more significant way. Zenia believed that Nasos and his mother were part of the resistance. Suppose Phaedon had made common cause with them. "Were there ever any rumors that Colonel Hero had double-crossed the junta? Sold guns to the leftists, maybe?"

"You make fables."

"Do I? You were an enemy of the junta, you and Galen Stavros. Did the Colonel funnel weapons to your side? Do you still have them?"

"Like your *gkomenos*, you ask too many questions and I have answered too many."

The heat from the sun was sweltering. Rivulets of sweat coursed down her neck. She had hit on a plausible source of the guns, but she wasn't a millimeter closer to finding Thor and the clock was running. "I don't care who's selling guns or forging identity cards. All I care about is finding Inspector Ramberg. Won't you please help me?"

"Guns are not my *apati* and I have nothing to do with the identity cards."

"What's *apati?*"

"A way to beat the system. The politicians and the bankers have rigged the game against us. If the people are to endure, we must out-cheat the cheaters."

"Will you at least tell me who can answer my questions? Who should I talk to?"

"A crow does not peck out the eye of another crow and a Greek does not put the knife in another Greek. I leave the Papas brothers to their business and they leave me to mine."

"Sergeant Papas has a brother?"

"Hector. The man with the mustache who guards the door. You are lucky he didn't find you. He has a bad temper."

So much for racial stereotyping. The man she'd pegged for Saddam Hussein's twin was Greek, not Iraqi. "Do you know who threw garbage on Marilita's house? Was it really Iraqis?"

"I don't know."

"Yannis, I understand that you don't want to make waves, that you and Alcina have to live here and you may be vulnerable to retaliation. But kidnapping a policeman is no penny ante *apati*. It's…kidnapping. If you have any idea where Thor might be or who has him, you had better come clean if you don't want to be regarded as an accomplice."

His face closed like a coffin lid. "You should go home. Your *gkomenos* is dead."

She felt the blood drain out of her face. "Why do you say that?"

"The *cthonioi*. Snakes are messengers from the realm of the dead. Your boyfriend has sent you a sign from hell."

Anger boiled out of her. She dug her nails into her palms to keep from slugging him. "If he's dead, you have no idea the messengers from hell that I will unleash."

Chapter Twenty-seven

The canopy of pine branches offered a respite from the heat of the sun, but with the internal heat generated by her anger, Dinah scarcely noticed. She was too angry to worry about snakes, at least not those of the creeping, crawling variety. An accumulation of two-legged, scam-running snakes had infested this island and her cynicism deepened by the day. How could a society function if no one trusted anyone and each individual believed that his survival depended on his ability to out-cheat every other individual?

She powered along the same trail she and K.D. had hiked two days ago and this time, she was itching for a head-on with Brother Constantine. Even if he hadn't seen the Peugeot take a nosedive off Pegasus Point, he would have smelled the smoke and heard the commotion and, if her instinct about him was right, he wasn't the kind of monk to mind his own business.

Her thoughts swirled around those missing American guns. The government obviously hadn't recovered them. Somebody had squirreled them away for forty years. She had read that Greek islanders tended to live for a long time, but by now the original thieves surely had croaked or passed their arsenal on to the next generation.

The trail split and she plowed ahead on the groomed trail, noting the spot where Brother Constantine had blocked her way before. He must have a set up camp somewhere in these woods.

She wished she had a clearer mental map of Kanaris and environs. She pictured the gorge as an elongated, wavy triangle. The coast road formed the base. The road up the mountain to Kanaris formed one side, and the road up to Zenia's house and Pegasus Point formed the other side. At the apex of the triangle and the narrowest part of the gorge was the abandoned marble quarry where Zenia's road dead ended. Thor's car had been coming down from the quarry when it went over. *I ought to search the quarry site, too*, she thought. *If there's a trail from this side, I'll go there after I've talked with Constantine.*

After a half hour of walking, the landscape changed. The area had obviously been ravaged by fire in the not too distant past. A swath of charred and blackened poles stretched in all directions. Without the umbrella of branches, the sun penetrated to the forest floor and new undergrowth flourished. The dread of snakes reasserted itself and she began to second guess her decision to go one-on-one with the outlaw monk on his turf. She should have brought backup, although the only backup she could trust, sort of, was a sixteen-year-old delinquent.

An unburned copse appeared off to her right. The beaten path led straight ahead through the burn. A sandy pig path meandered off through the unburned trees and brush. The wider trail showed a mishmash of shoeprints, the pig path none. Constantine had no reason to hide his camp since everybody knew he was here, but he would probably want a degree of privacy and shelter from the eyes of curious passersby. She sniffed the air. Her Seminole ancestors were supposed to be great trackers. Maybe subliminally, she had picked up Constantine's scent. She took the path less traveled. If it petered out, she could always turn around and take the other trail.

Slapping low-hanging limbs out of her face, she walked on for another five minutes. The trail ended abruptly in a wide, sun-dappled clearing dominated by a white canvas yurt stamped all over with blue fleurs-de-lis. Brother Constantine filled the door, his wiry beard billowing from his chest like a thunderhead. His black eyes projected a strong distaste for drop-ins.

"Hello, Brother Constantine."

"Dinah Pelerin. Have you taken another wrong turn?"

"No. I've come to ask if you saw the car fall into the gorge."

"You had no interest in my prophecies when last we met."

"I have no interest in them now. I'm asking if you saw or heard anything that will help me find Inspector Ramberg. He's missing, as I'm sure you know since you reported the fact to Yannis Thoma."

He hulked into the clearing, arms folded over his chest. "You doubt the power of Hera to confer the gift of prophecy?"

She wavered. Do not mess with a crazy person. Do not dispute the premise of his craziness and do not challenge him, especially if you're not sure you can outrun him. Constantine was fat, he smelled of beer, and he was wearing an ankle-length frock. She suspended her do-not-mess-with rule. "How do you square your soothsaying for Hera with your monastic vows?"

"I am catholic with a small c, encompassing all. May I offer you a beer? I'll bring out some folding chairs and we can talk."

"All I want is information about the car. Did you see it go over? Can you tell me anything about what happened to the man who was driving?"

"I may have information."

"What? Tell me."

"Have you not learned the first law of the land? Greeks must always be social before they speak of serious matters." He turned and went into the yurt.

He was baiting her. Her anger escalated.

He emerged with two folding director's chairs and two bright green bottles of beer. "Hold these while I set up the chairs." He foisted the ice-cold bottles into her midriff and opened the chairs. "Sit down. I'll get the church key." He laughed until his belly shimmied and lumbered back inside.

"Here we are." He returned, popped off the bottle caps, took one beer out of her hand, and sprawled in the chair across from her. The wood-framed chair screaked under his girth and one fat, bald knee poked through the opening of his cassock. He had anointed himself with a potent cologne and, on top of the stale beer smell and his natural musk, it nearly made her eyes water. "Sit down."

She gave him a smoldering look and sat.

"Cheers." He took a long draft and belched. "It seems your friend's presence in Kanaris has unsettled everyone."

"It's his absence that unsettles me. If you know something, just spit it out. Please."

"Have a drink of cold beer. It will quiet your mind."

She wished she'd brought the Zigana pistol K.D. had found in the cupboard. Until Constantine chose to speak, she was at his mercy. She glanced at the beer. Mythos. A fitting brand for the mouthpiece of Hera. She took a sip to moisten her throat.

He took another drink and stroked his beard. "The police asked me for my prophecy about what may have befallen your friend. They weren't able to make me an offer worth my while."

"You want something in return?"

"If I have useful information, a benefaction in return would be only fair."

"Jesus, Joseph, and Mary. Is everything in this country for sale?"

He guffawed. "The government is selling the train system to the Chinese. The Acropolis and the site of the Oracle of Delphi are available to rent. Two years ago the government planned to sell off a number of uninhabited islands to pay down the debt. The natives grew restive, so the politicians backed off. Instead, they will ask for long-term leases on the islands and public lands, but it amounts to the same thing. It is an auction. *Nè, málista,* in Greece, everything and everyone is for sale. The only question is price."

She thought, God forbid I should ever become that cynical. "You can't want money. Zenia Stephanadis says your monastery cheated the government out of valuable real estate and it made you rich. She says you've set off a treasure hunt in the gorge."

"She has tantalized the villagers with the idea of chests of buried euros." He threw back his head and laughed. "She would enjoy watching them shovel and sweat. Perhaps she has salted the earth with fool's gold. She is a vindictive woman. She blames the villagers for the satisfaction they took from her husband's murder."

"So you're not rich?"

"My money is safe in a Swiss bank. The brothers weren't the only ones to profit. There were those in the government who received their benefactions, as well."

"Did the other brothers leave the country with their loot?"

"Some. Others have chosen to remain in the monastery. To me, it is a waste to have so much money and live a life devoid of the pleasures money can buy."

"Living like a hermit in the woods doesn't seem much like a life of pleasure.

"You are right. Zenia gives me money for my immediate needs, but she can't give me what I need."

"Zenia gives *you* money? Why?"

"When I entered the monastery as a young novitiate, I shared a cell with a wily old monk named Demetrius. He told me that six months before Colonel Hero was murdered, he contracted a severe case of pneumonia and nearly died. A priest could not be found and Demetrius was called to hear the Colonel's confession and administer last rites. When the Colonel recovered, Demetrius came into a great deal of money. It was a double miracle." Constantine broke into another gut-shimmying laugh.

"Are you saying the monk blackmailed him?"

"Let us say, they negotiated. The Colonel's sins must have been splendid. I asked Demetrius for the details, but he declined to share. But all I had to do when I came to Kanaris was mention his name and our close friendship and Zenia could not do enough to help me."

Dinah felt a wave of revulsion, but she had ceased to be surprised. The corruption just kept coming. What horrible sins had Phaedon committed that Zenia would pay to keep quiet. Torture, rape, murder? Or had he confessed to being a closet commie who aided and abetted the enemies of the junta? To this day, that would be intolerable to a right-wing zealot like Zenia.

Constantine said, "The Norwegian was here."

She reined in her emotions. He would use any sign of desperation against her. "When?"

"The morning the car went over. At the marble quarry."

"What did you see?"

"What can you give me in return?"

Hot anger spurted. He was toying with her. The gorge and surrounding forest ran for miles. One fat, beer-swilling monk couldn't keep tabs on the whole area. "I can't think of a single 'benefaction' that I have or could get that would help you. My thoughts are actually running along the lines of having you drawn and quartered if you don't tell me."

"I want a card that will permit me to reside in the United States. I think I would like southern California."

She almost laughed. "Is the climate in the German Republic not salubrious enough?"

He frowned as if he missed the allusion and she didn't elaborate. "You're barking up the wrong tree. I'm not in a position to dole out U.S. green cards."

"You're an American citizen. Americans can appeal to their elected representatives. I've read about this. Your politicians are applauded for their beneficence. They will win good publicity for helping a man of the cloth."

"Why don't you buy a green card? All you have to do is invest a half million dollars in an American business and they'll let you in."

"With my legal problems, I would have to overcome too many obstacles. Say that I am being persecuted for my deviant orthodoxy. You will think of something."

"You've been specific about what you want. You've offered me nothing."

"I will show you something. If it helps you to find Inspector Ramberg, do we have a bargain?"

"How do I know you're not lying?"

"Because I will show you what I have found before you speak to anyone on my behalf. That is good faith, is it not? It is the Christian thing. Do you promise?"

"Yes. I'll do what I can."

"Let us go then. It's a short walk to the quarry, but steep."

Chapter Twenty-eight

Constantine's extreme corpulence and flapping cassock fooled Dinah. He bounded up the trail like a mountain goat. She found herself breathing hard to keep up. She was still chafing over Yannis' prediction that Thor was dead. She loathed Constantine, but she wanted desperately to believe that he could lead her to Thor, or some clue to his whereabouts. Constantine had prophesied correctly that the climb would create a serious thirst and he had supplied her with a bottle of water. She paused under an ancient rock wall and drank. Anxious as she was, she still marveled at the grit and ingenuity of the people who had planted olive trees up the side of this mountain and built these enduring terraces.

"The quarry is just ahead," said Constantine. He hurdled over a fallen log and turned back to wait for her.

She took a last drink of water and pressed on. He reached back over the log and offered her a hand. She ignored it. He grunted and continued to climb. She followed. The near perpendicular incline kept her eyes mostly on her shoe tops. When she looked up again, he had stopped. She drew alongside him and looked down into a deep rectangular pit, like an inverted skyscraper. She stumbled back from the edge, nearly falling into Constantine's arms.

He said, "The quarry dates back to ancient times. Some of the marble was used to build the Temple of Hera. When Zenia's husband bought the land in the mid-sixties, production ceased. It hasn't been mined for many years."

She inched forward and peered into the depths. Water had collected at the bottom. If Thor had fallen or been pushed…

She picked up a stone, threw it into the pit, and listened for the plonk. It seemed to take a long time. She edged around to the other side. There were two other pits, not quite as deep. None had barriers or warning signs. Driving heavy blocks of marble down that narrow, serpentine road would have been a hazardous job. The turnaround area had to have been wider when the quarry was operating in order to accommodate the trucks, but a thicket of pine saplings had encroached. Hillocks of tailings and fractured slabs of marble that must have been unsalvageable as counters and table tops enclosed the area and extended out into the road. A rusted-out dumpster overflowed with cans of lubricant and scrap metal and miscellaneous waste. It probably hadn't been emptied since the quarry was abandoned. A screen of trees along the edge of the road didn't quite hide a large area of clearcut.

"Yannis Thoma comes in the afternoons with his chain saw when Zenia is away at the theater. He steals the wood and sells it in the winter when people are cold." Constantine obviously didn't share Yannis' ethic about one Greek not sticking a knife in another.

She said, "I assume you didn't bring me here to show me an illegal logging operation."

"Here." He beckoned her toward the dumpster.

Her throat constricted. Dumpsters were notorious receptacles for dead bodies, butchered body parts, and horrors galore.

On the ground beside the dumpster, a black tarp had been spread like a shroud over something smallish. He lifted the tarp with his foot. The body part he uncovered was a forearm, gray-veined white marble. Her eyes fastened on the reddish stain on the outside of the elbow. Was it Thor's blood? Had somebody bludgeoned him with that arm and thrown his body into this dumpster?

She looked at Constantine with redoubled loathing. "Did you watch him beaten? Is that why you know about this…this thing?"

A suggestion of doubt flitted across his face. "I didn't see the man."

"You said that you did. Are you now saying you lied?"

"I saw his car. I know every car in the village and who drives it."

"You've put yourself at the scene of a crime. This arm links you to whatever happened here."

"I was harvesting honey in the forest. I saw the blue car. It was here and when I looked again, it was gone. I hiked up to see what the policeman had been doing and I found it."

"And thought you could use it for personal gain." She was quivering with rage. "Are you conducting an auction to see who'll give you the best price, me or the people who beat him up?"

"I am not someone you can shame, Miss Pelerin. If this object was used to club your friend, I have given you a valuable clue. There is only one man on Samos who owns fine sculpture. Mentor Rodino."

She had shelved Brakus' accusation because antiquities, stolen or not, seemed unrelated to Thor's investigation. Constantine's discovery seemed altogether too neat, but she couldn't process the implications at the moment.

She looked at the dumpster. It was unlikely that the kill… kidnappers would have unloaded all that garbage, thrown Thor inside, and heaped the garbage back on top of him. But this was a derelict site. Nobody came to collect the trash. She had to be sure. She set her water bottle down on a rock and turned to Constantine. "Help me empty the dumpster."

His head reared back in disbelief, but he appeared to recalculate and began to pull a few pieces of junk off the top.

"Set the plastic bags on the ground over here."

He reached in, hauled out a couple of sacks, and laid them at her feet. They weren't big enough or heavy enough to hold a body, but she pictured Yannis brandishing a chain saw and untied the string. Holding her breath, she dumped the contents on the ground. Cookie boxes, wine bottles, yogurt cartons, cigarette boxes, antifreeze cans, diverse gadgets. The heavier one contained a corroded car battery.

Constantine tossed out an empty propane tank and two more bags. She sifted through the garbage inside the bags as carefully as if they contained archaeological artifacts. Had Thor come here looking for weapons and interrupted a different crime? Somebody's secret *apati*—Yannis cutting down Zenia's trees, Papas peddling forged cards to refugees, Mentor lifting a stolen antiquity out of a hidey-hole?

Constantine wiped his hands on the front of his cassock. "That is as far down as I can reach. You can see that he is not here."

She chinned herself up on the side of the dumpster and peered over the rim. Caked mud and gravel, some sort of rusted cutting tool, a rotten rope.

He said, "Zenia will be at home today. She has no performance on Thursdays. I will walk down to her house and collect my weekly envelope. If I ask nicely, she may offer a poor brother a hot bath and a warm meal."

Dinah didn't know whether she felt more contaminated by the garbage or the brother. She said, "I'm surprised she hasn't shot you by now."

He laughed. "Whether you find your Inspector dead or alive, you have made a bargain. I will see you again."

He loped off down the road and she looked over the mess she'd made. The afternoon *meltemi* had begun to blow, sending yogurt cartons and cookie boxes flurrying. Mostly to give herself time to think, she gathered up the emptied sacks, spread them across the garbage, and weighted them down with rocks. She wrapped the forearm in the tarp. Why would the only man on Samos associated with fine sculpture break it and use it as a weapon, then leave it lying about like a personal signature? The thing must weigh close to ten pounds, more than enough to fracture a man's skull. She tried not to picture it swung against Thor's head, but she did picture it. She walked behind the dumpster and vomited.

When she was done, she found the water bottle, rinsed her mouth and hands, and took out her phone to call the police. It was dead. She'd forgotten to recharge it last night. Maybe it was a sign from the gods. She tossed the empty water bottle into the dumpster, slung the tarp with the forearm over her shoulder, and started down the mountain toward Kanaris.

Chapter Twenty-nine

"Pugh-ooh! You smell gross." K.D made a face of disgust. "Where have you been?"

"Dumpster diving with Brother Constantine." Dinah blew into Marilita's kitchen and laid the bloody forearm on the table. "Go upstairs and bring me some clean clothes, will you? Underwear, shoes, everything. And a towel."

"Why don't you go upstairs and take a shower?"

"No time." She kicked off her shoes and looked for her purse. Where had she left it? "Where's your phone? Give it to me."

K.D. set it on the table, but her hand remained closed over the screen. "There's private stuff in here."

"Sounds racy. I'll save it for the next time I'm bored."

"Jeez." She rolled her eyes and flounced out of the room.

Dinah sorted through her purse for the card Papas had given her. It listed both the main station number and his cell number. She called the main number. After a few rings, she heard a recorded message in Greek. She left a message in English to the effect that she had obtained new information regarding the disappearance of Inspector Ramberg and was on her way to visit Mentor Rodino. Damn. What call-back number should she leave? She covered the phone and shouted, "K.D., what's your number?"

K.D. shouted back from upstairs.

Dinah left both K.D.'s cell number and land line number and as an afterthought, stated the date and time.

She stripped off her shirt and shorts, filled the sink with hot water and suds, and gave herself a sponge bath. She scrubbed her hands and arms, but the bouquet of garbage seemed to have infused her pores.

K.D. returned with clean clothes.

"Where's Alcina?"

"Yannis came by and she left with him. I tossed her room, but couldn't find any letters."

"Did she tell you anything else about Nasos?" Dinah dried off and changed quickly.

"Only that she lights a beeswax candle for him every Sunday just like she does for her mother to light their way in the darkness." She lifted the edge of the tarp. "What's this?"

"It may be the weapon somebody used to bludgeon Thor."

"Jesus. He was bludgeoned?"

"I don't know." Dinah recalled Papas' reservations about the car wreck being staged for his benefit. She had a feeling that the discovery of that forearm had been staged for *her* benefit.

K.D. ticked a fingernail against the marble arm.

"Don't touch it. There may be fingerprints. If the police call the house, tell them about the arm and tell them they need to get a forensics expert to analyze it pronto." Dinah looked around for a place to hide the thing until the police arrived. Hastily, she shoved it behind the pipes under the sink. "If Papas shows up to take it, don't give it to him. Tell him I put it in the trunk of my car."

"Where are you going?"

"To pay a visit to Mentor Rodino."

"The guy with the zombie wife?"

"What?"

"You said he was going to dig her up."

"That doesn't make her a zombie. I'll take your phone with me. Put mine on the charger and I'll call you later."

"I want to come with you."

"Not a good idea."

"What if this Mentor dude is a killer? What if you need a decoy to lead him away from Thor while you do CPR or something?"

"I need you to hold down the fort here. In case the police call. Or N.C.I.S."

"That's lame."

"This isn't a game, K.D. I'm trying to keep you safe."

"I'm not like some feeb to be kept out of everybody's way. I have a brain. I can help."

Dragging a teenager into this was probably negligence bordering on child endangerment, but Dinah didn't believe that Mentor was a killer and she had ceased to think of K.D. as a child. If K.D. felt excluded, she might go into the village and jack a car. "All right. But no monkey business. You have to do exactly as I say. Clear?"

"Clear."

Since the vandals struck, Dinah no longer felt bound by Kanaris' prohibition against cars. She had driven through the village and parked the Picanto snug against the house, but there was no need to drive back the same way. Hiking down from the quarry, she had spotted another road that took off from the far end of Marilita's lane and appeared to intersect with the dirt road past Mentor's *kalivi*. It looked like a shortcut and she was in a hurry. She hustled K.D. out the door and the two of them drove off in a new direction.

The surface of the lane in this direction was less of a washboard and Dinah zipped along at good speed. But after a mile, conditions deteriorated to a rocky track that led up the mountain, over a ridge, and down in a series of hairpin turns carved around terraced vineyards and olive groves. She flung the car's front end around the tight curves as if she were schussing down a black diamond ski run.

K.D. said, "You're a maniac behind the wheel."

Dinah glanced at her, unbelted, a grin like an upturned horseshoe under her heart-shaped sunglasses. "Fasten your seatbelt."

"You're not wearing yours. Anyway, there are no cars to crash into out here."

"I'm the adult. Do as I say or I'll put you out of the car and you can walk."

"You're a mass of contradictions, you know that?"

To the extent that her head was crawling with contradictory thoughts and allegations, Dinah had to agree. She slowed down and scanned the hillside above for Mentor's additional *kalivis* full of Hellenistic plunder. There were a few scattered cottages. She wouldn't know if they were his without asking someone. At the next switchback, the track they were on joined the track she'd walked on that first day when she met him.

She'd forgotten how narrow the track was, barely wide enough for a midget like the Picanto to pass. As she neared the *kalivi* where Mentor hosted his harvest parties, the stone bench in front squeezed the track down even more. She steered the left front wheel over the lip of the track into the vineyard on the left-hand side to keep from scraping the fender against the bench on the right.

"You're still too close," said K.D.

She backed up and steered still farther to the left, craning her neck and straining to see in the right-hand mirror how much room she had. But the bench was too low for her to see and she had to rely on K.D. "How am I doing?"

"A smidgen more to the left," said K.D.

The grape vines had been planted right up to the edge of the track and there was a drop-off of several inches. She tried to estimate that smidgen and still keep the tires moving straight ahead on the verge.

"You're okay now. Straighten up and pull right."

Dinah tried to ease forward, but the left front tire slid off into vineyard, whacking into a vine and miring in the sandy soil. She tried to back up, but she couldn't get any traction. After spinning her wheels for a minute, she gave up. "I'll look inside the *kalivi* for a plank or something we can put under the tire."

"I can't open my door," said K.D., climbing across the gear shift and exiting on the driver's side.

Dinah edged around the front of the car, climbed over the bench, and entered the *kalivi*. No planks, no boards, no help. She started back outside to see if there was anything useful outside.

A droning sound caught her attention. It sounded almost human. She turned and peered behind the low wall where the barefoot pickers once trampled the grapes. Empty. She must have hallucinated the noise. She looked down just in time to avoid tripping on the stone slab that covered the well like a lid.

"I found a flat rock that may work," called K.D.

Dinah walked out the door and the sound came again. Like a moan. She turned back. The slab had been moved. The last time she saw it, there was a wider space between the edge of the slab and the edge of the well, wide enough to spit at the devil, as Mentor had joked. Now there was only a sliver, too tiny to see down inside the well.

She lay down on her belly and spoke through that sliver. "Hello?"

Nothing. Not even an echo. Her imagination was playing tricks. She pushed herself up. K.D. was standing in the door. "What are you doing?"

"I thought I heard a moan."

"Probably a bird. A dove or something."

The sound came again. Dinah lay back down and put her ear next to the crevice. "It's coming from under this stone."

It was definitely a moan. A person was down there. Thor? Panic seized her. She tried to slide the stone lid. "Give me a hand, K.D."

K.D. pitched in and the two of them pushed as hard as they could, but it was impossible.

"It must weigh a ton," said K.D.

Dinah spoke through the crack. "Thor? Is it you?"

No answer. Whoever was moaning down there was past speech.

"You think it's Thor?" K.D.'s voice echoed her panic.

"A fulcrum," said Dinah, jumping up. "We need a lever of some kind to wedge into that crevice. Maybe we can move the stone a few inches at a time."

"What can I...?"

Dinah gave her back her phone. "Call Alcina and tell her to call for an ambulance. If you can't get Alcina, call somebody else who speaks Greek."

Frantically, Dinah tore out the door and looked for a tool. One of Mentor's walking staffs had been left propped against the side of the cottage, but a wooden stick would break. She needed something strong enough to support that stone and pivot it around. She turned and her eye fell on the spit roaster. The bar was steel, strong enough to hold a goat or pig carcass. She yanked it out of its slot and ran back inside.

K.D. was talking to Alcina. Dinah pushed her out of the way and inserted one end of the bar into the crevice. She leaned on it with all her weight, pushed down with everything she had, wrenched to the right as hard as she could. The slab made a scrooping sound as it grated across the stone floor, but it moved only a couple of inches. K.D. put down the phone and reached for the bar.

"We need chocks," said Dinah. "Go find some small rocks, the rounder the better. I'll try to lift the slab an inch or two and when I do, you stick a rock under it."

K.D. set off in a run.

Another moan.

"Thor?" Dinah put down the steel bar and got down on her belly. The crevice had grown wide enough to see into, barely. It was dark, but she could make out Thor slumped against the far side of the well. His head hung limply on his chest.

"Thor, can you hear me?"

Apparently, he couldn't. If he'd been coshed with that marble arm, he would be severely concussed. He could have a blood clot or permanent brain damage. She jumped up and poured her fear into moving the stone. As she bore down on the bar, she prayed to whatever gods might be listening. She'd read that the stone that sealed Jesus' tomb weighed two tons. It had taken ten strong men to move it across his tomb and a single angel to roll it away. She prayed for an angel.

K.D. came back with an armload of rocks. Dinah managed to raise the slab enough for her to roll an apple-sized stone underneath. The two of them leaned hard on the bar and the stone slid another three or four inches. The opening was getting bigger, but it was nowhere near big enough to drag a man through it.

Dinah's arms ached and she was sodden with sweat and fear. Samos had experienced dozens of earthquakes over the centuries. It was an earthquake that caused it to break off from the Turkish mainland in the first place. Why couldn't God send a quake right now, a precision jolt for the sole purpose of sundering this one damned slab? "Did Alcina say she would call an ambulance?"

"Yes. The main hospital is in Samos Town. The ambulance will come from there."

Dinah pried the stone almost two inches off the ground and lugged right. "Do you hear that, Thor? The old grouch is trying to help us. We'll get you out of there. Hang on."

"That's the name of the play Zenia's acting in," said K.D.

"What?" Dinah straightened her back and mopped the sweat out of her eyes with her shirttail.

"*The Old Grouch.* I saw a notice in Zenia's kitchen in Greek and English. It's by a playwright named Menander."

When Alcina overheard Thor talking about the grouch, he'd been talking about Zenia's play. To whom? To Zenia? To his ally?

Thor moaned.

"There's almost enough room to pull him out," said K.D. "Let's both push down on the bar and shift right at the same time."

Dinah wiped her sweaty hands on her pants and nodded. "On the count of three."

They bore down on the lever with all their might and the stone lifted.

"One." Dinah felt as if her abdominal muscles would snap.

"Two." Her biceps burned and she didn't think she could hold the weight an instant longer.

"Three!"

They heaved and the stone slid almost a foot. Dinah would've collapsed except there wasn't time. Thor was white as paste and Samos Town was an eternity away. Now that she thought about it, she didn't see how a vehicle as large as an ambulance could maneuver down this twisty intestine of a track.

She lay down, raised Thor's head and leaned it back against the wall. Blood matted his hair and a rivulet of blood had flowed from his left ear down his neck and dried. He seemed to be breathing without difficulty, not that she would know. His skull didn't feel soft, but God only knew what damage had been inflicted on the inside. She lifted his eyelids and wiggled her fingers in front of his eyes. They didn't focus.

"Thor, wake up. Wake up now, okay? Please?"

Now that she'd already moved his head, she recalled that you weren't supposed to move a head injury victim unless it was absolutely necessary. You could end up doing additional harm, cause spinal cord damage, paralysis or death. "Sorrowing Jesus, what an idiot I am."

"What has happened?"

She looked up into the horrified eyes of Mentor's daughter Jacey. Standing next to her was a big man of about thirty, presumably her husband.

"An ambulance is on the way from Samos Town, but I'm not sure it can get here." She couldn't bring herself to add *in time*. She weighed the possible harm of acting impulsively and moving Thor versus the possible harm of not acting and waiting on an ambulance that couldn't get here. "Can you help me get him down this mountain to meet the ambulance on the coast road?"

"*Nè, nè, nè.*" Jacey spoke rapidly in Greek to the man, who answered and motioned with his hands.

Dinah saw him as a take-charge type and felt a surge of hope.

Jacey said, "Move your car out of the track. Leon will bring his truck from my father's house."

"Is the truck small enough to make it up the track?"

"*Nè, málista.* We will drive you down to the coast road. I will call and tell the ambulance where to meet us."

Leon handed Jacey his phone, added some further instruction in Greek, and started out the door.

"Leon says not to move him until he gets back. He will bring blankets and a board for his back." She dialed a number and went outside with the phone to her ear.

Dinah handed K.D. the car keys. "Do you think you can rev it out of the ditch?"

"I can do it."

"Back up until you find a place to turn around. Go to Kanaris and take the road from there to Samos Town. You'll have to find the hospital. I'll meet you there."

K.D. picked up her phone and cast a teary look at Thor. "Good luck," she said and left in a hurry.

Jacey finished her call and came back inside. "I don't understand. How could he have fallen into the hole? My father keeps it covered."

"He didn't fall, Jacey. Whoever it was bludgeoned him and buried him alive. Someone wants me to believe that somebody was your father."

Chapter Thirty

Dinah rode in the ambulance with Thor. She squeezed his hand while the baby-faced EMT who'd responded to the scene of the car crash monitored his vital signs. The siren wailed and the outside world went by in a blur. A succession of possible outcomes marched through her mind. Thor could wake up as good as new and they would sail away together into a lovely sunset. Thor could wake up brain damaged, amnesiac, unable to speak or understand language or feed himself. He could be crippled or paralyzed. He might vegetate for years in a coma or never wake up at all. She couldn't eliminate the possibility that they would die together in this screaming ambulance which heeled dangerously around every curve.

Thor's hand remained limp and she let go. By the time they reached the hospital, she had begun to anesthetize herself against bad news. Thor wouldn't be the first person she'd cared for and lost. In a few weeks or months, she would cordon off the pain and get on with her life. She always did. Mental detours around hard knocks were her specialty. If that made her seem callous, maybe she was. Maybe she didn't have the capacity for a "truly great love" as K.D. imagined. Not everyone did. Her mother didn't.

The EMTs transferred Thor inside and Dinah followed the gurney. As she entered the building, she was surprised to see Leon's small pickup turn into the parking lot. He looked as calm and cool as he had when dragging Thor out of the well onto the board. Jacey's face was a study in bewilderment.

The hospital registration process bewildered Dinah. Language wasn't the problem. The problem was insurance. The woman at the reception desk needed information that Thor couldn't give and Dinah didn't have. In Norway, every Norwegian citizen was covered by national insurance from cradle to grave. She had no idea how the Greek system worked. She said, "He needs a doctor right now. Go ahead and admit him for treatment and I'll find out about his coverage later."

"We must have the insurance information at the time of admission. It is the new rule." The young woman appeared sympathetic, but her position was adamant.

"Maybe that's the rule for non-serious cases. This is a freaking code blue. He'll die if he doesn't get treatment."

"I'm sorry. There is a list of doctors you can call to ask if they will see him."

"What about the doctors at this hospital? What is a hospital for if not treating emergencies?"

Leon walked up behind Dinah and touched her shoulder. "My father-in-law called an underground doctor to meet the ambulance. Come. He is waiting in the basement." He signaled the EMTs and they rolled Thor toward the elevator.

"Underground doctor?" Dinah hurried alongside him as they trailed after the gurney. "You mean a doctor who sees patients in the basement?"

"A doctor who sees patients who aren't insured. There is no more money for health care and hospitals demand proof of insurance or cash. But don't worry. If your friend needs drugs or hospital supplies, the underground movement will pay. My father-in-law will guarantee payment to the hospital and to Dr. Frangopoulos."

The elevator doors opened and they stepped inside.

Jacey jumped in a split second before the doors closed. "*Mpampas* is on his way to the hospital now."

Unless something incredibly convoluted was going on, it seemed less and less likely that Mentor had caused Thor's injuries. In fact, if Thor lived, it would be because of Mentor and his family.

The doors dinged open and the EMTs rolled the gurney out into the hall. A beefy man in a rumpled white coat was waiting for them. "I am Dr. Frangopoulos. How long has he been unconscious?"

"I don't know," said Dinah. "Possibly since early yesterday morning."

"Can he follow commands?"

"No."

The doctor pinched Thor's earlobe and yanked.

Thor grimaced and his eyelids flickered.

"A good sign," said the doctor. He opened Thor's eyes and shone a light. "Pupils sluggish."

The EMTs spewed a barrage of information and handed him a clipboard with their notes. Frangopoulos read over them. "Airways clear, heart rhythm normal. Alright, take him into room eight and let's take some pictures."

Thor mumbled.

"He's waking up!" Dinah caught his hand. "Thor?" She leaned over and put her ear to his mouth. "Thor, who did this to you?"

"Staff," he said.

"He's not comatose," said the doctor, "but there is intracranial swelling and probably bleeding. With this level of stupor, his thinking will be clouded and impaired. If you remain in the hospital waiting room, I will let you know when I have finished the neurological assessment."

Reluctantly, Dinah let go of Thor's hand and the EMTs wheeled him away.

A waiting room of any kind was a trial and waiting for life-and-death news about someone you care about was Dinah's definition of hell. Time dragged. She paced up and down and tried to take heart from the fact that Thor had come to enough to speak—a good sign, as the doctor said. But after four hours, it was hard to sustain her optimism. She felt as if she were trapped in her own version of *Waiting for Godot*, the only line of which she could recall was "Nothing to be done."

Leon and Jacey had left as soon as Thor was handed over to Dr. Frangopoulos. They were probably meeting with Mentor, putting him wise to what she had said about someone pointing the finger of guilt at him. She wondered if he would know automatically that it was Brakus. Irene Brakus' face lit up like a sunbeam when she looked at Mentor. Dinah would have chalked up Brakus' malevolence to jealousy were it not for one little word. *Staff.* Was Thor saying *staff* as in Mentor's walking staff or was it a meaningless utterance of an impaired brain?

She walked past a row of chairs. Absorbed by her own worries and woes, she had scarcely noticed the people waiting here for news of their loved ones. Her pacing no doubt exacerbated their nervousness. Feeling self-conscious, she sat down in the last chair and looked at the clock on the wall. Another half hour ticked by. Frangopoulos had promised to speak with her as soon as he'd finished the neurological assessment. It must be worse than he'd thought—a subdural hematoma or a cerebral hemorrhage or something that required brain surgery.

She bounced up again. There wouldn't be a qualified brain surgeon in a town this size. She needed to speak with somebody about airlifting Thor to Athens, or maybe back to Norway. She started down the corridor toward the nurse's station. Standing at the desk in earnest conversation with a nurse was Galen Stavros.

He saw her at the same time. "I came as soon as I heard."

The fight or flight region of her brain lit up. Had Thor been trying to say *Stav*ros? And where was K.D.? Why was she late? Dinah's feelings for the girl had warmed considerably over the course of this day, but she didn't trust her judgment. And she didn't trust anything at all about Stavros.

"Did he say anything in the ambulance?"

She shied away from him. "I don't see that's any of your business."

"I understand that you're frightened, but it's vital that we talk. Let's walk outside."

He took her arm, but she shook free. "Except for a traumatic brain injury, he's safe now. We don't need you or your 'well-placed connections' anymore. What we need is a brain surgeon."

"I've already sent for a neurosurgeon from Athens. He arrived an hour ago. He is with Thor as we speak."

She stared, speechless.

"You can be sure that I am on his side, Miss Pelerin. Could we please talk in private?"

Uncertain, she let him conduct her outside where a dark Mercedes was parked in front of the lobby entrance. A man in a police uniform stood in front of the car, an uzi resting loosely in the crook of one arm. His head turned slowly from side-to-side as he panned camera-like around the parking lot.

Stavros slipped a wallet out of his inside jacket pocket, flipped it open, and showed her a laminated identification card with his picture and some official looking insignia. "I am Lieutenant Colonel Stavros with the Special Anti-Terrorist Unit of the Hellenic Police, assigned to work with Inspector Ramberg to uncover a cache of stolen weapons."

She felt momentarily dazed. Stavros was the ally?

"I will ask you again, did he say anything to indicate that he'd found the weapons?" His peremptory manner bordered on intimidation.

She gave him a probing look. "Forget for the moment that you were not honest with me from the beginning. The only proof I have that what you say is true is an ID card that may or may not be for real. I've seen a dandy looking forgery run off by one of your Hellenic policemen."

"What kind of forgery?"

"An identity card. Issued by Germany."

His eyebrows practically levitated. "Did Ramberg show it to you?"

"No."

He pulled a card out of his pocket and showed it to her. "Did it look like this?"

She recognized the picture immediately. The name was Abrahem Fathi. "Yes."

Stavros said, "Ramberg took it off Fathi's body and gave it to me."

"For all I know, you could have taken the card from Thor after you tried to kill him." She remembered that when she showed Thor the business card Stavros had given her, he asked what he looked like. "Did you ever meet Thor? Because he didn't know you from a bale of hay."

"We met the day you went to meet young Katarina. We were supposed to have dinner, but you returned unexpectedly. I am his Greek liaison. I promise you that I am who I say I am."

"And just when I had convinced myself that you were Nasos Lykos, back from the dead."

For an instant, he appeared stunned. When he spoke, he was even more peremptory. "Sit down with me inside the car and we will talk."

She shook her head and backed away. She should never have let him inveigle her outside the building. It was that line about bringing in the neurosurgeon from Athens that drew her and it was probably a lie. Gulled again, she thought, as the man with the uzi panned around and looked at her.

She turned to go back inside.

"Wait." Stavros caught her arm and held her. He said something in Greek to the man with the uzi.

She wrested her arm free and was halfway to the door when the uzi guy walked around the car, pressed the keys into her hand, and returned to his vigil.

Stavros said, "From the time that Fathi was murdered, Thor planned to brief you about his investigation. I think it is time that we brief each other and combine our knowledge."

Whether from curiosity or exhaustion, she relented. "Did you really send for a neurosurgeon?"

"Yes. He is very good. He often treats policemen injured in the line of duty." He opened the back door of the Mercedes and gestured with his head. "You are in no danger."

"You first," she said.

He climbed in. She pocketed the keys and climbed in beside him. He removed his cap and said, "Nasos Lykos is dead."

"Dead men don't write poison pen letters."

His head jerked up. "I tell you, the man is dead."

"Zenia Stephanadis agrees. But somebody who claims to be Nasos is sending her threatening letters."

"How do you know about these letters?"

"I don't know how many there have been. I've only seen one. It's melodramatic and gothic, hinting at her past sins and warning that the wolf is coming to make her pay. Whoever wrote it hates her. Just like you do."

"Do you have it? Show it to me?"

She took it out of her purse and gave it to him. "This was hand-copied from the original."

He took a pair of horn rims out of his jacket pocket and read.

When he finished, she said, "I believe that Nasos Lykos or the person who's impersonating him is connected to the stolen weapons Thor was looking for."

"So he did confide in you."

She hedged. "Not in detail. After the house was vandalized, he became afraid for my safety. He told me he was here to investigate an arms smuggling operation for N.C.I.S and he thought he'd been betrayed. The only people who could have known that he was anything more than a Norwegian cop on holiday with his girlfriend are the Greek police."

"It was not I." He pulled the cap between his fingers inch by inch as if he were counting rosary beads. "When the Greek police were notified that vintage American weapons were being smuggled out of Samos, I knew they were the weapons Colonel Phaedon Hero had diverted for the liberation movement. My mother and I financed a number of the anti-junta groups."

"Then you are Nasos."

"I was. I have been Galen Stavros, a member of the Hellenic Police, for the last thirty-five years. I have a wife and children. I am a grandfather. I thought I had banished the hatreds of the past. I can't express quite how, but you remind me of Marilita and when you spoke about Zenia helping you, the bitterness that I felt surprised me. But I would never write such letters."

"Why didn't you let someone else handle this case? Why did you come back to Samos?"

"I knew I could give the Norwegians information they would not have found on their own. I didn't disclose my former identity or the fact that Marilita and I had worked together to oppose the junta. I told Inspector Ramberg only that Phaedon Hero had been the officer in charge of the armory in Samos Town and American weapons had been shipped regularly from Athens to that location for distribution to military units on the island."

"Why didn't you tell him that Colonel Hero was Zenia's husband?"

"I knew he would find out and I didn't want to reveal too much knowledge. I had no idea where he had hidden the weapons or who had begun selling them. This is the first time I have returned to Samos since I swam away from Megalo Seitani on June the ninth, 1973."

"You swam away with a head wound?"

"I would have drowned, but I was picked up at sea by a fishing boat. Yannis Thoma's fishing boat."

"Yannis said it was the junta that killed your mother and the Colonel."

Stavros held his left hand palm up in his right and traced his life line with his right thumb. "The assassins did not wear uniforms, although their speech and manner were military."

"How did they find out that you and Colonel Hero were supplying guns to the liberation movement?"

"I've asked myself that question a thousand times. The only person who could have known was Zenia."

"But how could she inform on her husband over a, a political difference of opinion?"

"She has always revered power and authority. It was why she married Phaedon. She thrived in the society of generals and colonels and Phaedon was a military rising star by the early sixties, destined for high rank and power."

"Why did he join the junta and why then turn against it?"

"Initially, he thought the Americans and the British would spur Greece to make liberal reforms. But as the U.S. increased its support of authoritarian governments and policies, he became disillusioned. After the junta assigned him to carry out the Prometheus Plan to eradicate the 'enemy within,' he knew he had to fight."

Dinah recalled Zenia's comment about the junta being the last legitimate government of Greece. "I don't think he would have told Zenia how he felt."

"He must have. And she killed him as surely as if she'd pulled the trigger, herself."

Dinah felt a sort of punch-drunk sadness for them all. "It must have been hell for you."

"Yes. My mother fought for justice all her life. She smuggled weapons to the Greek resistance during the German occupation and after the junta seized power, she began to set up a network of partisans. My father died before the coup, but he had left her very well off. Through her contacts, she found governments and dealers willing to sell her weapons and she arranged for our partisans to receive weapons training in Syria. She died fighting for what she believed in, but it was a terrible thing to see."

"You didn't have to see Marilita die."

"No." His face contorted. "We were never lovers, but she was as dear to me as my mother. When she was put to death and there was nothing I could do to stop it, I knew Nasos had to die. If he hadn't, he would have come back and killed Zenia." He replaced his cap over the scar. It was as if that cap served as a protective carapace, covering memories that were still raw.

A dull pain had begun to pulse behind Dinah's eyes. She was beyond weariness. It was too much to take in the tragedy of these old people. She needed to get back to the waiting room, to her own troubles, and yet she heard herself ask, "Who besides you would know about Zenia's sin? Who would want to make her pay?"

"No one," he said. "Only the dead."

Day 5

Chapter Thirty-one

At one o'clock in the morning, the neurosurgeon informed Dinah that Thor was stable following surgery to relieve the pressure on his brain. He was in the intensive care ward and the doctors wouldn't be able to assess his cognitive status for another twenty-four hours, or possibly longer. There was no reason for her to remain at the hospital and he advised her to go home and get some rest.

"I'll stay," said Galen Stavros. He had waited with her and this morning he looked haggard and ready to drop. "I cannot take the chance that his attackers will return."

"Can't you call someone to stand in for a few hours?" she asked.

"I will. I must make sure that my stand-in can be trusted."

His caution reassured her. And as there was nothing she could do here but pace and pray, she felt a duty to find out what had become of K.D.

Bleary-eyed, she let Stavros lead her back to the Mercedes. The man with the uzi had been replaced by a different man with an uzi.

Stavros opened the rear door for her. "I've arranged a driver for you. His name is Antonis."

A man with long brown hair stepped out of the shadows, saluted Stavros, and took his place behind the wheel.

She settled into the back and said to Stavros, "You'll call if he wakes up?"

"Of course. And call me if Katarina has not returned home. Unless she has done something very reckless or gone clubbing in Samos Town, there is not much to fear. I've instructed the local police that I will take charge of the sculpture you found. Antonis will bring it back with him tonight." He started to close the door.

"Wait." She reached in her purse and pulled out the card that K.D. had filched from Papas' car. "Here's another forged ID for you. Sergeant Papas and his brother Hector use the wine co-op as their studio. Most of their clientele have Arabic names."

His mouth quirked up on one side. "With so many in our ranks harassing the refugees, it is a twist that one policeman is helping them, but by his help, turning them into criminals and fugitives."

She said, "They can't all be smugglers and terrorists."

"No, but the sergeant and his cards may help us to narrow the field."

He closed the door and the car glided off into the night. She curled up, hugging her knees to her chest, and reflected on her conversation with the reincarnated Nasos. She had guessed right about Phaedon. He had been supplying weapons to opponents of the junta. At first, he procured guns through backdoor channels from the Soviets. But as a glut of American weapons poured into the country, he began to divert a portion of each shipment. The stolen weapons were never missed and no one suspected his duplicity, or so he thought until masked assassins showed up at the beach that day and demanded the location of his stockpile. When he refused, they shot him point-blank and turned their guns on Nasos and his mother. Marilita had flown at them, screaming and clawing. Wounded, Nasos ran onto a rocky promontory and dived into the sea. The gunmen fired after him, but missed.

She asked him where Alcina was during the shooting, but he had lost track of her and he never saw Aries Brakus at all. Aries had been out of the army for several years and Stavros had no doubt that the only person who could have known about Phaedon's treason and informed against him was Zenia.

Dinah looked out at the whitecaps ruffling the water like memories rolling in from the shores of a distant past. Nasos had created a new identity for himself and a narrative that he could live with. Had he been powerless to save Marilita? Maybe. Who was she to judge? Memory wasn't a videotape. It was the story you told yourself so you could sleep at night. Sometimes the gory details had to be deleted and the failures of courage glossed over to make it bearable. If Zenia had done what he said she did, she must have contrived some major historical revisions to make her feel good about herself.

The driver's gap-toothed smile appeared in the rearview mirror. "I will drive you through the village to your house. You must tell me where to turn."

"Fine. Thank you." She hadn't noticed when they left the coast and now they were on the climb to Kanaris. Lost in thought, the road had slipped away, along with his name. Antony? Antonis? She closed her eyes. What would she do if K.D. hadn't come home? More than concern for her safety or anger at her high jinx, she wanted her company. Even if she fell asleep, she didn't want to be by herself.

The Mercedes cruised through the silent village. There were no street lights and all of the houses were dark. Even the Marc Antony had closed and gone dark.

"Turn here," she said.

The Mercedes swung into the lane, hardly registering the rough cobbles. The glaring lights and antiseptic smells of the hospital had seared her senses. She let down her window and breathed in the sweet night smells. The cicadas were singing and the moon was full. Antonis turned into Marilita's driveway and parked behind a blue Vespa. The Picanto was nowhere to be seen and the house was dark.

He got out and opened the door for her.

She had seen that Vespa somewhere before, hadn't she? She chewed her lip. "Will you come inside with me? I don't know who is here."

He slid a gun out of his inside jacket pocket, held it low at his side, and walked ahead of her to the front door. He turned the knob, pushed the door open, and stepped inside. There were no lights. She clung to his back like a shadow. They looked right, down the hall to the kitchen, then left, toward the living room. Music wafted from that direction.

...sunk in pain
Obsessed with love and clouds and rain...

Antonis raised his gun and whispered. "When we enter the room, can you find the light?

"Yes."

The two of them skulked down the dark hall in tandem. They crept into the living room and Dinah hit the light switch. K.D. was lying on the couch, her head resting in the lap of the young man who had given Dinah directions to Mentor's house after her tires were slashed. The boy saw Antonis' gun and his eyes stretched wide as saucers.

K.D. raised her head off his lap and gave Dinah a wan smile. One of her eyes glistened with tears. The other was red and swollen shut. "I wrecked the car," she said, sitting up and holding a wet cloth against her forehead. "This is Farris. He gave me a ride home."

Sorrowing Jesus, thought Dinah, and went to examine her injuries.

Farris leapt to his feet and shut off the music. "I tried to take her to the hospital but she would not go."

"I didn't want to cause you any more worry," said K.D., her voice quavering. "How is Thor?"

"Still unconscious." Dinah ran her fingers over the goose egg on K.D.'s forehead.

"Ouch!"

"Did you black out or feel disoriented?"

"No. I was clear as a bell, wasn't I, Farris? I know I should've been wearing a belt, but..."

"Hush. How about the other car? Anyone hurt?"

"There wasn't another car. I swerved to keep from running over this old lady. There was no crosswalk and it was really her fault. I ran into the side of a building and the shop owner didn't speak English and I was so lucky because Farris came along and gave the police your name and number and somebody will call you tomorrow."

"Are there any cuts? Anything that needs stitches?" Dinah lifted K.D.'s swollen eyelid.

"No."

"How long ago did this happen?"

"About nine hours," said Farris, looking sheepish. "I have been taking care of her."

"I'll bet." A loving parent would have rushed the kid to the hospital for observation, but Dinah wasn't a loving parent. She was a barely functioning nanny with too many troubles on her mind and she was utterly depleted. "It's up to you, K.D. You might have internal bleeding and not realize it. This gentleman," she waved a hand behind her toward Antonis, "will drive you to the hospital if you want to go. If not, I can't make you."

She said, "I'll be okay. Daddy always used to joke that the Dobbses have harder heads than most people. I guess I'm living proof."

Dinah frowned.

K.D. put her hand over her mouth. "Oh."

Farris retrieved his helmet from behind the sofa. "I will go now. I will come to see you tomorrow, Katarina."

"I will go, too," said Antonis. "Tell me where the sculpture is, please."

"Wrapped in a tarp under the sink," said Dinah.

Farris left and Dinah followed Antonis down the hall. He looked inside the tarp at the bloodstained arm and whistled. "This would have caused much damage."

"Yes."

He blushed and appeared eager to get away. "I will come back and drive you tomorrow when you are ready. Lock the door when I leave."

"I will. *Efkharistó*."

She heard the door close and leaned her arms on the table. Her biceps ached from the strain of all the lifting she'd done. There wasn't a muscle in her body that didn't ache. Her nerves were pulsating and her thoughts tangled in knots. A glass of wine would relax her and probably put her right to sleep. K.D. would have sore muscles, too. No one who's been conked on the head should drink or go to sleep, but it had been hours since the accident and Dinah had already abdicated the role of minder. K.D. had passed the point where she could be managed.

She uncorked a bottle of wine, took out two glasses, and carried them back to the living room—pausing en route to bolt the door.

K.D. sat prim and erect on one end of the couch. "How is Thor?"

"Stable. Prognosis uncertain." She poured two glasses, handed one to K.D., and curled up on the other end of the couch. "Thank you for what you did this afternoon, K.D. I couldn't have done it without you. If he pulls through, it's because you were there to help. You are definitely not a feeb."

Her open eye glazed with tears, which she was quick to hide. "Did he say anything after I left?"

"Nothing coherent." Dinah was still puzzling over that one word, *staff.* It was probably just a neural glitch. Or if he'd had a moment of lucidity, he was trying to call Stavros' name, perhaps to let her know that he was a friend. She lay her head back and stared up at the ceiling, its plaster crazed by a web of minute lines. It seemed as if reality itself was crazed. There was no pattern, no coherent whole, just a mosaic of pieced-together recollections and fleeting perceptions—Stavros', Alcina's, Thor's, and hers.

K.D. said, "Thanks for not chewing me out about the accident."

"We've both had a rough day." Dinah picked up a CD sleeve on the coffee table, *Memory Comes Back.* "Farris looks familiar to me."

"He gave you directions to Mentor's house, don't you remember?"

"Yes, but I saw him somewhere else. In the airport the day you arrived. He was wearing a "Raining Pleasure" T-shirt and you gave each other a flirty look. Did you meet him on your flight from Athens?"

K.D. pressed the cloth over her eyes with both hands. "Yes."

"It was serendipity that he showed up so promptly that morning. He was probably prepared to offer you a ride into Karlovassi on the back of his scooter."

K.D. made a little soughing sound through her nose.

"Did you ask him to slash my tires?"

She lowered the cloth and tears streamed from both eyes. "I'm sorry, Dinah. Truly, I am. But he and I just so totally bonded, like instantly. We couldn't let Fate separate us before we had a chance to truly know one another. I didn't know he would slash *all* of the tires. And it turned out for the best, didn't it? Thor might have died if we hadn't stayed on the island, right?"

"You didn't know that, K.D. And self-justification is a dangerous habit."

"God, I'm such a hopeless git."

"Don't beat yourself up, K.D. Your instinct about Galen Stavros was right. It turns out he's a policeman."

"I knew I was right about him. I went online and looked up that Sextus Empiricus dude he quoted. Sextus was all about suspending judgment, which is how everybody ought to be but totally is not. Sextus said some pretty heavy stuff, but it was sort of like, everybody's different and no two people see a thing the same way. Like you didn't see Galen the way I did and my mother doesn't see anything the way I do and the police, not Thor, but I mean the Atlanta police, are total morons. I'm not making excuses. I know I have to take responsibility, but it's enervating."

Dinah straightened up and drank a few sips of wine. The painting of the Spanish knight held her attention. It was crazed and crackled, too. Either it was very old or the artist had wanted it to look old. Her brother, a budding art forger, used a craquelure varnish on some of his paintings to effect the illusion of age.

She got up and went to look at the knight more closely. Marilita had told Nasos, aka Galen that the face reminded her of someone she couldn't be with, probably Alcina's unnamed father. Alcina had the same prominent eyes and drooping lower lids. That had to be a hereditary trait. There were computer apps that could show what someone would look like as he aged. Dinah tried to imagine what the knight would look like as an old man. His high forehead, long neck, and high, rounded hairline resembled Egan. The aging resins had darkened the skin tone to brown, like Stavros' skin, and it was possible to see something of Stavros' character in the bleak smile. But the raptor-like nose, thin lips, and square chin brought to mind the photo of Phaedon hanging next to the front door in Zenia's house. The knight's face was a Rorschach test.

And suddenly she saw it. "I can't believe how blind I've been."

K.D. got up and joined her in front of the painting. "What is it? What do you see?"

"The whole shebang," said Dinah. "Call Farris back. I need to borrow his scooter."

Chapter Thirty-two

The Vespa growled to a stop in front of Zenia's house. Dinah turned off the ignition, unbuckled her helmet, and dismounted. There were no lights in the house, but moonlight illuminated the curved stairs and bathed the boulder in a silvery glow. She rolled her borrowed conveyance behind a tree out of sight and crept down the paved drive toward the garage.

She held the beam of her flashlight low until she reached the garage. She killed the light and waved her arms up and down in front of the door, but there were no motion sensors. No lights flashed on. She was relieved, but a little surprised. Zenia had bought a gun to scare off the wolf, but she hadn't installed the simplest of safeguards. Or so far it seemed so.

Zenia had opened the door with a remote control device. Most modern garage door openers had a wireless, keyless entry system. Dinah shone her light along the side of the garage looking for an outside keypad. Bingo. The little box was attached to the inside of the jamb on the right-hand side, a few inches below eye level. With luck, Zenia had been equally negligent when setting the security code. Dinah lifted the cover, punched in the last four numbers of Zenia's telephone number, and hit enter. That wasn't it. She tried 1-2-3-4, the typical sequence used by people who didn't like to burden themselves with complexity. That didn't do the trick and she tried 4-3-2-1, then repeated combinations of each number, which also failed.

She kicked herself for not knowing Zenia's birth date, but the year was 1928. That didn't work, either. The numerical equivalent for the name Hero had too many digits. The road was known simply as Quarry Road and the house had no number. If she had a coat hanger, she might be able to reach the emergency release lever inside the garage and open the door, but she didn't have a coat hanger. Grudgingly, she supposed that if she'd brought K.D. along, she'd have finagled her way inside like abracadabra. But K.D.'s expertise wasn't available and time was wasting. Already, it was four in the morning and she didn't want to take the chance that either Zenia or Egan was an early riser.

Frustrated, she circled around looking for a window to break or a back door to force, but the garage appeared to have been hollowed out of solid rock. She returned to the keypad and the answer came, as K.D. would say, like "duh." Of course. Everything related back to that bad day at the beach. She entered the numbers 6-9-7-3 and the door began to rise, more noisily than she would have liked, but neither Zenia's ears nor Egan's were lynx-like.

No interior light came on, another security omission that worked in her favor. She left the door open and shone her flashlight into the darkness. She walked past the Isotta and headed straight for the arched stone doorway into the underground passage. Once inside, she found the main switch and a dozen recessed lights snapped on in the niches that lined the tunnel. Light didn't alleviate the feeling of being in a catacomb. When she had followed Zenia through here the first time, she had paid scant attention. This time she knew what she was looking for.

In the first niche on her left stood a large, two-handled amphora, probably for storing olive oil or wine. It depicted two warriors, one with his spear raised over his head, poised to slay the kneeling other. Across from the amphora, on her right, was a pair of disembodied marble feet. The figure they supported must have been colossal. The next object on her left was an exquisitely painted pot which Dinah recognized as a loutrophoros. She had seen ones like it in the Louvre. Such vessels were used in funerary rituals and placed in the tombs of the unmarried. She could see nothing about the thing that would make it more applicable to unmarrieds than marrieds, but she wasn't a pottery wonk.

The next sculpture was a swan—its wings enfolding a terrified woman, Leda. In Greek myth, Zeus was forever turning up in disguise to rape some hapless hottie. With the king of the gods, it was one perfidy after another. No wonder Hera had been jealous and resentful.

A whooshing sound behind her made her jump and she pasted herself flat against the wall between the amphora and the funeral pot. She heard another whoosh like fluttering wings punctuated by a loud thud. She pictured a large bird, an owl or a hawk, driving a smaller bird into something hard, the back of the Isotta, perhaps. More fluttering and then silence. In her mind's eye, the hawk was flying away to its aerie, prey held tight in its talons.

She let out a breath and continued her tour. The next statue was the one she had come to see. Asclepius, the god of medicine. In his right hand, he held his serpent-entwined rod. The Staff of Asclepius. The staff symbolized healing and the serpent symbolized the sloughing off of old age in the way that a serpent sheds its skin. This was the staff that Thor had meant. There could be no doubt. The left arm was broken off at the elbow.

She made a quick inspection of the remaining niches and statuary. She had no idea how valuable these pieces were, but she felt sure that this subterranean hideaway was more than a private museum. Phaedon had designed it to be the repository for the weapons he diverted from the armory in Samos Town. Thor had figured it out and come here looking for them. There must have been a fight and Asclepius fell out of his niche. Someone had picked up the broken arm and clobbered Thor, then took the weapon a short distance up the mountain to the quarry and tossed it. He couldn't afford to be seen driving Thor's car, so he pushed it off into the gorge, stuffed Thor in the trunk of his own car, drove to the *kalivi*, and entombed him in the well in order to incriminate Mentor.

The only problem with that scenario was that the guilty party had to be Egan. Other than Zenia, he was the only one with unfettered access to this cave. He would have been in the house on the morning when Thor drove up here. He looked old and innocuous and could have sneaked up behind Thor. But Egan didn't look strong enough to lift a wet sponge, let alone push a Peugeot off a cliff or move that heavy stone from the *kalivi*. Lifting Asclepius back into his niche would have given Hercules a hernia. Constantine must have been in on it. If he didn't take part in the actual assault, he was paid to "discover" the bloody arm and put his brawn into the heavy work. She still wasn't sure about Brakus and Papas, but one thing at a time.

Where were the weapons? Was there a secret panel? She ran a hand from the serpent's tail up to its mouth and tongue and from the top of the staff to the bottom, but there were no magic buttons or levers. She squatted down and felt around the feet and in the interstices of the cloak. She could find no hidden mechanisms. She was in the process of standing when she banged her knee against the edge of the niche and lost her balance. As she fell backward, she grabbed onto the staff and Asclepius swiveled sideways—throwing her onto her bum.

When she righted herself, she saw that the rear wall of the niche had opened out to reveal another tunnel or room. She leaned her head and shoulders inside. It was dark and emitted the earthy fug of a crypt, but the floor had been swept clean and far in the back, a dehumidifier thrummed. Her flashlight picked out a bank of wooden crates stacked on pallets. Each crate bore a stenciled "United States of America."

"What are you doing there?"

Dinah's heart knocked against her chest. It wasn't the voice she'd expected. She turned to see Zenia, cocooned in an oversized yellow kimono from which the barrel of her pistol emerged like the proboscis of a wasp.

"I should have known you'd come back." Without her lipstick and eyebrows, she looked blank, like an unfinished cartoon. She held up the trailing skirt of her robe and minced around for a better look. "What is that?"

"The storeroom where your husband kept the weapons he stole from the junta."

"No such thing." Keeping a firm grip on the pistol, she bent over and cocked her head inside. "I don't see any weapons." She stepped back and scrunched her eyes. "What have you done to Asclepius? His arm is gone."

Dinah weighed the possibility that she didn't know about the guns. "Are you covering for Egan, Zenia? That arm was broken off the statue when you and I walked past it on the morning Thor disappeared. I didn't realize that anything was amiss, but you noticed. You looked furious. Did you ask Egan about it?"

"Someone broke in. Those Iraqi vandals."

"Is that what he told you? Maybe it was Nasos Lykos. Like he said in that letter he wrote to you, the wolf is at the door."

She bobbled the gun, but recovered immediately and backed away. "Don't be absurd."

"Have you considered that Egan might be writing those letters?"

"Nonsense."

"Is it also nonsense that Egan is selling Phaedon's guns to terrorists?"

Her mouth worked but no words came out. She edged around and tried to look inside the storeroom again.

"Had you read Phaedon's journals before you gave them to Egan? You must have. Did Phaedon describe in his private papers how he'd turned your private museum into a secret armory?"

"There was nothing in the journals about guns. Only maneuvers and security operations, the military hierarchy."

"Maybe you didn't know how to decode the military jargon. Egan did. He found these guns and he's been selling them." Dinah gripped her flashlight and mulled her chances of batting the pistol out of Zenia's hand before she could pull the trigger. If only she would move a bit closer. "Egan almost killed Thor with the arm of that statue. Do you remember the heavy coat

Egan wore the morning you brought me here? It was probably hiding a bloody shirt. He changed clothes before he left the house with me."

Zenia backed farther away, her facial muscles writhing. "I don't know about any of this." Dinah had discarded the notion that Zenia didn't lie, but the fuddled look in her eyes was no trick of the Stella Adler school of acting. She was confused. Dinah didn't know if that made her more or less dangerous.

"When did your husband tell you about his political change of heart?"

"Phaedon died a patriot."

"That's a lie, Zenia. He was a traitor."

"Pah."

"He was a traitor, but it wasn't his disloyalty to the junta that made your blood boil, was it?"

"I don't know what you're talking about."

"Yes, you do. It was his infidelity that infuriated you. You probably could have ignored a passing indiscretion, but he didn't just have a meaningless fling. You believed he had fallen in love with your sister and she with him. That's why you obsess over Marilita's carnality and her disdain for all things right and proper. That's why you informed on Phaedon and his fellow travelers. But tell me this, Zenia. Did Phaedon know in the end that he was murdered for adultery rather than for treason? Did Marilita know that you were her executioner by proxy?"

"She was a murderess. That's why she was executed."

"You have to own the truth one day, Zenia. You sent the murderers."

"I did nothing wrong, nothing any other patriot would not have done. Nasos and Marilita were aiding the communists to make war against their own government. They had to be stopped. Marilita brought radicals and communists into our house. She killed my husband."

"No, she didn't. The junta killed him and framed Marilita. It probably didn't matter who took the blame so long as the junta wasn't seen as assassinating one of their own. But why did they kill him on the beach at Megalo Seitani?"

"There's no road. It's a long walk. There would be no one to see." She seemed to be tiring, her will to deny winding down.

Dinah urged her on. "It sounds like the perfect spot for a group of insurgents to meet. You knew that everyone you wanted dead would be on the beach that day."

"I wanted no one dead. I wanted them arrested and put in prison. I wanted Phaedon to see them led away, to know that Marilita was dangerous to him and to all of us."

"Then your revenge went farther than you'd planned. Did you not stop to consider how the junta would react to even the suspicion that they had been double-crossed by one of their members? It would be worse than embarrassing. It would undermine their authority."

"The government investigated. Phaedon had not been a part of the conspiracy. He was exonerated."

"Of course he was exonerated and the propaganda machine set to work to smear Marilita and lionize Phaedon. To do less would be to cast doubt on the legitimacy of the entire government."

"I have no regrets. I reported a meeting of anti-government extremists to the authorities. No one could have foreseen that Marilita would murder everyone."

Dinah wasn't surprised that Zenia had absolved herself of guilt, but she couldn't believe that she held to the fiction that Marilita was the shooter. "What made you suspect an affair between Phaedon and Marilita?"

She lifted her chin and her eyes cleared. "I saw them whispering together behind my back. He laughed at her impudence and her audacity. It was obvious she had seduced him. After his illness, when the priest began to blackmail him, I knew."

"Why didn't you shoot him then?"

"A tawdry domestic drama would have diminished us both."

The sleeve of the kimono fell over the gun. She pushed it back up and her black eyes narrowed to slits. Dinah tried to guess what she was thinking. *She does get it, doesn't she? She* understands that this is the end of her pretense? She said, "Shooting me won't do you any good, Zenia. You can't keep the truth from coming out now."

"I'm eighty-five. No one will question an old woman who shoots a burglar. I have spent half my life defending my husband's good name. I will not permit you to undo everything I've worked for and humiliate me."

"Don't you understand, Zenia? The junta was a bunch of tyrants and torturers. Betraying them was what made Phaedon a true hero. It's not his good name you're defending. It's your pride. All you have is hubris, just as the wolf says. If you shoot me, you'll still have to pay for Marilita. He will make you."

She raised the gun. "Be quiet. I need to think."

Tell me about it. Thinking madly, Dinah looked over Zenia's shoulder toward the open garage door. Her insurance policy hadn't shown and it sank in that she should be seriously scared. "It's not as easy to kill someone when they're standing right in front of you as it is to have other people do it for you."

"Go inside there." She gestured toward the crypt behind Asclepius with the gun.

"I can't. I'm claustrophobic."

"Go on, get in or I'll shoot."

Dinah threw her eyes over Zenia's shoulder and cried, "Thank God, you're here!"

Zenia turned her head and Dinah dived for the gun. As the two of them toppled onto the stone floor, Dinah wasn't sure whether the pop she heard was the report of the gun or the sound of a hip breaking. In the melee, she couldn't tell whether it was her own or Zenia's. The pistol was loose and tangled up in the slick folds of the kimono. She felt like a brute whaling away at a brittle old woman, but this was no time for mercy. Zenia was groping for the gun with one hand and clawing at Dinah's eyes with the other.

Dinah rammed her knee into Zenia's midsection and floundered amidst the layers of yellow for the gun. Finally she latched onto the grip and struggled to her feet. She checked the safety on the pistol and tucked it in her jacket pocket.

"Are you hurt, Zenia? Is anything broken?"

"Of course, I'm hurt, you fool."

When Mentor walked in, Dinah was helping her to her feet and checking her over for broken bones.

Chapter Thirty-three

"This woman is beating me," said Zenia.

Mentor looked between Zenia and Dinah, visibly confused.

Zenia was tottery and Dinah forced her to sit down in the niche next to the funeral pot. "Come in, Mentor. Zenia and I were just reminiscing about the past and you can answer some very important questions for us."

"I don't know how your friend came to be in my *kalivi*, Dinah. I have not wanted to speak with you because I have no explanation. It is beyond thinking."

"It's what Thor would call a setup," said Dinah. "Your good friend Brakus told me that you deal in stolen antiquities and hinted strongly that you would do anything to keep the police from discovering your illegal trove."

"I can't believe Savas would tell such a lie. I date and catalog sculptural fragments and artifacts for museums. I translate the inscriptions from the ancient Greek. I write the descriptive cards. That is how I supplement my pension."

"Finally someone with an innocent *sympliroma*." Dinah sat her bruised hip down gingerly on top of one of the marble feet. "But you can't be surprised that Brakus gossips. He spread the rumor that Zenia casts the evil eye and poisons the village cats."

Mentor looked chagrinned. "No one actually believes in the evil eye."

"You believed the story about the cats," said Dinah. "Your mother believed it."

Zenia gathered her kimono around her and sneered. "The village is full of superstitious fools. If anyone poisons the cats, it is Brakus' wife. She has a plague of them begging and mewling about her kitchen."

"Irene would not poison a cat. And to say that I steal, that is a calumny."

Sitting hurt her hip and Dinah stood up again, which also hurt but not as bad. "I believe you, Mentor. The weapon that struck Thor came from that statue of Asclepius." She pointed. "Is it a stolen masterpiece?"

He inspected the statue. "The pitting on the cheek is wrong. Achieved with acid or a very fine chisel. I would guess it to be a not-very-good replica of the beardless Asclepius on display in the 'Braccio Nuovo' hallway of the Vatican."

Zenia sneered. "Phaedon did not trifle with replicas."

Dinah had the sense that she was watching a performance. The actress had undertaken a certain role and she couldn't deviate from the script in even the smallest way. "You have an unfortunate relationship with the truth, Zenia. You fabricate grievances and grudges. None of the villagers in Kanaris had anything to do with Phaedon's murder. And you fabricated an affair between Marilita and Phaedon. Did you ever ask Phaedon why he paid blackmail or learn what terrible sin he confessed to Brother Demetrius? Maybe he confessed to the awful things he did while implementing the Prometheus Plan."

"Rubbish."

"The thing that puzzles me is why you continue to let Constantine blackmail you when he doesn't even know what embarrassing information he's supposed to have."

"Donations to the clergy are not blackmail."

"You couldn't understand why Marilita didn't resent Nasos seeing other women, why she didn't want to get married, why she and Phaedon had so much to say to each other in private. And there was that painting of the knight that she loved so much. You were jealous and you saw in it what you expected to see, Phaedon's face. The way she looked at that painting must have seemed like a taunt."

"None of what you say is true."

"For once, you are right. I've asked Mentor to come here this morning and set us both straight." Dinah thought she knew what Mentor would say, but she wasn't a hundred percent sure. Whatever his answer might be, she needed to know. She didn't think that need sprang from a desire to punish Zenia, but she wasn't sure about that either. She'd have to think about it later. "Tell us, Mentor. Zenia and I would like you to verify the fact that Phaedon and Marilita were not lovers and Phaedon was not Alcina's father."

"Why do you think I would know...?"

"Because your mother told you all about Marilita. She adored her. They were like mother and daughter. Marilita confided in your mother and I'm guessing that your mother confided in you. She didn't believe that Marilita murdered anyone. And after that awful *mnimosyno,* she must have been angry. She told you about Zenia's heartlessness. She would have told you who else attended the *mnimosyno.* She would have told you if Alcina's father was there and how he reacted to Zenia's contempt for the deceased."

Zenia stood up. Her skin had a waxy cast and the faintest augury of doubt skirred across her face.

Mentor said, "Mother went to visit Marilita in the hospital in Athens when Alcina was born. The father was there. Mother had the impression that he loved Marilita, but he was married to another woman and for whatever reason, he could not or would not divorce her."

"Who?" asked Zenia.

"Aries Brakus. He and Marilita were secret lovers until her death."

When Oedipus learned about his mistake, he gouged out his eyes. Zenia received the news with a stoical calm. Either she was incredibly brave or incredibly unfeeling. On a professional level, the old tragedienne would surely appreciate the irony. But whatever she was thinking, Dinah's thoughts were already rushing forward to a conversation with Egan, whom Zenia had thrown out of the house last night. She had guessed that it was Egan who was sending her the Nasos letters. This morning didn't seem like a good time to confront her with yet another misunderstanding.

Chapter Thirty-four

Dinah looked at the bloodshot eyes staring back at her in Zenia's bathroom mirror and frowned, but she wasn't the least bit sleepy. It was as if she had crossed over into a permanently insomniac state, but her thinking had never been clearer. The lines zoomed between the dots like lasers, connecting everyone and everything into a comprehensible constellation. She felt acutely perceptive, as if she might begin speaking Greek spontaneously.

She splashed cold water in her face. "You are punchy, you know that? Go back to Kanaris before you do something monumentally stupid."

She went into the kitchen where Mentor had brewed a pot of tea. She helped herself and wandered out into the living room. Mentor followed with the tea pot and the two of them sat down and sipped in silence. She had telephoned the hospital. Thor remained fast asleep. No change. Stavros had posted guards he could trust and gone back to his hotel in Iréon for a few hours rest. Zenia said that Egan had called for a room at the same hotel when she ordered him out. On Samos, coincidence was the norm. It would be interesting if Egan were to bump into Stavros in the hotel lobby. Out of context, he probably wouldn't recognize him as Nasos.

Egan had apparently left the house peaceably. He probably saw no reason to argue with Zenia. He could come back for his guns anytime. Maybe he'd already sold them and the buyers had simply been told to come and pick them up, or he could be content to cut his losses and move on.

Good grief. What if he had decided to hop a flight to Brazil? All of a sudden it seemed urgent that Stavros be brought up to speed. What she had to say was too complicated and there were too many attendant questions to communicate over the phone. Everything on Samos was close by. She would make a quick run to Iréon and talk to Stavros in person before returning to Kanaris.

She inhaled a second cup of tea and phoned K.D. to reassure herself that she had made it through the night. K.D. sounded chipper, possibly too chipper, but Dinah didn't bother to cross-examine her. She would get into the contraceptive issue later. "Put a bag of frozen peas on that shiner," she told her and hung up.

Mentor said, "Zenia has taken to her bed and I have called Dr. Frangopoulos, just in case."

"Thanks, Mentor. After the doctor leaves, will you stick around for a while to make sure she doesn't lapse into a fit of suicidal remorse or call Egan and warn him that Asclepius has given up his secret?"

"Nè, málista. But where are you going? You are tired. You should not take crazy chances."

"I don't plan to," she said, and left the house the same way she had entered, through the underground passage.

It was a Day-Glo sunrise. Fiery fingers of red stretched across the sky and tinted the treetops with a reddish glow. The air felt heavy and muggy. The old adage "red sky at morning sailors take warning" passed through her mind. Maybe Samos would see a little rain this afternoon. She rolled Farris' Vespa out of its hiding place, buckled her helmet, and looked up at the menacing sky. If it rained before she reached Iréon, she was in for a soaking.

Iréon was the site of the Temple of Hera, the Heraion. Before her idyll on Samos went to hell, Dinah had looked forward to spending a day there. She had read all about it. The early Samians worshipped Hera more than any of the other gods and at the beginning of the sixth century, they built a magnificent Ionic temple in her honor. An earthquake demolished it and they built an even more magnificent temple in its place. It had a hundred and fifty-five marble columns more than sixty feet tall. An elaborate wall carved with battle scenes and sphinxes protected the altar. Giant statues lined the Sacred Way from the ancient city to the temple and worshippers invoked the goddess' blessings by bringing rich votive offerings. Today the sanctuary lay in ruins, but in spite of everything, she still hoped for a passing glimpse.

As she coasted through Pythagório, there were no cars or pedestrians. She had to remind herself that it was too early for the shops and restaurants to be open. She followed the signs to Iréon. The road cut across a flat, marshy plain where the Imbrasos River emptied into the Aegean. The sky had darkened to sepia and a stiff wind whipped the tops of the tamarisk trees and roughened the sea. The sharp, salty zing of ozone filled her nostrils. Thunder rumbled in the distance and a bank of ominous black clouds gusted in from the sea. Suddenly, she did not want to be sitting on this scooter like a lightning rod.

The Heraion was just ahead. Discretion being the better part of valor, she decided to take shelter while she could. She pulled into the empty parking lot as a bolt of lightning unseamed the clouds and a spate of pea-sized hailstones rained down on her. They pinged off her helmet and stung her arms and shoulders through her thin jacket. She dismounted, removed her helmet, and looked around for a building of some kind, or at least an overhang.

No one was manning the ticket booth, but it was locked and she hurried on past a trio of headless female figures into the hallowed sphere of Hera. There was no one in sight for acres around and all that was left of the temple was a field of broken stones and one lone remaining column. Its precarious, misaligned disks jutted up like a disjointed finger. She had expected a deal of destruction and despoliation, but these ruins were extravagantly ruined. It looked as if the previous heap of ruins had been freshly bombed. Zenia had mentioned an ongoing excavation, but Dinah saw no sign of it. Weeds and bushes cropped up around the broken stones and added to the sense of neglect.

The hail shelled her and it didn't just tingle. It hurt. She rapped herself for being a dummy. *I should have kept the helmet. I should have kept going to one of the waterfront tavernas or on to the hotel. I should have given Stavros the lowdown over the phone and gone straight back to Kanaris and hit the sack.* This is what comes of too little sleep and poor impulse control.

Another bolt of lightning rived the sky and the fusillade of hailstones intensified. She spotted a stone building at the end of a long alley of broken stones and capitals and ran for it. A sign posted above the lintel said *"Mouseio,"* which she translated as Museum. The door was unlocked and she ducked inside. There were two long, glass display cases containing jewelry and bowls and implements. On the facing wall was a mural and a poem dedicated to Hera from the Homeric Hymns. An interior door opened into a second room with more display cases.

Thunder boomed and the little building trembled on its foundation. Hail spatted against the roof and windowpanes. She looked out the window behind her as a jagged shaft of lightning ripped the heavens. Angry waves battered the sea wall, no more than a dozen feet from the museum door, and where the hail-stones splashed into the sea, spouts of white water jetted up like a thousand fountains. Once again, Greece had surprised her.

She walked around the cases, too tense to give the contents more than a cursory look. Shivering, she sat down cross-legged on the floor behind the second glass exhibit case, leaned her head back, and looked up at the mural of Hera. Scepter raised, she promenaded with her sacred peacock in front of a cloud-swathed Mount Olympus. Above the mural just under the roof was a long, horizontal window through which she could see and hear the successive salvos of hail. The plaque with the Homeric hymn read:

> *To Hera, Queen of the immortals, of supreme beauty,*
> *Sister and Wife of Zeus, the loud-booming glorious one,*
> *whom all the blessed ones on long Olympus revere and*
> *honor no less than Zeus whose sport is the thunderbolt.*

Another thunderbolt struck quite close and rattled the windows. It sounded as if Hera and Zeus were having a knock-down-drag-out, but Dinah found the pelting hail and peals of thunder romantic. So long as she wasn't being bombarded or drenched, she loved storms. She wished that Thor were here to put his arm around her. She could go to sleep listening to the bluster outside. She felt a pang of guilt. She should be waiting at the hospital instead of hunkered down in a drafty museum doing nothing. She took out her phone to call the hospital again.

The door blew open. "You've made a dog's dinner of it."

The door slammed shut. She eased back down on her haunches and powered off her phone. Egan had come to her.

"You didn't have to kill Fathi. For taking one gun?"

"It wasn't the gun," said Brakus. "It was his mouth. If I hadn't killed him, we'd be in jail." He said something else in Greek.

Dinah had assumed that Egan was the murderer. So much for her acute perceptiveness. She flashed to Fathi walking past the taverna trying to sell Yannis a gun. Brakus had heard and, as soon as he saw his chance, he must have bolted out the back door after him. Brakus had been a runner, an eight hundred meter man. He caught Fathi, took the gun away, and shot him. But he must have pulled a muscle or a tendon during his run. That's why he was gimpy when he followed her back to the body.

Egan said, "You were smart not to let Fathi know you were my partner, but killing him was disastrous. You could have scared him off, bought him off, anything. Attacking Ramberg was the last straw. I'm not staying to find out if he recovers. I want my money now."

"No!" Something—a fist—whomped the top of the exhibit case and Brakus launched into an angry harangue in Greek.

Dinah slid Zenia's pistol out of her jacket pocket. One of them was walking up and down on the other side of the exhibit case. She didn't dare to move. They lowered their voices and Egan reverted to English. The drumming hail made it hard to hear.

The sound of footsteps stopped. Her heart stuttered.

"*Blakas*." Egan imbued the word with maximum condescension. Dinah thought at first he had said Brakus' name, but Brakus exploded and she decided that *blakas* was an insult.

"Pathetic," said Egan. His recurrent use of English seemed calculated to annoy Brakus. "You have involved too many refugees and now that unsavory monk. With the Ramsberg business, the national police will swarm over the island. We can't take the risk."

Brakus answered in Greek, interspersed by more whomps on the top of the exhibit case.

"Oh, for Christ's sake." Egan sounded tired and peevish. "You didn't have to hit him."

"When he…" A clap of thunder derailed the rest of sentence and then, "…could have acted shocked to see the guns. Have you never heard of *acting*? It's Zenia's house, no connection to us. But you had to get rough."

"If I hadn't stopped him, he would have taken the guns."

"You should have let him. It's too risky to move them now or to make any more sales. Even Zenia is suspicious. She didn't believe my story that vandals broke the statue and that Pelerin woman has her thinking I sent letters pretending to be Nasos Lykos. I'm leaving on the four o'clock to Athens. I'll wait for you at the Sunrise until two and you'd better not be late."

"*Deilos*. Coward. Whiner."

"Do what you want, Savas, but I found the guns and I want my…"

"This is what you get."

"Good God, you're as mad as your father."

A shot rang out.

Dinah's skin shrank. She heard the sound of something sliding across the floor. Egan's body? Brakus was dragging him behind the display case. She had to do something. She looked up at the window over the mural and raised the pistol. What did Papas call the police? She racked her brain. *Asty*-something…*asty*…

"*Astynomia!*" She shouted and fired three shots through the window. Glass and hail rained down. She scrambled to the end of the display case and took cover. All she saw when she peered around was Brakus' back as he charged through the adjoining room. She heard wood splinter and glass break and she fired another shot to make sure he kept going.

"Like a bad movie," said Egan and laughed his dry, raspy laugh.

She took off her jacket, pressed it against his wound with one hand, and phoned Stavros with the other. When Stavros understood the situation, she rang off and pressed both hands against Egan's wound. Brakus' aim must have been shaken by the thunder because the bullet had missed the lungs and heart and gone into Egan's left shoulder. "I think you're going to live, Egan. Since I probably saved your life, will you answer a question for me?"

"What's that?"

"Were you really going to make a movie about Marilita's life or were you just stringing Zenia along to gain access to Phaedon's papers and his house?"

"Afraid poor old Zenia was deluding herself about the film. She's gone rather cuckoo, maundering about ghosts and letters from the dead."

Day 6

Chapter Thirty-five

Dinah slept most of the day. When she woke up, it was to good news. Stavros called to tell her that Thor had woken up and the surgeon reported that there were no observable neurological sequelae or cognitive deficits.

She felt a flood of relief and then guilt that she hadn't been there throughout his ordeal. "Does he remember what happened?"

"He seems to have total recall. He learned that Greek notaries maintain records of all building construction and additions. Thinking that Phaedon had built a storehouse for the weapons he stole, Thor located the notary who handled the construction of Phaedon's house and discovered the blueprints for an underground tunnel. He went to ask Zenia to show him, but she had driven into Kanaris and Egan and Brakus were the pair he found. He said they 'got the drop' on him, which I interpret to mean that he was overpowered."

She laughed. "It's an American idiom. From old TV westerns."

"What about Brakus? Did you find him?"

"Yes. I can't claim much credit for that. He had gone back to Kanaris to pack his money and his toothbrush. He is not a very intelligent criminal, but few are. I believe Egan Vercuni was the brains of their operation."

"Is Egan going to be all right?"

"He is doing well for a *giriatrikos*."

"Geriatric?"

"Nè. His days in prison will be short. He hopes to shorten them even more by cooperating with the police."

"Did he pay somebody to vandalize Marilita's house?"

"Yes. Sadly, there are too many in need of a few euros and willing to do most anything."

"What about Brother Constantine? Have you found out what his role was?"

"Primarily passing information, says Vercuni. Always for a price. He helped Brakus move Thor and bury him in the *kalivi*, which makes him complicit in the crime of kidnapping. My men have been unable to find him at his usual campsite and he may have left Samos. We are still searching. He has been wanted for questioning in connection with his real estate fraud for over a year."

She broached the next subject somewhat tentatively. "I know who wrote Zenia those letters, Galen."

There was a long pause. "Who?"

"You were right when you said that only the dead would know or care about Zenia's sins. Your impersonator was Aries Brakus. Irene Brakus told me that he died in a mental institution about ten years ago. After he attended Marilita's *mnimosyno* and heard Zenia's rant, he started to obsess about Marilita's death. For whatever reason, jealousy or madness, he started to believe that he actually *was* Nasos. Savas found a packet of unmailed letters among his belongings after his death. Irene didn't know what he had done with them. Savas may have sent them just to get back at the high-and-mighty woman who despised him and his father as peasants. You'll have to ask him."

"Perhaps that element of the case is best left unanswered, but I thank you for telling me." His voice brightened. "Thor has been looking at his watch and asking where you are. What shall I tell him?"

"Tell him to keep his gown on. I'll be there in an hour."

Day 10

Chapter Thirty-six

Thor walked his chair back farther under the awning and grinned. They were celebrating the successful conclusion of his mission and discharge from the hospital in a fancy restaurant in Kusadasi. He was still bothered with pain from his broken shoulder blade, but his brain was intact and he was unusually animated. He said, "Both Papas and Egan have agreed to turn over the names of all of their buyers in exchange for a more lenient sentence and they'll testify against Brakus. Between you and Galen, you've earned me a promotion in E-Fourteen. I just got the offer this morning."

"You're not going to take it, are you, Thor? After what happened? It's too dangerous."

"Sure I'm going to take it. I'm flying to Oslo tomorrow to have my head examined by the home team. I have to fill out some paperwork and after that, it will be official. I'll be stationed in Berlin." He reached for her hand. "Will you come with me?"

"You know how I feel about cold weather."

"It won't be cold for months yet. And when it does get cold, it'll be a blast. I'll buy you a pair of electric socks and take you skiing in the Alps at Christmas."

"I don't think you should take the job."

"Why not?"

"Police work is dangerous. You could have been permanently brain damaged. There are lots of other professions you could get into. You could go to law school and practice law."

He arched an eyebrow. "I've heard your views on lawyers and the legal profession."

"Become a history teacher then. You like history."

"I like police work better."

"You're being a blister. It pays poorly, you have to rub shoulders with terrible people all the time, and it's hazardous to your health."

"Seems we're having our second fight. But two fights in ten days isn't bad."

"You were unconscious for three of them."

He laughed. "Only two, really. In *The Rockford Files*, Jimbo is knocked unconscious in every other episode and he's always fine."

"Life isn't a TV show, Thor."

"Too bad. TV improves on reality, knotty cases cracked in an hour and no real blood spilled. I confess that I've missed TV here in Greece."

She gazed back across the strait toward Kanaris. "For Zenia, it's been a real-life Greek tragedy. I can't help but wonder how the story would have turned out if she'd simply asked her husband and her sister if they were having an affair."

"From what you've told me, she was too proud and consumed by jealousy. How did you figure out that Marilita's lover was Aries Brakus?"

"The eyes. The face in the painting had unusually prominent eyes and so does Alcina. Brakus, too. It's a hereditary trait. They are brother and sister and never knew it. A tendency to mental problems may be another hereditary trait. Stavros told me that Savas didn't sound any too sane when the police questioned him."

"He's just trying to convince everyone that he's nuts so they'll go easy on him."

"Why, Thor, I didn't think you had a cynical bone in your body."

"I hope the influence is mutual. Have you been feeling more optimistic by any chance?"

"Yes, I have. Knowing that your head isn't broken has made me very happy. And things have worked out happily for my friend Mentor. Irene Brakus has hired his daughter and her husband to work in the taverna now that she's on her own and all that family togetherness is bound to lead to a match between Mentor and Irene. I think they'll make a lovely couple."

"Speaking of the couple thing. You haven't forgotten that there's a question pending, have you?"

She hadn't forgotten. "My dig begins in September and it could go for months."

"I'm not asking you to give up the thrill of legendary Troy. It'll take a few months for me to get established in Berlin. You could move in over Christmas."

"I hate leaden skies and frozen tundra."

"Berlin can't match Greece for blue skies, but there's no frozen tundra."

"Moving in together for real is a lot more complicated than basking in the sun for a few weeks on a Greek island. I'm not easy to live with. I'm prone to moods and doubts and I have fickle genes. As you know, my mother has been married and divorced seven times."

"Didn't I hear you lecturing K.D. that children don't inherit their parents' defects?"

"Don't quote me back to myself. Sometimes they do and sometimes they evolve mutant defects of their own."

"You're going to list for me your mutant defects now?"

"No patience, a sarcastic tongue, poor impulse control, and I smoke. I wish I had a cigarette right now. I know it's a filthy habit, you don't have to tell me."

"I wasn't going to."

"I've quit twice. I'm a backslider. And a dilettante. I have no stick-to-it-ivity. I can't finish my dissertation. I can't hold a job. I can't stay in one place for longer than a few months. I'm a flibbertigibbet."

"My phrase book's not handy. Help me out."

"Flighty and...flibberti...I don't know. Flighty."

He smiled. "I've known you were a flight risk from the first day we met."

Her eyes followed a ship pulling away from Kusadasi, embarking for Patmos or Kos or Rhodes, maybe even Alexandria or Beirut. Places she'd never been. She turned back to Thor. "I hate lutefish."

"Lute*fisk*."

"Whatever. And aquavit. It makes my teeth hurt."

"Akevitt is mother's milk to a Norwegian, but it's not a deal breaker."

"Small things matter," she said. "They add up."

"If you list them one by one, they do." He replenished her wine. "You haven't mentioned that you tend to jabber quite a lot, especially when you drink red wine."

She scowled. "I'm serious, Thor. I've crossed lines you wouldn't cross, done things you wouldn't approve of."

"What things?"

"I don't know. Broken faith, shirked duties, lacerated feelings." She drew the line at telling him about her Uncle Cleon's drug money in Panama. "I've lacerated a lot of feelings."

"Now you're bragging. Why are you running yourself down like this?"

"Before you ask a person to live with you, you should know. And you were right when you said I lied. I lie all the time."

"But not to people you care about, as I recall. I think I can live with the problems you've enumerated so far. Are there others?"

"One other and it's a doozie." She took a large swallow of red wine. "You'll have to rent a two bedroom apartment in Berlin. I've told K.D. she can hang with me for a while if her mother agrees to let her miss a year of school."

"Even after the kid lied to you about not being able to return to Atlanta because her mother had gone to Switzerland?"

"Particularly after that. I'm not the best role model, but I may be the best she can find in the short term."

"The short term seems to be your forte." His eyes grew serious. "Look, Dinah, I'm not dragooning you. This has to be because you want it, too."

This was it. Now or never. A bubble of fear floated up from her innermost depths. She flashed to what he'd said about her being the least cautious person he'd ever met. Maybe it was true. She closed her eyes and thought about Geronimo jumping his horse off a four hundred foot bluff into the unplumbed depths of Medicine Creek. Sometimes you have to take the plunge. If she didn't, she'd be asking herself "what if" for the rest of her life.

"Okay," she said. "Let's give Berlin a whirl."